Percy Hetherington Fitzgerald

The Life and Times of John Wilkes, M. P., Lord Mayor of London,

and Chamberlain

Percy Hetherington Fitzgerald

The Life and Times of John Wilkes, M. P., Lord Mayor of London, and Chamberlain

ISBN/EAN: 9783337429058

Printed in Europe, USA, Canada, Australia, Japan

Cover: Foto ©Raphael Reischuk / pixelio.de

More available books at **www.hansebooks.com**

THE LIFE AND TIMES

OF

JOHN WILKES, M.P.,

LORD MAYOR OF LONDON,

AND

CHAMBERLAIN.

BY

PERCY FITZGERALD, M.A., F.S.A.,

AUTHOR OF 'THE LIFE OF GEORGE IV.,' 'LIFE OF GARRICK,' ETC.

' With thee Good-humour tempers lively Wit,
Enthron'd with Judgment, Candour loves to sit;
And Nature gave thee, open to distress,
A heart to pity, and a hand to bless.'
CHURCHILL.

WITH FOUR ILLUSTRATIONS.

IN TWO VOLUMES.

VOL. I.

LONDON:
WARD AND DOWNEY,
12, YORK STREET, COVENT GARDEN, W.C.
1888.

CONTENTS OF VOL. I.

PREFACE.

THE prominent incidents of Wilkes's career are well known : his struggles with Ministers on the General Warrants, and his desperate contest with the House of Commons for his seat. He is familiar also as the noisy, successful demagogue, who was the cause of much turbulence and rioting. Not so well known is his share in the conflict which raged for many years between the King and his Ministers on the one side, and the City Fathers on the other, when the latter displayed an intrepidity and resolution that was worthy of all praise. This curious episode is now for the first time recorded in detail in these volumes, and will be found, I think, an interesting contribution to the 'History of London.'

The course of Wilkes, moreover, was so chequered, and his character such a mixture of good and evil, that his adventures, as they may be called, furnish much entertainment. There is something piquant, too, in the contrast between the excellence of his cause and the reckless and unscrupulous means he adopted to support it. Whether full justice has been done in treating this singular character, it rests with the reader to determine.

The materials have been abundant, for, curious to say, this attractive subject has not been fully treated before the present attempt, except in a short but comprehensive sketch by Mr. Fraser Rae, entitled 'Wilkes, Fox, Sheridan.' His voluminous papers are to be seen in the British Museum, and on these I have drawn largely. The most interesting portion is the correspondence with Churchill, hitherto unpublished, which exhibits the friendship, as well as the reckless profanity, of the two rakes. Wilkes figures largely in the contemporary memoirs, and was found by his contemporaries, as he was by Lord Mansfield, to be the most agreeable man of his time. It was this attraction, found in his letters, and even in his violent proceedings, that conciliated the most hostile, and has made the writing the life of the dissipated, unscrupulous, but gay and good-natured, Wilkes an agreeable task.

ATHENÆUM CLUB,
January 20, 1888.

PEDIGREE OF THE WILKES FAMILY.

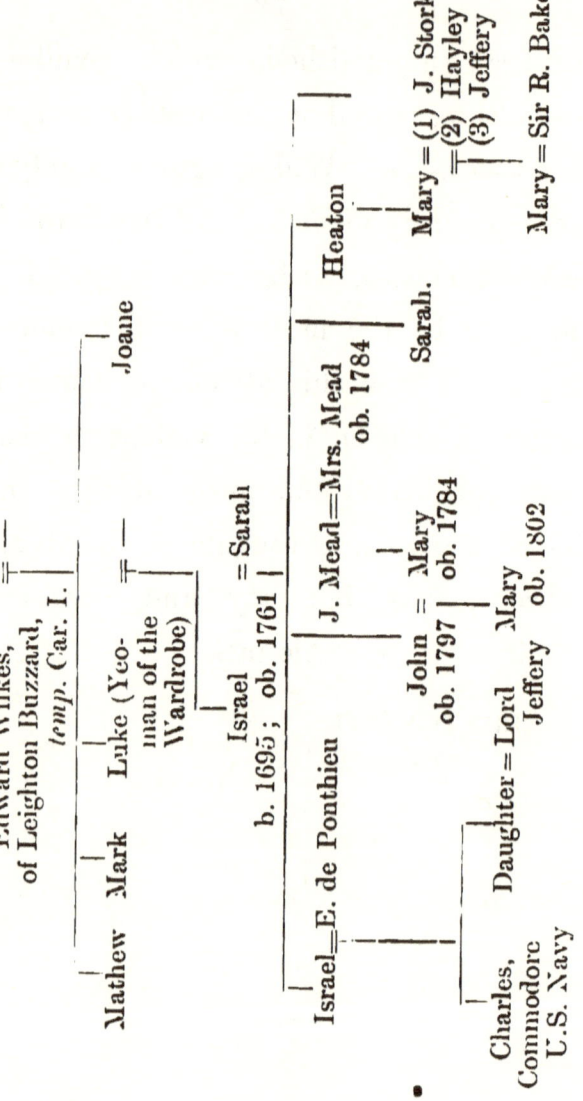

Edward Wilkes,
of Leighton Buzzard,
temp. Car. I.

Mathew   Mark   Luke (Yeo-
                  man of the
                  Wardrobe)   Joane

                  Israel   = Sarah
                  b. 1695; ob. 1761

Israel = E. de Ponthieu   J. Mead = Mrs. Mead   Heaton
                                         ob. 1784

                               John = Mary   Sarah.   Mary = (1) J. Stork
                               ob. 1797 ob. 1784   (2) Hayley
                                                                         (3) Jeffery

Charles,   Daughter = Lord   Mary
Commodore   Jeffery   ob. 1802   Mary = Sir R. Baker
U.S. Navy

THE LIFE OF JOHN WILKES.

INTRODUCTION.

At Ludgate Circus, where the London traffic is busiest, and getting across the street is a business of anxiety and risk, the foot-passenger is at little liberty to note the two mean and stunted obelisks which stand in the road. One of these is a token of the City's love and gratitude to John Wilkes, sometime Alderman, Lord Mayor, and Re-membrancer of the City of London. The other is in honour of one Waithman, a noisy, troublesome Alderman, who advertised him-self well by taking up the cause of the unlucky Queen Caroline. Wilkes also adver-tised himself well, but it was his own par-

ticular interests and cause. Yet though his
exertions were not tainted with any sort of
corruption, he could hardly be styled a ' pure '
patriot. His services to the State and Constitution were of an extraordinary and valuable
kind. He ' settled,' or caused to be settled—
' paying with his person '—points of constitutional law affecting the liberty of the subject.
He confronted the arrogant pretensions of
despotism in a coarse, rough, and violent
way, the most effective for the purpose; and
fought the battle with an insolent scurrility
and courage that roused the nation. Yet,
notwithstanding these services, we feel that
the idea of a STATUE to John Wilkes somehow
shocks the sensibilities, and it would be felt
to be the celebration of a victory won by
violence in the cause of selfishness.

Towards the close of his life, Wilkes began
a sort of autobiography, which if it makes
us lament that the scheme was not carried
out, supplies evidence of one curious note in
Wilkes' character, his amiable, good-humoured
vanity, for which no man ever received more
indulgence. Had the performance been carried

out in this spirit, it would probably have
been little more than a continued stream of
self-laudation, and we should find that his
contemporaries were more satisfactory judges
of the career of the patriot than he was
himself.   He was, in truth, an extraordinary
character, full of energy and buoyancy, never
checked by the most disastrous repulses.
As was said of Foote, he was 'incompressible.'   No agitator or indeed politician was
ever so successful.   Whatever he set his
heart on, he was certain to reach, sooner or
later.   He baffled all his enemies—King,
Ministers, the two Houses, the Courts,
creditors, and private foes; and this success
was continuous, attending him to the last
years of his life.

CHAPTER I.

WILKES, in this MS. fragment of autobiography to be seen in the British Museum, thus complacently reviews his own adventurous career:

'In my time a private person has stood forth, who by the fond voice of his countrymen has been equalled to the patriots of former ages. He has likewise experienced the same fate. He was hated, persecuted, and driven out of his country by a Court faction and a despotic Ministry, yet all the while beloved by the nation to a degree of enthusiasm, and honoured with repeated marks of popular favour. This person is Mr. Wilkes, whose life I now undertake to write, because no other man can have had equal opportunities with myself of knowing

every part of his conduct, both in public and
private, or of being so well acquainted with
the real and secret motives of all his actions.
I have been intimately connected with, and I
even made a part of his family, several
months before his birth; nor have I ever
quitted him since.'

Wilkes, too, was one of those mixed
characters which invariably excite interest.
Though he was one of the most debauched
beings that ever existed, pursuing pleasure *on
principle*, yet there was no effeminacy in his
nature. He was brilliant, entertaining,
clever, and sagacious, and moderate even in
his violence; an admirable, vigorous writer;
liked by all, even by his enemies, save
perhaps by his Majesty; a charming companion and a cultivated, classical scholar.
The career of such a man is likely to be interesting, and such, I hope, it will be found
in my hands.

Wilkes, when commencing his story, of
which he never wrote more than a few
pages, thus solemnly moralizes over his own
career:

' There is a dignity and mild majesty in
the independency of private life, which is not
indeed so dazzling, yet affords more pure
and unalloyed pleasure than all the glare
of title, power and pomp. I am in reality
more interested in scenes of this kind than in
the cruel and sudden reverse of fortune in
kings and princes, because the other is
brought home to my own case as a private
gentleman, or even one of inferior but independent condition. I know that there is
no probability of my being ever a sovereign.
The propriety, therefore, of conduct in a
prince interests me very little; but all the
actions of a private gentleman and every
event of his life may be similar to my own.
I shall never command my own army, lose
an important battle, be taken prisoner, and
have to deliberate what sacrifices I am to
make for the recovery of my liberty. I may,
however, be oppressed by a despotic Minister,
thrown into prison by a wicked favourite, and
though, by the vigour of the laws and the
integrity of the judges, I regain my freedom,
I may have to spend the remainder of my life

in unavailing struggle against a prevailing faction.'

After lamenting that historians only thought of recording the showy achievements of conquerors and warriors, while those conspicuous in arts and sciences are 'consigned over to the biographer,' he urges that, 'next to the satisfaction which the mind feels in consequence of a virtuous action,' is the thought of being handed down to posterity. 'I wish my countrymen had a Plutarch. Of Hampden, Lord Russell, and Sydney, for instance, how little do we know!'

The Wilkes family came originally from Bedfordshire, where it had been settled in the days of Charles I. At this period we find at Layton Beausert, which few will recognise as Leighton Buzzard, Mr. Edward Wilkes, who had four children, oddly named Matthew, Mark, Luke, and Joan. Luke's son was Israel, a distiller in Clerkenwell, who married a Miss Heaton, and died in 1761. His children were Israel, Heaton (who through his life seems to have shared the pecuniary difficulties of his brother, without his abilities), two

daughters—Sarah and Mary—and the remarkable subject of this memoir, the well-
known JOHN WILKES, who was born on
October 17, 1727.

Israel Wilkes, his father, came into possession of Hoxton Square through his wife.
He lived, we are told, in splendid style, and
went to church in his coach-and-six. He
kept an elegant and sumptuous table for his
friends. No wonder that John, from his
infancy, imbibed notions of extravagance.
The lady was a rigid Dissenter, and occasionally persuaded her husband to attend
meeting with her. The other children did
not much distinguish themselves. Israel, the
eldest, was placed in the business house of
Mr. de Ponthieu as partner, and married
Miss de Ponthieu; but the business not
prospering, he went to America, and settled
in New York.

Israel settled in America about the year
1782, and brought letters to the Governor
from many important persons in England.
To this person he looked for place or
office. He eventually went into business,

and hoped to obtain the 'agency of British Packets' through his greater brother's interest, but failed. His son Charles became cashier in the United States Bank. From this branch sprang a celebrated Commodore of the United States navy, a dashing officer and man of science.

The youngest son seems to have been a 'poorish creature' enough, never succeeding in anything. In his hands the distillery failed. He then, like Mr. Micawber, turned his attention to coals, but could make nothing of *that*. His life seemed to be generally spent in striving to persuade his important brother to 'do something for him.' As might be expected, he died 'not in affluent circumstances.'

The two daughters seemed to have had a tinge of oddity, or of something worse. On this was, indeed, suggested a character of Dickens'. The eldest died unmarried. 'She lived secluded from the world for many years, in Hart Street, Bloomsbury. She had apartments up two pair of stairs; with thick blinds before the windows, to keep out the day-light : and she burnt either a lamp or a candle continually.'

The second daughter married a Mr. Storke : and we find that Sir R. Baker was a cousin of the family.

There was in her odd history much that suggested her brother, though with little of his redeeming merits.

But in the next generation there was one member who was to do credit to the family. Israel Wilkes, when advanced in life, had a son born, Charles Wilkes, who became a man of science, a commodore in the American Navy, made exploring expeditions of much interest, and was more particularly famed for having stopped the English steamer *Trent* on the high seas, and taken out the two Confederate Agents.

Young John Wilkes was early found to be a sprightly boy and of great promise. His father was both fond and proud of him, and spared no expense upon his education. An important lady of fortune, Mrs. Mead, and a particular friend of the family, was also partial to the boy.

Mr. Wilkes, senior, must have possessed some of that lively spirit for which his son was later to be celebrated. Long after, Mr. Wilkes, writing to his ' Polly,' recalls a touch of this paternal humour : ' I had a father, a perfectly good-humoured man, who loved laughing : he said one day to me, "Jack, have you got a purse ?" My answer was, "No, sir." "I am sorry for it, Jack," said my father ; "if you had, I should have given you some money to put in it." I soon got a purse, and in two or three days my father asked me again, "Jack, have you got a purse ?"—"Yes, sir."—"I am glad of it," said my father ; "if you had not had a purse, I would have given you one." This was mere fun in my father, for he was exceedingly generous, and gave me all I could wish.'

He was presently—as he tells us in his short MS. sketch of his boyhood—sent with his two brothers to a considerable school in Hertford, ' kept by Mr. John Worsley.' This was a celebrated place of education for Presbyterians, to which creed his mother belonged. This, however, seems to have had no influence on his profession, as such formal religion as he retained through life was of an orthodox cast; and he was always fond of attending Church on Sundays with tolerable regularity.

After remaining here five years, he next passed under the care of another Presbyterian, Mr. Matthew Leeson, who kept a school at Thame in Oxfordshire, where he stayed but a year. His instructor, he tells us, in his recollections, ' was one of those teachers who are fond of every paradox and heresy. He was persecuted even by his own little sect, because he did not hold the received opinion of the ' Trinity, original sin, redemption, etc. At last the dissenting congregation created him so much uneasiness that he was obliged to quit the ministry; and he likewise left the town soon after.' Dr. Carlyle, however, in his pleasant memoir, gives an amusing account of this breach. ' This man,' he says, ' a Mr. Leeson, or Lyson, had been singled out by the father as the best tutor in the world for his most promising son, because, at the age of three-score, and after studying controversy for more than thirty years, he told his con-

gregation that he was going to leave them,
and would tell them the reason next Sunday;
when, being fully convened, he said that
with much anxiety and care he had examined
the Arian controversy, and was now convinced
that the creed - he had read to them, as his
creed, was false, and that he had now adopted
that of the Arians, and was to bid them farewell. The people were shocked with this
creed, and not so sorry as they would have
been otherwise to part with him, for he was a
good-natured, well-meaning man.'*

His youthful pupil—who early showed
signs of precocity—was not likely to have
been influenced by such a character.

'He then came to Aylesbury, and the pupil
attended him. He lived there,' goes on the
account, 'in a house belonging to a widow
lady, whose name was Mead.

'The family were new converts to Presby-
terianism, and actuated by the warmth so
frequent after a change. He continued there
for two years, and no rent was ever asked.
He seemed to be under the protection of so

* 'Autobiography,' p. 168.

opulent a family, and they were vain of the
patronage and of the credit it gave them
among the sectarians of the Capital.'

' Mrs. Mead was the widow of a dry-salter
who had made money and carried on business
on London Bridge.   Her maiden name was
Sherbrooke, and she was the daughter of a
gentleman of considerable property, living at
Cheneys, in Bucks.   All her brothers and
sisters dying, this considerable property became hers.'   The celebrated Dr. Mead was
nearly related to the family ; and his daughter,
Mrs. Nicholls, was long after declared by Miss
Wilkes to be her mother's ' nearest relative
after me.'

Mrs. Mead, the widow, was a person likely
to be well considered in Aylesbury, being a
pillar of the Dissenting interest.   One reason
for young Wilkes following his preceptor to
Aylesbury, was the furthering of a plan which
the parents of both families had set their
hearts upon.

Mrs. Mead had an only daughter, who
would be an heiress, inheriting from both
sides of her family ; and ' it was the warm

wish,' we are told, ' of Mrs. Mead's that an
intimacy might grow up between her daughter
and young Mr. Wilkes.' Mrs. Wilkes and
Mrs. Mead were ' upon terms of the purest
affection.'

They were both Dissenters. The young
lady was, certainly, ten years older than
Mr. Wilkes; but this was not considered a
serious objection. From this early familiarity
with a strict sect of Dissenters the young
Wilkes no doubt acquired his disgust to
religion, and even to decorous behaviour.

His father next proposed to send him
abroad, to the University of Leyden, which,
for some reason, had grown into fashion with
the English and Scotch. It will be recollected that, some twenty years later, Boswell
set off to prosecute his studies at the same
seat of learning. It happened that the clever
and vivacious Dr. Alexander Carlyle was at
the University at the same time as young
Wilkes, and to him we owe a lively sketch of
the young student at Leyden:

' There were at this time about twenty-two
British students at Leyden, of whom, besides

the five at our house already named, were the
Hon. Charles Townshend, afterwards a distinguished statesman; Dr. Anthony Askew; John
Campbell, junior, of Stonefield; his tutor, Mr.
Morton, afterwards a professor at St. Andrews;
John Wilkes, his companion, Mr. Bland, and
their tutor, Mr. Leeson; Mr. Freeman, from
Jamaica; Mr. Doddeswell, afterwards Chancellor of the Exchequer; Mr. Wetheral, from
the West Indies; Dr. Charles Congalton, to
this day physician in Edinburgh; an Irish
gentleman, Keefe, I think, in his house;
Willie Gordon, afterwards K.B., with four or
five more, whose names I have forgotten, and
who did not associate with my friends.

'On the first Sunday evening I was in
Leyden I walked round the Cingle—a fine
walk on the outside of the Rhine, which
formed the wet ditch of the town—with John
Gregory, who introduced me to the British
students as we met them, not without giving
me a short character of them, which I found
in general a very just outline. When he
came to John Wilkes, whose ugly countenance
in early youth was very striking, I asked

earnestly who he was. His answer was, that he was the son of a London distiller or brewer, who wanted to be a fine gentleman and man of taste, which he could never be, for God and nature had been against him. I came to know Wilkes very well afterwards, and found him to be a sprightly entertaining fellow—too much so for his years, as he was but eighteen; for even then he showed something of daring profligacy, for which he was afterwards notorious. Though he was fond of learning, and passionately desirous of being thought something extraordinary, he was unlucky in having an old ignorant pedant of a dissenting parson for his tutor. His chief object seemed to be to make Wilkes an Arian also, and he teased him so much about it that he was obliged to declare that he did not believe the Bible at all, which produced a quarrel between them, and Wilkes, for refuge, went frequently to Utrecht, where he met with Immateriality Baxter, as he was called, who then attended Lord Blantyre and Mr. Hay of Drummellier, as he had formerly done Lord John Gray.

'This gentleman was more to Wilkes's taste than his own tutor ; for though he was a profound philosopher and a hard student, he was at the same time a man of the world, and of such pleasing conversation as attracted the young. Baxter was so much pleased with Wilkes that he dedicated one of his pieces to him. He died in 1750, which fact leads me to correct an error in the account of Baxter's life, in which he is much praised for his keeping well with Wilkes, though he had given so much umbrage to the Scotch. But this is a gross mistake, for the people of that nation were always Wilkes's favourites till 1763, thirteen years after Baxter's death, when he became a violent party-writer, and wished to raise his fame and fortune on the ruin of Lord Bute.'

The friendship here alluded to is interesting, as affording evidence that Wilkes had been able to attach to himself at least one virtuous and enlightened friend. Baxter afterwards wrote to him thus : ' We talked much on this, you may remember, in the Capuchins' garden at

Spa. I have finished the *Prima Cura ;* it is in the dialogue way, and design to inscribe it to my dear John Wilkes, whom, under a borrowed name, I have made one of the interlocutors. If you are against this whim (which a passionate love for you has made me conceive), I will drop it.'

' Wilkes,' goes on Carlyle, ' was fond of shining in conversation prematurely, for at that time he had but little knowledge except what he derived from Baxter in his frequent visits to Utrecht. In the art of shining, however, he was much outdone by Charles Townshend, who was not above a year older, and had still less furniture in his head ; but then his person and manners were more engaging. He had more wit and humour, and a turn for mimicry; and, above all, had the talent of translating other men's thoughts, which they had produced in the simple style of conversation, into the most charming language, which not only took the ear but elevated the thoughts.'

At Leyden then he pursued his studies with much ardour, acquiring a good know-

2—2

ledge of the classics, which late in life he turned to profit, in editing with success some fine editions of Catullus and other writers. He cultivated those easy manners, and that convivial vivacity which afterwards so distinguished him. When he had completed his course, he set off on a tour through Holland and part of Germany.

Returning to England in 1749, he found that an arrangement had been made for him, and it was expected that he should commence his suit to the young lady destined for his wife. Being now a young gentleman of elegant manners and of 'conversation gay and interesting,' he had, to use the phraseology of his time, no difficulty 'in carrying the fortress' already prepared to surrender. He paid many visits to Aylesbury House, and his suit prospered so rapidly that in October, 1743, they were married, as Mr. John Almon, the bridegroom's friend, tells us cautiously, 'to the apparent satisfaction of all parties.' Mrs. Mead gave the newly-married pair her house at Aylesbury, and removed to another

residence of her own in Red Lion Court,
behind St. Sepulchre's Church, where they
came occasionally to stay with her. Thus
was the married life of the pair to commence,
which was to prove a short and ill-omened
connection. Unhappily they started, as
Sterne would say, with many an ass's load of
discordant elements on their backs. The
lady was of the ripe age of thirty-two ; the
husband about twenty-two. She was a strict
dissenter ; Mr. Wilkes, in spite of all his
training, was ostentatiously a member of the
Church of England. He, however, went with
her occasionally to meetings, but ' he always
communicated ' in the orthodox church. Still,
as his friend tells us, he was not a man
likely to quarrel with a lady on the score of
religion. But the real cause of dissension
was his taste for pleasure and amusement,
the lady being of an indifferent and serious
temperament. But had she been more indulgent, her forbearance would have been
strained to the uttermost. There were other
numerous reasons for discordance. He dis-

liked the mansion in Red Lion Court;
the situation and neighbourhood were disagreeable ; he wished to reside in the fashion-
able part of the town. He soon removed this
cause of contention, by taking one of the
handsomest houses in the West End, and
launching out into all kinds of expenses.

His new house in Great George Street,
Westminster, required an expensive establishment. ' A variety of company, and splendid
dinners almost every day, were indeed such
scenes of dissipation as must be distressing to
mind that had from early life been habituated
to economy. But, what was infinitely worse,
and beyond the power of forbearance, was,
his introducing into his house a number of
juvenile, gay bacchanalians, of dissolute
manners and vulgar language. Mrs. Wilkes
remonstrated ; he retorted : she abandoned
his table, and left him to treat his guests as
he pleased.' Later Mr. Wilkes, rather un-
generously, laid the blame on the lady when
defending himself from an attack in the papers.
' I have heard some of his friends remark, that
she is perhaps the woman in the world the

most unfit for him; and the only one to whom he would not have been an uxorious husband, for he loves a domestic life; she was certainly a large fortune; but, unhappily, half as old again as Mr. Wilkes, when he married her. I have often dined with them, both in town and country. He was admired as an extremely civil and complaisant husband; rather cold, but exactly well bred: and set an example of polite and obliging behaviour in his family, which many of those who find fault with him would do well to imitate. *Her reputation is unspotted;* and she still possesses Mr. Wilkes's esteem, though not his tenderness.'*

Long after, writing to Mrs. Stafford, on March 4th, 1778, he described his marriage: ' In my nonage, to please an indulgent father, I married a woman half as old again as myself; of a large fortune—my own being also that of a gentleman. It was a sacrifice to Plutus, not to Venus. I never lived with

---

* This, though written in an assumed character, was Wilkes' own sketch of himself. He was fond of thus speaking of himself.

her, in the strict sense of the word ; nor have I seen her for nearly twenty years. I stumbled at the very threshold of the temple of Hymen.'

CHAPTER II.

WHEN a general election, in 1754, was approaching, Wilkes was encouraged to look for a seat. He was now twenty-seven years old, and, being assured that there was an opening at Berwick, he determined to try his fortune there. It was curious that he should have selected a Scotch seat, considering his later antipathies. But, as we have seen, at this time he was friendly to that nation. In his address he assured the electors that he came before them because of their ' steady attachment to the cause of liberty,' which he always had ' nearest his heart.' ' Gentlemen,' the address proceeded, ' I come here *uncorrupting*, and I promise you I shall ever be *uncorrupted*. As I never will take a bribe, so I will never offer one. . . . I have no private views : my sole ambition is to serve my country, and to contribute to the preservation of the invaluable privileges which this nation enjoys beyond any other in the world. I shall rest steadily on these principles.'

All his family were vehemently against this project, which they knew was unsuited to his means and position. His father, wife, and mother-in-law all joined in the opposition, believing that it would be his ruin, and farther tend to the destruction of all domestic peace. He was positive, went to the poll, and was defeated — obtaining 192 votes. Notwithstanding his heroic utterances as to coming there 'uncorrupting, and uncorrupted,' the contest involved him in a large outlay—reaching, it was said, to between three and four thousand pounds! These vexations and consequent embarrassments led to fresh domestic differences, and the disappointed candidate, forsaking his home, sought for sympathy and dissipation among congenial friends. It was at this time, indeed, that he seemed to have flung aside all restraints. Yet all that he could find fault with in his much-tried wife

was the neglect of his table and ' of the inferior articles of some domestic duty.' It was
characteristic, however, that a man of such
tastes, who spent his time with gay boon
companions, should excuse his absence from
home by the humdrum arrangements he found
there.

As is often common in such cases, he laid
the blame of his own defeat and disappointment on his wife, and complained ' that he
had not met that tender reception at home he
had a right to expect.' He admitted that her
behaviour on the whole had always been
' strictly moral, seriously rational and consistent.'* His own life was ' irregular, dissipated, and licentious.' He spent his time
with loose friends, and abandoned his house.
Under such conditions his neglected wife,
who had ventured on some ' reproaches,' at
last insisted on a formal separation. Mr.
Wilkes was not at all indisposed to this step,
which would restore him to his liberty; but
Mrs. Mead took the side of her daughter, and

* This, again, is Wilkes' own account, given to a
confidential friend—Almon's ' Life,' vol. i., 28.

being of so 'serious' and decent a life,
naturally wished to rescue her from so painful
a state. The arrangement was accordingly
made; but she had to sacrifice to him a large
sum, of her receiving in return a small an-
nuity of two hundred a year.

Sir C. Wentworth Dilke, in his ' Papers of
a Critic,' has warmly taken up the defence of
Wilkes in this transaction, pleading that here
was a young man married to a woman ten
years older, of strict and austere principles,
who was uncongenial to him, he, in his turn,
being all that was clever and brilliant. To
this it may be replied that had his wife been
a paragon of seventeen, the same result would
have followed. He was a rake on principle,
and with such it would be difficult for the
most accommodating of wives to live, even if
we leave out the question of his wasteful
extravagance, which would have beggared
both.

Unfortunately the sequel of this transaction
is still less to Wilkes' credit, and supports the
case of his unhappy wife. So enslaved was he
by his spendthrift tastes—and no one ever

so developed the science of spending money,
without having it, or making others pay for
him—that he took the step of trying to
snatch from his wife the pittance he had
settled upon her. Application was made to
the Courts with this view, under the guise of
a writ of *habeas corpus*, but it was refused.
As he could not have hoped to have succeeded, it was probably intended to put
pressure on her to make further sacrifices, or
to cause her annoyance. The reported case
shows the view taken by the Court of this
discreditable proceeding :

‘ *Rex* v. *Mary Mead.*—Mrs. Mead now
brought her into court. The substance of
the return was, that her husband (*having used
her very ill*) did, in consideration of *a great
sum*, which she gave him out of her separate
estate, consent to her living alone ; executed
articles of separation ; and *covenanted* (under
a large penalty) *never to disturb her*, or any
person with whom she should live ;—that
she lived with her mother, at her own earnest
desire ; and that the writ of *habeas corpus*
was taken out with a view of seizing her by

force, or some other bad purpose. The Court
held this to be a formal renunciation by the
husband of his natural right to seize her
or force her back to live with him : and they
said that any attempt of the husband to
seize her by force and violence would be
a breach of the peace. They also declared
that any attempt made by the husband to
molest her in her present return from Westminster Hall would be a contempt of the
Court ; and they told the lady she was at
full liberty to go where, and to whom, she
pleased.'*

Thus emancipated, Wilkes had now full
scope to plunge into all the enjoyments of the
town without restraint. His social gifts had
attracted to him a number of men of similar
taste, and who, indeed, might be said to be
at the head of their profession of pleasure-
seeking. They were, indeed, an edifying
company. Foremost among them, was
Thomas Potter, an extraordinary being,
who enjoyed the credit of having effectually
" poisoned his friends' morals '; Lord Sand-

* Burrowes's ' Reports.'

wich, the most notorious of *débauchés;* Sir Francis Dashwood, afterwards Lord Le Despencer; Paul Whitehead and Mr. John Hall Stevenson.

These were rakes of the first water. Wilkes was one of those characters who study pleasure, and live for pleasure, a vile, bestial principle. Potter was the son of the Archbishop of Canterbury, a depraved sensualist, and yet, strange to say, an intimate friend of Mr. Pitt's, with whom he lived on affectionate terms. Notwithstanding his epicurean tastes, he was a skilful politician, an official, and Member of the House of Commons —no doubt from his association with Mr. Pitt.

To the same set belonged Sterne (though this was a few years later), and Sterne's friend and neighbour, John Hall Stevenson, of notorious memory, whose seat was Crazy Castle, at Skelton, in Yorkshire.

There was one singular ' note ' in the professional licentiousness of this period : it was joined with a very high cultivation of mind and wit, and set off with classical adornments. These rakes and gamblers could turn elegant

verses to each other, as the occasion suggested; while their letters—such as those of
Lord March, 'Gilly' Williams, Storer, and
others—are full of a charming vivacity,
spirit, and even wit.

This opens a perplexing speculation; for
indulgence in coarse pleasures is commonly
supposed to dull the more refined tastes and
instincts.

Storer was a highly-cultivated amateur,
delighting in collecting prints and in 'Grain-
gerising'; Lord Carlisle had elegant tastes;
while Hall Stevenson possessed, at his 'Crazy
Castle,' a fine library of rare antique volumes,
chiefly French—'Bruscambilles,' and others
of that class—which his friend, the Curate
of Coxwold, made abundant use of to add
piquancy to 'Tristram Shandy.' The six
volumes of the 'New Foundling Hospital for
Wit' are filled with pleasant occasional *jeux
d'esprit*, addressed by these lively men of
pleasure to each other, showing cultivation
and elegance in the 'turn' of thought and
expression.

The most *bizarre* result of these combine 1

tastes was exhibited by an artistic society which still flourishes, viz., The Dilettante. It consisted of a number of cultivated amateurs, who wished to encourage the study of artistic antiquities. This was done by grants of money, missions to Greece and Italy, the publication of works on newly-discovered objects of art, and commissions for pictures, portraits, etc. One of their odd rules was, that any member, on his marriage, or promotion in official life, should pay the society a 'percentage' on the additional emolument that thus accrued from the lady's fortune, or salary of the office. This tax might be compounded for, in anticipation, by a fixed sum; and the books show that it was somewhat rigorously enforced, and cheerfully paid. Another regulation was, that each member should contribute his portrait to the gallery of the society; and the result of the rule was to be seen in the Thatched House Club in St. James's Street. Their home, at the present moment, is at Willis's Rooms, where are works by Sir Joshua and other good masters.*

* Sir Frederick Pollock, a member of the society, has

The society included among its leading men most of the ' fast ' men of the day, evidence of which is an extraordinary picture, still in their possession, and associated with the scandalous orgies of the Medmenham Monks. The society, in its earliest days, met at a tavern in Palace Yard, known as The King's Head, and in the large room was hung a picture of Sir Francis Dashwood, head of the order, and which he had presented to the society according to the regulation. He was portrayed in the habit of a ' Franciscan Monk,' kneeling before a nude Venus, and holding a goblet in his hand.*

Many are the traditions of this society, to have belonged to whom is one of the worst scandals in Wilkes's course. The mind that could turn a mere convivial association to such uses must have been base and depraved indeed. It only wanted hypocrisy and the Tartuffe element to make the whole complete. It seems incredible, but the spectacle actually

---

written a very interesting and agreeable account of the collection.

* This picture is still in the possession of the society.

was to be furnished of these debauchees
' rounding,' as it is called, on one of their
associates and upbraiding him with pious
horror for his offences against decency.

Mr. Wilkes, after he had quarrelled with
the 'Abbot' of the Society, wrote a description of Medmenham Abbey, in illustration of
his deceased friend Churchill's poems. ' Medmenham,' he says, ' is a very large house on
the banks of the Thames, near Marlow in
Buckinghamshire. It was formerly a convent
of Cistercian Monks. The situation is remarkably fine. Beautiful hanging woods,
soft meadows, a crystal stream, and a grove
of venerable old elms near the house, with
the retiredness of the mansion itself, made it
as sweet a retreat as the most poetical imagination could create.'

Sir Francis Dashwood, with other gentlemen to the number of twelve, rented the
abbey, and often retired thither in the sum-
mer.* Among other amusements, they had

---

* There has always been a certain mystery as to the
names of the twelve monks of Medmenham. But it has
been stated that among them were Churchill the poet,

sometimes a mock celebration of the rites of
foreign religious orders ; of the Franciscans
in particular, for the members had taken
that title from their founder, Sir Francis
Dashwood.   Whitehead was secretary and
steward to the order.   No profane eye has
dared to penetrate into the English Eleusinian
mysteries of the *chapter-room,* where the monks
assembled on all solemn occasions.

' Over the grand entrance, was the famous
inscription on Rabelais's abbey of Thelème :
Fay ce que voudras.   At the end of the
passage, over the door, was : *Aude, hospes,
contemnere opes !*   At one end of the refectory
was Harpocrates, the Egyptian god of silence ;
at the other end the goddess Angerona, that
the same duty might be enjoined to both
sexes.'

Wilkes, Robert Lloyd, Sir Francis Dashwood, Bubb
Dodington, Lords Melcombe and Orford, Paul Whitehead, Collins, Dr. Bates ; to which might be added
John Hall Stevenson, and perhaps Potter, which would
nearly fill up the number.   Sir J. Aubray was heard to
say, some forty years ago, that he had attended a few
meetings as a guest, but was thought *too young* to be
formally admitted.

In a lively novel, ' Chrysal; or the Adventures of a Guinea,' which enjoyed extraordinary popularity in the last century, the author, Charles Johnston, gave some curious sketches of the members and proceedings of the scandalous society.*

Among them, described with particularity, were Sir Francis Dashwood, Lord Orford, and Mr. Wilkes. He imputes a particular and settled design and purpose to these orgies, which was to bring religion into contempt, and with some acuteness, says that the most effectual way of silencing the occasional remonstrances of conscience is the force of ridicule applied to sacred things. In this view an elaborately sacrilegious system of the mocking and parodying all that was sacred was contrived with a horrible ingenuity, and there was set up at every corner some hideous perversion of either the texts of Scripture or the most sacred truths. And as this ribaldry

---

* Disguised under fictitious names; but the author furnished a written key to Lord Mount-Edgcumbe and others of his friends, which was printed by Davis in his "Olic."

is of exactly the same description as that found in the notorious 'Essay on Woman,' it is not unfair to presume that it was the debauched wit of our hero who was responsible for it.* No servants were employed to attend on the members; but there was a sort of second order of Probationers, who waited on the regular monks. The 'Abbot' is described as ' a person of flighty imagination who possessed a fortune that enabled him to pursue these flights, cloyed, too, with common pleasures, and ambitious of distinguishing himself among his companions. He had resolved to try if he could not strike out something new.' All members, on entering, assumed a name. Wilkes's was ' Archbishop John of Aylesbury.' Solemn rites attended the admission of the neophytes, which was carried out with great mystery and secret rites.

' John of Aylesbury' seems to have been the ' life and soul,' as it is called, of the com-

* A further proof of this is the relish and minute particularity with which Wilkes, in his notes to his friend Churchill's Poems, describes all the mottoes and other objects which were disposed about the abbey.

munity. 'He had,' says Johnston, 'such a flow of spirits that it was impossible ever to be a moment dull in his company. His wit gave charms to every subject he spoke upon ; and his humour displayed the foibles of mankind in such colours as to put folly even out of countenance. But the same vanity which had first made him ambitious of entering this society, only because it was composed of persons superior to his own rank in life, still kept him in it, though upon acquaintance he despised themselves. His spirits were often stretched to extravagance to overpower competition. His humour was debased into buffoonery, and his wit was so prostituted to the lust of applause that he would sacrifice his best friend for a scurvy jest, in which he was also assisted by a peculiar archness of disposition and an expertness in carrying his jests into execution.'

One of these practical jokes was in Mr. Wilkes's most obstreperous style. He secretly introduced a large black baboon, and shut him in a huge chest in the room where the brethren assembled for their rites. By an

ingenious arrangement he contrived that by
pulling a cord the animal should be suddenly
released.   At a critical moment of 'the in-
vocation' this was done ; and the animal,
jumping from its concealment, threw the whole
party into convulsions of terror.   All roared
out, '*The devil ! the devil !*' and fled from the
room, tumbling over each other in a style
that did little credit to such sceptics.   The
animal then leaped on Lord Orford's shoulders,
from whence it could not be dislodged.   This
exhibition turned the rage of the members on
the contriver of the joke, who, according to
the novel, was then expelled the society.*

* It is often an incident in the demagogue's course to
find him reviling some brother demagogue with whom
he had formerly been on terms of affectionate intimacy.
Wilkes and his Abbot presently fell out, and it is amusing
to find the former 'monk' giving an account of a visit
paid to his former friend's house, and ridiculing him for
the profanities with which he had set off his domain.
He says, 'I passed a day in viewing the villa of Sir
Francis Dashwood, now Lord Le Despencer, and the church
he has just built on the top of a very steep hill, for the
convenience and devotion of the town at the bottom of
it.   The word *memento* in immense letters on the steeple
surprised and perplexed me.   I could not find the *mori*,
or perhaps the other word was *meri*.'   After surveying

It has been mentioned that one of the most
extraordinary incidents in the career of these
libertines was their assumption in public of
airs of decorum. A working member of
the order was Paul Whitehead, a mediocre
poet, who left remains, published by a friend
of his, Captain Thomson, with an affectionate
memoir. The superficial reader musing on
these panegyrics, and the 'works' of the
person thus celebrated, would conceive that
this was some amiable being, not very pre-
tentious in his gifts, and unrecognised by the
world, and that his obscurity had been re-
deemed by a certain faithfulness and conscientiousness. His friend, the captain, dedicated his 'remains' to Sir F. Dashwood, now
Lord Le Despencer, F.R.S., LL.D., in a touch-
ing inscription: 'As his virtues,' says his friend,
'were better known to your lordship than to

---

the extraordinary statues and other objects set up on
the grounds, Mr. Wilkes says, ' I retired to my inn, full
of astonishment that any man should take so much pains,
and be at so great an expense, only to show a public
contempt of all decency, order, and virtue.' It was
said that Whitehead's heart was placed in the ball of
the steeple ! Hence the '*memento.*'

any other person, to whom can his compositions be addressed with so much propriety?'
This being was the secretary to the infamous
society, and Sir Francis's obsequious tool.
Churchill, also supposed to be one of the
fraternity, took special pleasure in ' gibbeting '
him :

> ' He, like a thorough, true-bred spaniel, licks
> The hand which cuffs him, and the foot which kicks,
> He fetches and he carries, blacks my shoes,
> Nor thinks it a discredit to his muse.'

And again :

> ' May I (can worse disgrace on manhood fall ?)
> Be born a Whitehead, and baptized a Paul !'

The last incident in his life was of a truly
grotesque sort.   By his will he left a precious
bequest to his patron.   After directing his
body to be opened, ' that the faculty may, if
possible, discover after I am dead, what they
seemed totally ignorant of while I was living
—the cause of my death,' a sarcastic stroke
at the doctors—he ordered his heart to be
taken out, adding : ' I give the *heart aforesaid*
to the Right Honourable Lord Le Despencer,
together with £50, to be laid out in the

purchase of a marble urn, to be placed, if
his lordship pleases, in some corner of his
mausoleum, as a memoir of my warm attachment.' Lord Le Despencer accepted the
legacy, and contrived a queer pageant, half
pagan, half religious. The urn was carried
in procession by a number of grenadiers of
the yeomanry regiment. After proceeding
through the grounds it was laid on a pillar.
An oratorio in the church with a sermon
wound up the proceedings. Later it found
its way to the steeple.

This Sir Francis Dashwood was not without his merits. He had travelled a good
deal in Italy, and was an almost fanatical
dilettante. He was well accomplished, and
could paint well. This is shown by the
frescoes on the walls of his mansion at West
Wycombe, now almost mouldered away, but
which were his work. He was credited with
plain, good sense, though he lacked application, as might be expected.

Lord March, afterwards the notorious
' Old Q.,' had his regular preacher and
chaplain, the Rev. Mr. Kidgell, of whom we

shall hear more presently.   Lord Sandwich
played in oratorios.   Churchill, Horne Tooke,
Sterne, and Dodd, offered an extraordinary
specimen of the dissipated and clever parson,
all unfrocked, more or less.

Lord Sandwich is chiefly associated with
the unfortunate incident in which Miss Ray,
the actress, lost her life ; who, as is well
known, was assassinated at the theatre by a
clergyman.   This nobleman had undoubted
abilities, and sentimental tastes and accom-
plishments.   His concerts at his house,
where the unfortunate Ray was prima and
he himself modestly took the kettle-drum,
were well attended.   He had a certain official
ability, and was almost as ugly as Wilkes,
yet more common-looking.

Churchill has sketched him in some terrible
lines :

'From his youth upwards to the present day,
  When vices more than years have mark'd him gray,
  When riotous excess, with wasteful hand
  Shakes life's frail glass, and hastes each ebbing sand,
  Unmindful from what stock he drew his birth,
  Untainted with one deed of real worth,

Lothario, holding honour at no price,
Folly to folly added, vice to vice,
Wrought sin with greediness, and sought for shame
With greater zeal than good men work for fame.'

Wilkes's connection with Aylesbury had found him friends of a more reputable sort, among whom was Lord Temple, who has been drawn by Macaulay in the most virulent and, it must be said, prejudiced colours.

'The head of the Grenvilles,' he writes in his essay on Lord Chatham, 'was Richard, Earl Temple. His talent for administration and debate were of no high order. But his great possessions, his turbulent and unscrupulous character, his restless activity, and his skill in the most ignoble tactics of faction, made him one of the most formidable enemies that a Ministry could have.' And again in grosser terms, 'Those who knew his habits tracked him as men track a mole. It was his nature to grub underground. Wherever a heap of dirt was flung up, it might be suspected that he was at work in some foul crooked labyrinth below.'

We are familiar with Macaulay's anti-

thetic method, and the exhaustive method
of research which enabled him to declare in
thousands of instances alike that 'no man
was ever more,' etc., and yet 'no man was
ever less,' etc.　Lord Temple, no doubt,
was fond of working the threads of political
intrigue, but this went little beyond writing
or inspiring anti-Ministerial pamphlets; and
he tried to get back to power by the various
devices in favour with statesmen out of
office.　But he was a fond husband, a firm,
affectionate, and sincere friend, a man of
good abilities, who was treated ill by the
various parties.　It is, at least, by good
natured actions that we can track him in
his relations with Wilkes, and not by those
' heaps of dirt' alluded to by the great
historian.

This nobleman was Lord - Lieutenant of
Bucks, and took an interest in the concerns
of his county.　Among ·other plans he was
eager to raise a militia regiment, in which
he was supported with much ardour by
Wilkes.　There was a good deal of opposition, but the scheme was successfully carried

out, Sir Francis Dashwood being appointed colonel and Wilkes lieutenant-colonel. Here for many years Wilkes found himself at home, taking delight in his military duties, and greatly liked by his men, and popular with the officers and country gentlemen from his social gifts. As Lord Temple said on his dismissal, he had endeared himself to all; and Gibbon, who was prejudiced against him, bears this remarkable testimony to his gifts and vices. In the month of September, 1762, he tells us:

'Colonel Wilkes dined at our mess. I scarcely ever met with a better companion. He has inexhaustible spirits, infinite wit and humour, and a great deal of knowledge, although profligate in principle as in practice, his life stained with every vice, and his conversation full of blasphemy and indecency. These morals he glories in; for shame is a weakness he has long since surmounted. He told us himself that at this time of public discussion *he was resolved to make his fortune.* This proved to be a very debauched day. We drank a good deal both after dinner and supper; and when at last he had retired, Sir Thomas Worsely and some others broke into his room and made him drink a bottle of claret in bed.'

When Sir Francis Dashwood resigned the command of the regiment, Wilkes became its colonel.

On this double promotion, Dashwood to the peerage and he himself to be colonel, Wilkes wrote his congratulations:

'*To Sir F. Dashwood.*

'June 17, 1762.

' DEAR SIR,

'I was three times the last week to pay my respects to you in Hanover Square. . . . Your letter (to the regiment) is highly honourable to us all, but I am sure deserves my most grateful acknowledgments. It shall always be my endeavour to merit the obliging things you was so kind to say of me, and I shall esteem myself peculiarly happy if I can in any way alleviate the loss which the whole corps must sensibly feel. I feast my mind with the joy of promotion, and hope to

indemnify myself there for the noise and non-
sense here.' *

This intimacy with the Temples, Dash-
woods, Sandwichs' and other men of mark,
and his own gradual advance in the social
scale—he was now Colonel of Militia, Fellow
of the Royal Society, and had served as
High Sheriff in 1754—led him to turn
his eyes persistently to the chances of the
political world. He was eager to seize the
first opening of getting into Parliament, which
seemed to offer more difficulties in his case
than are usually found in that of a young
man of such talent and good connections.

The election of 1757, which was to bring
him into Parliament, also opened for him
a chance of patronage and advancement, in a
rather fortunate way. His friend Potter was
member for Aylesbury, in Buckinghamshire,
and, having been appointed Vice Treasurer
of Ireland, had to vacate his seat. At the
same time, Sir Robert Henly, who had been
appointed to another lucrative office, left

* MS. Brit. Mus.

a borough—that of Bath—open. It was
contrived, with much secrecy and plotting,
that Mr. Pitt, who sat for an obscure place
called Okehampton, should be returned for
Bath, and that Potter should take his place at
Okehampton. Thus was Aylesbury left to
Mr. Wilkes.

' The business,' we are told, ' was very
adroitly managed. It may be said,' adds
Almon, who had it from Wilkes, ' with the
strictest truth, that this affair, from its com-
mencement to its conclusion, cost Mr. Wilkes
upwards of seven thousand pounds—for he
was the person who paid all—to obtain one
seat in Parliament, and that for only three
years. He might, at that time, have purchased a borough for the whole septennial
period, for less money.'

This foolish and desperate business had no
doubt one compensation, for it brought him
into a sort of community of interest with Mr.
Pitt, as all three were concerned in this
chasse croisée. But the difficulties that
oppressed him in consequence, and the
enormous cost of the transaction, drove him

to the most serious extremity for money. His friend Potter supplied him with a fatal mode of extrication, by introducing him to Sylva,* and other accommodating Jews, from whom he secured advances on annuities, and by other ruinous modes of raising money. Characteristically, Mr. Wilkes laid the blame of these embarrassments on his friend, who, he said later, was ' plunged much deeper than me in annuities, and gave me the worst advice.' Such reproaches are common incidents in boon companionship.

Wilkes' characteristic declaration to Gibbon at mess will be recollected : ' he was determined to make his fortune ;' a purpose that flowed with strict logic from his fixed determination to secure all the pleasures that life offered. This could not be carried out without the possession of money or place, which he lost not a moment in trying to secure. Within a week of his election, Mr. Wilkes

---

* It should be added, however, that Sylva's claims were discharged by public subscription, made some years later.

had hurried to St. James's Square, to offer
his services or devotion to the Minister, and
a few days later he, as it were, formally
registered his fealty and hopes of future pretensions in a singular letter, the meaning of
which cannot be mistaken. The underlined
passages will be noted :

' *Wilkes to Pitt.*
                    ' Aylesbury,
                        ' July 14th, 1757.

' The day after my election, I had the
honour of paying my respects in St. James's
Square. I was desirous of so early an
opportunity of saying how greatly I wish to
be numbered among those who have the highest esteem and veneration for Mr. Pitt. I
am very happy now to contribute more than
my warmest wishes for the support of his
wise and excellent measures, and my ambition
will ever be to have *my Parliamentary conduct
approved by the ablest Minister, as well as the
first character of the age.* I live in the hope
of doing my country some small service, at
least ; and I am sure the only certain way of

doing any, is *by a steady support of your measures.* I beg leave to assure you that *I shall never depart from these sentiments,* and shall always endeavour *to distinguish myself with the most entire zeal* and attention. Sir,

'Your most devoted, humble servant,

'J. WILKES.'

Nothing could be clearer and more unmistakable than this fulsome appeal. To this tone of flattery, however, the great minister was well accustomed. This may be considered the patriot's first formal step in politics, which he took with much promptitude and decision.

CHAPTER III.

ONE of the most curious surprises in this career is our finding this prime 'rake' of a sudden transformed into the political *littérateur*.

This taste is unusual in the case of professed men of pleasure, who can ill spare the time and study necessary to pursue the niceties of composition. The difference between his day and ours must not, however, be forgotten. A vigorous trenchant pen was then what a vigorous trenchant tongue is now. The speech did little work, because reporting was imperfect, or did not exist at all; but the pamphlet, the article, the 'address,' and the poem—these were read greedily, and were certain of good circulation.

Wilkes soon found that he had the gift of carrying on political warfare with his pen.

But what led him more directly to adopt these methods was the acquaintance he made with a few writers—some of mark, others attached to Grub Street.

Belonging to the former class were Churchill and Smollett; to the latter, Churchill's friend, Robert Lloyd, Dr. Armstrong, Bonnell Thornton, and a few others. Of these Robert Lloyd had been educated at Westminster School, where also Churchill, Bonnell Thornton, and other promising lads had been scholars. Later, he had become an usher in the school, while his friend Churchill, who had taken Orders, became a curate in the district. The pair, though having little to live on beyond the pittance furnished by their respective vocations, were addicted to loose pleasures, which they followed with an almost frantic ardour. Lloyd appears to have been the prompter of Churchill's excesses, who soon became bankrupt, and abandoned his wife and his profession.

They then both adopted ' literature ' as a profession—much as a spendthrift in the lower classes, when he has spent his last shilling, enlists in a regiment.

It is curious to find that, as in Wilkes' case, the blame of this *débacle* is laid at the door of the wife and his 'ill-considered marriage' —her 'imprudence kept pace with her husband's.'

Wilkes became acquainted with this pair of *viveurs*, and joined in the round of debauch. We are told, on the authority of his friend, that ' Mr. Lloyd was mild and amiable in private life, of gentle manners, and very engaging in conversation. He was an excellent scholar, and an easy, natural poet. His peculiar excellence was the dressing up of an old thought in a new, neat, and trim manner. He was contented to scamper round the foot of Parnassus on his little Welsh pony, which seems never to have tired.'

But it was to Churchill that Wilkes was early drawn, by the most affectionate regard and sympathy. He made his acquaintance in an odd way. One Armstrong, a military doctor, with literary tastes, had published a complimentary poem, addressed to Wilkes, whom he styled ' gay Wilkes,' and in which he attacked Churchill.

Wilkes's attention was thus at once drawn to Churchill, and he sought his acquaintance forthwith, disdaining the incense thus offered to him.

Smollett was working on the *Critical Review*, and accepted Wilkes' overtures to co-operate with him in ' a league, offensive and defensive.' ' Nay,' adds the novelist, in a letter to him, ' I consider myself already a contracting party, and have recourse to the assistance of my allies.' The novelist found that his friend was likely to have extraordinary and increasing influence with the ruling powers, and the sworn follower of Mr. Pitt was likely to be a useful ally. When, in 1759, Dr. Johnson's famous black servant was ' pressed ' for the navy, Smollett wrote: ' You know what matter of animosity the said Johnson has against you, and I dare say you will desire no other opportunity of resenting it than that of laying him under an obligation. He was humble enough to desire my assistance on this occasion, though he and I were never cater-cousins; and I gave him to understand that I would make application to my friend

Mr. Wilkes, who, perhaps, by his interest with Mr. Hay and Mr. Elliot, might be able to procure the discharge of his lacquey.'

What the mysterious ' matter of animosity ' that Johnson had against Wilkes at so early a period was, it is difficult now to determine ; for it could not have been aroused by a trifling pleasantry uttered by the gay Wilkes.* Wilkes, good-naturedly, applied to an influential friend at the Admiralty, and was successful ; and Johnson, as we see, was content to accept the obligation. In consequence Smollett assured Wilkes he was ' his, with the most inviolable esteem and attachment.'

Later, when the *Review* was threatened with a prosecution for an attack on Admiral Brown, Smollett again appealed to his friend to interfere, adding significantly that, ' if the affair cannot be compromised, we intend to kick up a dust and die hard. In a word, if

* On a passage in Johnson's 'Grammar,' prefixed to the 'Dictionary,' 'It seldom, perhaps never, begins any but the first syllable,' Wilkes quoted some instances to prove the falsity of Johnson's remark. 'The author of this observation must be a man of quick appre-hension, and of a most compre-hensive genius.'

the foolish admiral has any regard to his own character, he will be quiet.'

The Ministry of Lord Bute, now prime favourite, and the consequent odium which attended both the King and his favourite, or rather vizier, furnished the most tempting opportunity for the talents of the pamphleteer and the lampoonist. This is a well-known and oft-told tale. For Wilkes, it was exactly the opportunity he desired. He was much pressed for money. A dissolution was announced for the spring of the following year, 1761, and the election was again to tax his resources. He had, however, duly 'prepared' the borough for a contest.

'Every fortnight he invited select parties of his constituents to dinner at his house, whom he entertained with the greatest hospitality ; and he paid the most polite and constant attention to all the inhabitants. Thus his election was tolerably secure ; but not without the usual *gratifications* to those who were accustomed to expect it.'

No wonder he used 'frequently to remark to his friends, that he never would advise any

gentleman to represent the town he lived at;
for his constituents would be a heavy and
perpetual incumbrance on his table and his
cellar.'

He was elected without opposition.

This idea of a ' favourite ' has always been
odious to the nation, and the odium which
attended Bute was further intensified by the
unmistakable partiality with which all offices
and honours were lavished on the favourite's
countrymen—the abuse which so excited the
ire of Johnson during his later life.

It seems likely enough that what more
directly inflamed Wilkes was the direct interference with his advancement from the Scotch
influence, which was not only hostile to
himself personally, but operated by re-
moving his patrons from power. This was
the more exasperating, as he might fairly look
for some sort of provision, such as his friend
Potter had obtained. Pitt's brother-in-law,
Temple, was his warmest friend; and as Grenville and Temple were Pitt's colleagues, from
the joint interest of the trio he might hope
much. It will be interesting now to follow

his steps in the direction of that 'taking care of himself' which was the first object of Mr. John Wilkes, pursued steadily and without flagging through his whole life. He seemed to hold that as real war was bound to support war, so patriotism must support the patriot, and complete success was destined to crown his efforts. That he had obtained a promise of advancement from Mr. Pitt seems likely, as we find him in a letter written three or four years later reminding him that ' it was his pride to have Mr. Pitt his patron and friend.' His exertions at this time were directed to this one aim.

So diligently did he apply himself to the cultivation of this interest, that in the year of the death of the King, in 1760, we find him applying for place on no less than *three* openings! Little objection could be made on the score of character, as three of this Medmenham fraternity, Lord Sandwich, Sir Francis Dashwood, and Mr. Potter, were to be heaped with honours, and occupied high offices of state.

In 1760 the Embassy at Constantinople

had just fallen vacant, owing to the resignation of Sir J. Porter, and Wilkes boldly applied for it. It was 'a situation perfectly suited to his wishes, as it would put him out of the reach of disagreeable applications of all kinds.' He found reason to suppose, however, that his success in this matter was prevented by Scotch interference, Lord Bute being probably displeased at the channel through which Mr. Wilkes's request came—which was, through Mr. Legge, to the Duke of Newcastle.

Mr. Wilkes also thought that Mr. Pitt, who was at this time the Secretary of State, showed him some neglect in the matter ; but this suspicion does not seem so well founded as the former. As their brother, Mr. Henry Grenville, who had already been in the diplomatic service, was a candidate, Lord Temple and Mr. Pitt naturally secured the place for him. Nothing daunted, Wilkes in the following year tried his fortune again. ' It was thought that Canada would be restored to England during the negotiations for peace, and the Government of that great province immediately caught the attention of Mr.

Wilkes, who mentioned it to his friend, Lord Temple ;* and it is certain that, had the negotiation taken a favourable turn, and peace been the consequence, he would have been appointed to this honourable situation, for both Lord Temple and Mr. Pitt gave him the most flattering assurances.'

This idea of a foreign governorship was before him for many years, even after his great struggle with Ministers had set in. He no doubt fancied that by making himself ' a thorn in their side ' they would be glad to get him out of the country. When the Rockingham Ministry were in power, he renewed his solicitations, but fruitlessly,†

---

* Hume was appointed secretary at the English Embassy in Paris. Dr. Douglas was eagerly expecting promotion. Macpherson was another protégé. Ramsay, a Scotch painter, received all the Court patronage.

† In a letter to Horne, he wrote : 'As to the Rockingham Administration, I do not owe a pardon to them, although I warmly solicited it during the whole time of their power. Soon after they came into employment, I wished to have gone in a public character to Constantinople.' And in a letter from Paris to Mr. Cotes in 1764, ' If they ' (the Ministry) ' would send me ambassador to Constantinople, it is all I should wish.' And again in 1765,

all which seems incomprehensible, for it is
unlikely that Wilkes would have aimed at such
high offices, without some serious encouragement; and yet the idea of sending out an un-
tried, inexperienced, and debauched young man
as ambassador or governor seems preposterous.

But however this may have been, the change
in the political situation that came with the accession of the new King in 1760 showed him
that his hopes of embassies and governor-
ships were all the idlest of dreams. No
Ministry dared now to venture on such an
appointment. That Mr. Pitt's encouragement
had been of a substantial kind, is shown by
yet another attempt of Wilkes to secure place,
made in the same year. He wrote to his
patron limiting his desires modestly to what
an Irish patriot once styled 'an emolumentary
situation' at home. He would be satisfied
with the Board of Trade, and he thus appealed

'If I am to give my opinion, Constantinople is by far
the most eligible.' In a letter from Paris, dated October
13, 1765, he says: 'I am still in the same idea as to
Constantinople.' And in one from Paris, dated July
20, 1766, 'I wished to have gone to Constantinople. I
would go to Quebec, and perhaps I might be found in no
mean way useful there.'

to his patron : ' May I for a few moments draw
your attention from the interests of your
country to the concerns of an individual
whose pride it is to have Mr. Pitt his patron
and friend ? I do not mean to be importunate,
or to cause the least embarrassment ; but to
submit to you every wish I have, and every
desire I feel, entirely acquiescing in your ideas
of the propriety of what I am going to
mention.

'I am very desirous of a scene of business
in which I might usefully, I hope, to the
public, employ my time and attention. . . .
I wish the Board of Trade could better state
a place in which I could be of any service.
. . . among all the chances and changes of
the political world, *I will never have any obligation in a parliamentary way but to Mr. Pitt
and his friends.* May I take the liberty of
hinting that if the thing he proposed be
thought fit and proper, it might take place
in the interval between the two Parliaments ?'
There is here again the tone of obsequious
devotion, and also of confidence, which shows
that the writer might reasonably hope to be

gratified by what he calls ' some scene of business ' which would provide for him. However, this application brought nothing.

It is scarcely a surprise to find that he began to think that Mr. Pitt was rather cold in pressing his interest; but it is likely enough that it was considered that Mr. Wilkes had done little or no service to entitle him to reward. Had he now been suitably provided for, it is likely enough that the turbulent Wilkes might never have given trouble, and ' Wilkes and Liberty ' never have been joined in one cry. On the other hand, such turbulent, intrepid spirits rarely accommodate themselves to the dull current of official life, and he might likely enough, at this early period of his life, have fallen out with his colleagues. But in aid of the former supposition is the fact that, when late in life he found a chance opening, no one showed himself more eager to be a placeman, or, when in office, behaved with more order and decorum.

These various unsuccessful attempts are mentioned in anticipation. For many years Wilkes fondly clung to the idea that ' some-

thing would be done for him.' Nay, it will
be seen that long after, even when *au prises*
with the Ministry, he was still open to such
propitiation.

This is somewhat disheartening for admirers of what is called 'pure patriotism.' But
where the patriot lives for pleasure, it is difficult to join a stoical self-denial with unruly
Capuan indulgence.

One of the first Ministers to be discarded
by Lord Bute was Mr. Legge, who was a
warm friend of Wilkes, and who the latter
insisted was supported in but a lukewarm way
by Pitt and the Duke of Newcastle. In
October these two Ministers had to follow
him into retirement. They had urged that
the war with Spain should be prosecuted, but
being opposed by Lord Bute, gave in their
resignation. Wilkes seized on the occasion to publish a pamphlet, which had
extraordinary success, and which he entitled,
'Observations on the Papers relative to the
Rupture with Spain.' It was a vindication of
his friends—Mr. Pitt and Lord Temple; and
exposed the folly, cowardice, and imbecility

of the Ministry, in losing the opportunity of reducing the power of Spain so far as never to become formidable. A good and telling pamphlet was a regular element in political warfare, and often did excellent service. Now the political pamphlet is extinct, and falls as flat as does the prologue before an old comedy. This appeared in January, 1762, and it is said that he was assisted in its composition by Lord Temple. It was attributed to many writers.*

* A pleasant instance of Wilkes' humour, not untinctured, however, with some malice, is associated with this publication. A report was circulated that it was the work of the worthy Dr. Douglas, later Bishop of Salisbury. This ecclesiastic, being one of the Scotch 'division,' was much annoyed at the rumour, because, as he frankly confessed, 'it would be prejudicial to his interests.' Wilkes, meeting a friend in the Park, said he heard that Dr. Douglas had written it. He was now implored to give up his authority, so as 'effectually to stop the progress of a report which, if at first propagated only wantonly, will, I fear, if not traced to its source, in the end have the same bad effects as if it had come from the most determined malice.' Wilkes must have been much tickled at this, and wrote back gravely in this strain : 'I am entirely satisfied with your authentic assurances on this subject, and on every occasion will contradict so groundless a report. There is not a man

Wilkes, having thus lost all his friends in the Cabinet, found himself without the slightest prospect of advancement. He had made an attempt to put himself in communication with the favourite, having attended his levee ' with an intention of speaking to him;' but after being kept waiting two hours, went away. It was not unnatural that he should have found himself gradually forced into an attitude of hostility to the favourite. Apart from his behaviour to his friends and patrons, he was disgusted with the partiality now introduced, which bestowed all patronage on the lucky countrymen of the Minister. The Homes, Mallochs, Smolletts, Adamses, and others, were all taken into pay and service. It is not uncharitable to suppose that Wilkes was inflamed by the largesse bestowed on this tribe, and who, it must be said, provoked the war, by turning on their former friends.

---

in this country who more honours your superior literary abilities than I do ; or more warmly wishes, for the dignity of our Church, to see them rewarded in an eminent and distinguished manner.' There is a pleasant sarcasm in all this, as he takes care to show clearly that he understood the reason of the clergyman's nervousness.

It was thus that the author of ' Peregrine Pickle' had been his most eager ally. We have seen how he had taken his side against Johnson; and this feeling found vent in the following effusion :

' My warmest regard, affection, and attachment, you have long ago secured ; my secrecy you may depend upon. When I presume to differ from you in any point of opinion, I shall always do it with diffidence and deference. Meanwhile I must beg leave to trouble Mr. Wilkes with another packet, which he will be so good as to consecrate at his leisure. That he may continue to enjoy his happy flow of spirits, and proceed through life with a full sail of prosperity and reputation, is the wish, the hope, and the confident expectation, of his much obliged, humble servant.'

The homage which ingratitude usually pays to decency, follows the stages of a gradual and progressive change ; and the person who from motives of interest or dislike wishes to shake off the sense of obligation usually takes the trouble to proceed by steps, shading off his behaviour, as it were, allowing indifference to ripen into offence. Few changes of this kind, however, have been made so coarsely as this of Smollett's. The effusive protest, just quoted, had been uttered in March, 1762, and within nine months we find Smollett writing of his friend in this strain :

'I would ask if common honesty can reside in the breast which is devoted to falsehood and dissimulation ; if one virtue of humanity can warm the breast which swells with perfidy, with hatred, and unprovoked revenge? Or if the duties of a good citizen can ever be performed by the hired voluntary instrument of sedition ? No! Such should not escape unpunished; he does not deserve to breathe the free air of heaven, but ought to be exiled from every civilized society.'

Smollett had by this time disposed of his pen to the Minister; but though the attack should not have come from a friend, it was directed against a paper quite as scurrilous from the hand of Wilkes, who had begun to contribute to a paper called *The Monitor.**

* He seems to have written eight papers in all : Nos. 340, 358, 373, 376, 378, 379, and 380. See *North Briton*, vol. iii., p. 53, note.

The two numbers, those of May 22 and June 12, are conceived in the most offensive strain, and deal with but one subject, ' King's Favourites.'　In the first, a degrading picture is given of the 'King of Saxony's subjection to Count Bruhl'; in the second, that of ' Louis XV. to the Pompadour.' It might indeed be said that these are more objectionable than the famous ' No. 45,' but it shows that Wilkes had been deeply engaged in this sort of controversy before he had undertaken *The North Briton.*　Not so well known is it that for these two numbers written by him the printers were, later, taken up and cast into prison.

To this conspicuous instance of ingratitude Wilkes was indebted for all the exciting incidents which brought him his reputation. The scurrilous, venomous attack on him had appeared in a paper called *The Briton,* specially founded to support the Court and Bute party. It bore the Royal Arms conspicuously on its front, and Smollett had been entrusted with its direction. The first number appeared on May 29, 1762. Wilkes,

we are told, was ' incensed ' at the attacks of
this mercenary print upon himself and his
friends, and determined to found a paper to
oppose it. Accordingly, on June 5, *The
North Briton*, more celebrated for its single
number, ' No. 45,' made its appearance.

CHAPTER IV.

PARTNERSHIP WITH CHURCHILL.

THE paper was originally written in the assumed character of a Scot, whose praises of Lord Bute, and arguments for the advance of his countrymen, were intended to have an ironical cast. This was soon found too cumbrous a piece of literary mechanism, and after a few numbers it was abandoned for a more trenchant mode of attack. It has been often repeated that *The North Briton* was scarcely of sufficient importance to have excited the commotion it did, and that it would have been more prudent to have treated it with contempt. But the truth is, as we read it now, it is found to be a very stirring, vigorous and dangerous opponent, written with much pungency, wit, and even vivacity. This may be imagined, when it is stated that

Wilkes had found so valuable a coadjutor as Charles Churchill, who contributed not only his prose but also his verse. Wilkes was often absent, and eventually the whole burden of the paper fell upon Churchill. He must at least have written half of the numbers, and, as Mr. Forster says, 'wherever it shows the coarse, broad mark of sincerity, there seems to us the trace of his hand.' The correspondence between them during the progress of the paper shows Wilkes to be full of an unbounded admiration for his friend's powers, and his gratitude for his assistance corresponds with his generous appreciation, which certainly was beyond the merits of the work.* He is perpetually calling him 'not to forget Saturday,' and the next number; and everything Churchill (who seems to require these constant stimulants) sends is received with an affectionate delight and unbounded gratitude. Thus, on June 15, he wrote from Winchester :

---

* These letters between Churchill and Wilkes, lately added to the stores of the British Museum, were of course unseen by my late friend, Mr. John Forster, when he wrote his essay on Churchill.

'As the devil would have it, no contrivance of time would answer till now to send you *The North Briton.* Pray keep your excellent complaints to the archbishop, etc., for an entire paper, with all the pomp of quotations, etc., from the prayers.' He then asks him to consult some lawyers, 'for fear I have got too near the pillory. As to this number, add, subtract, multiply and divide it as you like.'

It is shown by these letters that Churchill had been recently initiated into the Medmenham fraternity. In this month he was expected on a visit at the Abbey. 'Next Monday,' writes his friend, 'we meet at Medmenham.' On this occasion he was not able to attend, but he shows in a letter full of coarse and even shameless allusions that he was more than qualified to join in the orgies. As to the paper, he said he 'had not wrote a letter of it, according to my usual maxims of putting everything off till the last. But you may be certain,' he adds, 'of its being done in time. I have the cause too much at heart to let it be out of my head.'

He then explained that he was reformed in his disorderly conduct, having settled down with a new connection. In reply, his friend banters him, saying that he was not at all pleased with the news. ' Now you are so reformed, how I should have relished you ! Perhaps it might have caught, and I might have been converted by you—the first-fruits of your ministry. How you would have exulted ! We have never yet had a St. Charles. Already I honour you more than St. Andrew, St. David, or St. Denis, or any saint but St. George, whom I honour beyond all the rabble that people call the third heaven ' — allusions to the Medmenham hagiology, where saints' names were profanely adopted by the members. We find Wilkes ardently prompting him to ridicule the bishops. ' I could hear your hints in the post-chaise about the thanksgiving of my Lords Bishops. How droll it would appear to the regiment when I open your letter and show them a form of prayer, etc.' No. 8 of *The North Briton* was an attack on Lord Bute, on the text of Mortimer, a favourite

form with Wilkes, and often handled by him,
and reiterated in rather wearisome fashion.

A redeeming feature in Wilkes's nature was
his devotion to this friend, and all through
their interesting interchange of letters this
was shown with most affectionate partiality. Everything Churchill did or wrote
seemed to be of the best. The coming of
Churchill to dine or to stay was looked
forward to as to some gala day. But when
Churchill proposed dedicating his new eclogue
to his friend, the latter, in a tumult of gratitude, wrote to him : ' I am beyond imagination proud that the eclogue is to be inscribed
to me. I desire all mankind to know that I
am honoured by your friendship. I live to
merit it.' Still, the other, absorbed in his
pleasures, showed some neglect. ' You and
Lloyd are the most faithless of men,' wrote
Wilkes in amiable reproach, ' and more
fickle than any woman. You have managed
The North Briton incomparably. You ride
that fierce steed with the truest spirit and
judgment.' Which again shows that the real
inspiration and direction of the paper, Wilkes

being so much away from town, was that of
Churchill. An extraordinary incident now
showed that the Government could venture to
intimidate this dauntless journalist.

‘Oct. 25.

‘ Lieutenant-Colonel Barrie, the scalper,
is coming here to-day. You guess for what
purpose Barrie is sent. All eyes will be
on me. I will not give up an inch of the
pass to him. I am impatient to see our
names together in print, and would have the
world know I have the happiness of being
loved by Mr. Churchill.’

By December the attacks of the paper had
grown so daring that the printer grew alarmed.
‘ I wish,’ wrote Wilkes, ‘ you would learn to
write a good hand. Nature’s chief master-
piece is writing well, and you are micro-
scopical. Mr. Bindley only should print you.
I have seen Leach, whose printer, Peter Cock,
had the terrors of the Lord of the Dale so
strong before him that he has fallen ill to
avoid printing the paper. Kearsly, however,
has got it done. I passed three hours to-day

in Pitt's bedchamber at Hayes.   He talks as
you write, as no other man ever did or could.'

' Why will you not let me see you or hear
from you ?   I had rather you would come and
abuse me for hobbling prose, than stay away and
give me immortality in the poem I long to see.
I dine alone to-day, and wish much for you.'

' I wish you would breakfast here to-morrow
to correct Saturday's *North Briton;* there is
combustibility enough in it.'

' As I find *The North Briton* has deviated
into the primrose paths of downright poetry,
I shall leave him to pursue that sweet track
till Saturday se'nnight, when I shall bring
him back to the dull hobbling road of insipid
prose.   The conducting *The North Briton*
through this sweet poetical country belongs
to you, the sovereign of it.   I have read
your verses over fifty times with rapture.'

It seems evident that the partners were
all along trying to provoke the Ministers into
taking some such violent action as was
attempted later, and Wilkes was preparing in
advance, even to the possibility of having to
withdraw from the kingdom.   In view of a

like contingency he thus generously provided
for his friend.

On March 8th he wrote :—' I am impatient to see you, and to submit to you my
feeble productions. I have left you, and
am got over by Bute, who has converted me.
and I have accordingly dedicated to him in
the highest strains of love.' And a few days
later :—' I have ordered in all the straggling
parties of General Churchill, which had
Flexney at their tail. The contributions
they have levied on the public will amount
to £120. Let me beg you not to draw on
Flexney, but draw on me for any sum whatever to what extent you will, and give it a
few days after date ; I will pay it. You have
me in everything warmly yours. I am settling
my affairs that we may neither of us want
money in the other kingdom—of France, not
of Heaven. Again, my dear Churchill, draw
for any sum you will ; you may have it at a
few days' notice, as you choose. I am more
than I can express.'

These impending dangers did not, however,
affect his spirits. ' You will receive by to-

morrow's coach, directed to you (but save
some for Saturday), three dozen of Rhenish,
of which you are unworthy. First—*lie*,
because you said I should certainly *lie* at
Walsh's last night; whereas I lay here.
Second—*lie*, because you said I should be
drunk with him that very night; whereas I
was sober here alone—thou duplicate, com-
plicate of—— I have only time to tell you
and to ascertain of the Post-office what kind
of man you are to my sartin nolidge.'

The attack on the Scotch, 'A Prophecy of
Famine,' which so enchanted Wilkes, appeared in January, 1763, and had the effect
of enormously increasing the antagonism to
the intrepid pair. This bitterness inflamed all
the Scotch against them. But, as if unsatis-
fied with such dangerous enemies, they were
to rouse another—Hogarth, who, one of the
jovial coterie, had even been on a visit at
Medmenham. Early in the year Wilkes was
with his regiment at Winchester, guarding
French prisoners, when he received notice
from a friend that the painter was on the eve
of publishing a caricature in which he, with

Pitt, Lord Temple, and Churchill, were to be ridiculed. The meaning of this Wilkes later expounded in bitter terms.*

'In 1762 the Scottish Minister took a variety of hirelings into his pay, some of whom were gratified with pensions, others with places and reversions. Mr. Hogarth was only made serjeant-painter to his Majesty, as if it was meant to insinuate to him that he was not allowed to paint anything but the wainscot of the royal apartments. The term means no more than house-painter, and the nature of the post confined him to that business.'

This was, of course, but an outburst of spleen. Wilkes sent to remonstrate with Hogarth, and was assured that he only intended attacking the two Ministers. A reply was sent, warning the painter that if Wilkes's friends were attacked, he would, on the following Saturday, revenge this blow by sending a paper to *The North Briton;* 'that is,' he adds, 'if he thought the proprietors would insert what he sent.' Hogarth disdained this appeal. *The Times,* as the print

* 'Letters to and from Mr. Wilkes,' 1769.

6—2

was called, appeared on Sept. 9, with figures
of Churchill and Wilkes introduced.

'Hogarth has begun the attack,' wrote
Wilkes to his friend on that day. 'I shall
attack him in hobbling prose. You will, I
hope, in mostly verse.'

In a fortnight, on September 21, appeared
Wilkes' onslaught, which spared nothing, and
ranged over the artist's life, who, he said, had
failed in every art but low grotesque. Here
are some choice specimens of this bludgeon-
like style :

' After " Marriage à-la-mode " the public
wished for a series of prints of a " Happy
Marriage." Hogarth made the attempt, but
the rancour and malevolence of his mind
made him very soon turn with envy and disgust from objects of so pleasing contempla-
tion, to dwell and feast a bad heart on others
of a hateful cast, which he pursued, for he
found them congenial, with the most unbating
zeal, and unrelenting gall.'

' *Gain* and *vanity* have steered his little
light bark quite through life. What a despic-
able part has he acted with regard to the

society of *arts and sciences!* How shuffling
has his conduct been to the whole body of
artists! There is at this hour scarcely a
single man of any degree of merit in his own
profession, with whom he does not hold a
professed enmity. His insufferable vanity
will never allow the least merit in another,
and no man of a liberal turn of mind will
ever condescend to feed his pride with the
gross and fulsome praise he expects. To this
he joins no small share of jealousy.'

He then shows how the painter had ridiculed
the Guards in their ' March to Finchley,'
dedicating it to the King of ' Prusia,' that
' it might be as offensive as possible to his
sovereign.' We shall see what was Hogarth's
retort.

In No. 12, Johnson was attacked in gross
terms, on the score of his pension; definitions
being extracted from his ' Dictionary ' in a very
scurrilous but amusing style. Among these
was the definition of a favourite as ' a mean
wretch, whose whole business is by any
means to please.' That of a pension, on the
same authority, was ' an allowance made to

anyone without an equivalent,' and ' paid to the state hireling for treason to his country ;' a ' slave of a state, hired to obey his master.' No wonder the lexicographer always spoke of ' Jack Wilkes ' with horror and dislike.

The attacks on the favourite, however, never relaxed for a moment. Nor was the King spared, nor his Majesty's mother. It was not surprising, therefore, that by December, 1762, the town began to expect that some step would be taken to crush the ' libeller.' In No. 27, he wrote :

' Almost every man I meet looks strangely on me—some industriously avoid me—others pass me silent—stare—and shake their heads. Those few, those very few, who are not afraid to take a lover of his country by the hand, congratulate me on my being alive and at liberty. They advise circumspection—for, they do not know—they cannot tell—but— the times—Liberty is precious—Fines—Im-prisonment—Pillory—not indeed that they themselves—but—then—in truth—God only knows——'

But the editors did not find their course

quite smooth, and the course of the paper was to be marked by some curious incidents.

The Government had not the courage to grapple with Wilkes and Churchill, but they ventured to deal with smaller prey. The two papers on Historical Favourites, which had appeared in *The Monitor* of May and June, seem comparatively inoffensive. Some pressure had indeed been attempted on *The North Briton ;* for on November 26th the writer speaks of ' an unexpected disappointment, arising from the fears of a printer, who trembled at the thoughts of imprisonment, and had smarted under a severe private reprimand. *The North Briton* will never tamely give up the glorious cause in which it is engaged ; it will never be drawn away by the arts of a subtle man, nor intimidated by the menaces of a wicked Minister ; it will always be ready to stand forth for its king and country.'* But in November Lord Halifax issued a warrant against Arthur

---

* These manful words seem to have been Churchill's. As a substitute for the expected prose he supplies some verses in ridicule of Oxford.

Beardmore, an attorney, described as 'the
author or one concerned in the writings of
several seditious papers,' which contained
gross and scandalous reflections and inven-
tions upon his Majesty's Government and
upon both Houses of Parliament. Several
other persons—printers—were arrested. But
the proceedings were carried out in a half-
hearted way. Wilkes scornfully proclaimed
that there was no intention of carrying the
thing further, that bail was given merely for
a colour, and that 'some private conditions
were settled.' A shallow and imprudent pretence he called it. And it so fell out, and
the matter was allowed to drop. So anxious
was he to bring the matter to an issue, that
he used every exertion to induce the attorney
to bring actions against the Ministry, offering
a sum of money as a guarantee against the
costs. The other, however, prudently
shrank from the conflict. Within a few
months he was doing battle from his cell in
the Tower with Ministers in the courts, had
fought two duels, was eager to arrange
for a third, and was in actual conflict with

both Houses of Parliament! Unlike many a
demagogue, therefore, he showed no intention
to shrink from 'paying with his person.'*

While carrying on these attacks he was
encouraged by Lord Temple, from Stowe,
who, while encouraging, moderated his ardour
by judicious advice and warnings that were
prophetic. Wilkes, in an excited strain,
informed him of all his plans—sending him
doggerel verses, such as a song on Lord Bute
receiving the Garter—

'The King gave but one : but like t'other Scot, Charters,
All England to hang him, would give him *both* Garters,
And, good Lord! how the rabble would laugh and
    would hoot,
Could they once set a swinging this John, Earl of ——'

—which his lordship did not approve,
declaring 'it was a d——d song, and he
wished it burnt.'

* Lord Temple seems to have been concerned in this
plot. Beardmore was the attorney. The under-sheriff,
having exempted Shebbeare from standing in the pillory,
was fined and imprisoned, and Wilkes paid him from
Lord Temple £150. 'He wants £250 more,' wrote
Wilkes.

In the October of this year, 1762, Temple

was conjuring him to restrain his political
sentiments for the sake of the regiment he
commanded. 'Forgive the liberty, and be
assured it proceeds from the best intentions.
You have lately sent me several scraps of
verses. I would beg you send no more.
Anything of the least delicacy ought never
to be conveyed by the post' — a caution
warranted by the proceedings of Ministers.
Those who would hire spies to record
Wilkes's movements would not scruple using
the *Cabinet noir*. ' The contents of your letter
do not please me. I beg you to weigh your
own conduct very maturely,' he wrote in the
month following. 'We have to deal with a
very strange world.' And again, ' My dear
Marcus Cato, I cannot sufficiently admire
Marcus Cato this week. All Stowe salutes
you with the highest applause, affection, and
esteem.'

The Colonel was as effusive on his side,
and well he might be, for this liberal friend was
one of those whom Wilkes taxed abundantly
for his necessities. This was one of the
invariable incidents in Wilkes's friendships.

He began with small sums, but after a time became bolder. 'If I do not put your lordship to inconvenience, I would beg a last sum of £400 or £500,' for which he would settle at Michaelmas. 'I make no apology to Lord Temple. I am proud to have an obligation to Lord Temple, and I have none to any other man.' Even then thus early there seems to have been a subscription spoken of for him, for he complained that little money was paid in. 'I am worse off than the Duke of Newcastle or anybody, for I cannot be in anybody's debt without reading a history of it in the newspapers.' He sends him a lively sketch of himself and his friend Churchill.

'I have most successfully got through the long list of patriotic toasts, and the *nasty wine* of this borough (Aylesbury). I have only a little headache, but Churchill is half dead. He was so violent against my Lord Mayor at Missenden that I was forced to drop that part of my toast. . . . I had the honour of being escorted into the town by every man who had or could hire a horse.'

But alas! all this patriotic manfulness seems to have been controlled by the one wish of his life, viz., to secure office or emolument. A strange incident is recorded by Mr. Malone, which shows what Wilkes's position was at this time, and how open he was to an advantageous treaty. When *The North Briton* was beginning to attract attention, 'he was dining one day with Mr. Rigby, and after dinner honestly confessed that he was a ruined man, not worth a shilling; that his principal object in writing was to procure himself some place, and that he should be particularly pleased with one that should remove him from the clamour and importunity of his creditors. He mentioned the office of Governor of Canada, and requested Mr. Rigby's good offices with the Duke of Bedford, so as to prevail on that nobleman to apply to Lord Bute for that place. Mr. Rigby said the Duke had not much intercourse with Lord Bute; neither could it be supposed that his lordship would purchase Mr. Wilkes's silence by giving him a good employment. Besides, he could have

no security that the same hostile attacks
would not be still made against him by Mr.
Wilkes's coadjutors, Lloyd and Churchill,
after he had left England. Wilkes solemnly
assured him there need not be the least
apprehension of that; for that he would
make Churchill his chaplain, and Lloyd his
secretary, and take them both with him to
Canada.

'The Duke, at Rigby's request, made the
application. Lord Bute would not listen to
it, and even treated the affair with contempt.
When this was told to Mr. Wilkes, he
observed to Mr. Rigby that Lord B. had
acted very foolishly, and that he might live
to lament that he and his colleagues had not
quitted England, as much as King Charles
did that Hampden and Cromwell had not
gone to America.' Some sort of treaty had
been attempted with him as to office or place,
and he now actually proposed revealing to
the public this latter treaty with Mr. Rigby,
and consulted his friend Cotes, who dissuaded
him from his purpose.

'I have weighed what you mention about

Mr. Rigby : and would give it to the public ;
but my friend seemed to think there was so
much of private conversation mixed with it,
the world would say, there was a betraying
of that, in an unjustifiable manner. Many
of the phrases are too remarkable to be
forgot—" anything now, to any amount, not
ostensible "—and a promise of Canada—
when that government is settled, he shall
be the first Governor of Canada — another
fallacy, for Murray is made Governor of
Canada : *vide* Gazette.'*

This shows that this rather unscrupulous
official must have made him some offers. It
may seem a bit of political gossip, but it
has an air of probability. Some corroboration,
however, is found in the fact that in No. 31
of *The North Briton* there is a violent attack
on Rigby, who is assailed in the bitterest
terms.

* 'Maloniana,' p. 362.

CHAPTER V.

ATTACK ON LORD BUTE.

THIS reckless bludgeoning was, however, not to pass with impunity. At this time the Lord Steward at the Court was Lord Talbot, a violent, passionate, and indiscreet nobleman—who, in some riot at the Palace gate, went out and fought the mob in person. Devoted to the King and the Court faction, he was infuriated at the attacks made by Wilkes on the Court. A scurrilous onslaught on himself gave him an opportunity. In the twelfth number, published in August, 1762, appeared some offensive ridicule of the Earl's display of horsemanship at the coronation.*

---

* 'A politeness equal to that of Lord Talbot's—horse ought not to pass unnoticed. At the coronation he paid a new, and, for a horse, singular respect to his sovereign. Caligula's horse had not half the merit. We remember

The haughty nobleman, after a few weeks'
delay, sent Wilkes a cartel, demanding if he
avowed or disclaimed the authorship of the
paper ?   Wilkes, later, made merry over this
composition, which was signed like an official
document, ' Talbot,' without the usual form of
' your humble servant, etc.'   A sort of contro-
versial argument followed.   The one contended,
' I must first insist on knowing your lordship's

---

how nobly he was provided for. What the exact proportion of merit was between his lordship and his horse, and
how far the pension should be divided between them, I
will not take upon me to determine. The impartial and
inimitable pen of Cervantes has made Rosinante immortal as well as Don Quixote. Lord Talbot's horse,
like the great planet in Milton, danced about in various
rounds his wandering course. At different times, he was
progressive, retrograde, or standing still. The progressive motion I should rather incline to think the merit
of the horse, the retrograde motion, the merit of the lord.
Some of the regulations of the courtiers themselves for
that day had been long settled by former lord stewards.
It was reserved for Lord Talbot to settle an etiquette for
their horses. I much admire many of his lordship's
new regulations, especially those for the royal kitchen.
I approve the discharging of so many turnspits and
cooks, who were grown of very little use. I do not,
however, quite like the precedent of giving them pensions
for doing nothing.'

right to catechise me about an anonymous paper. If your lordship is not satisfied with this, I shall ever be ready to give your lordship any other satisfaction becoming me as a gentleman.'

The other, in reply, urged with some propriety, that he knew that 'every gentleman who contributes to support periodical papers by his pen is not answerable for all the papers that appear under the title of that which he assists, but I cannot conceive that any man should refuse to assure a person who hath been the object of the wit of any paper, that he was not the author of a paper he did not write.'

With an air of banter the other answered that he still had 'the misfortune of not yet seeing your lordship's right of putting the question to me about the paper of the 21st of August, and till I do, I will never resolve your lordship on that head, though I would any friend I have in the world, who had the curiosity of asking me, if it was in a civil manner. Your lordship says, that if I do not deny the paper, you must and will conclude I

wrote it. Your lordship has my free consent
to make any conclusions you think proper,
whether they are well or ill grounded ; and I
feel the most perfect indifference about what
they are, or the consequences of them.'

After this it only remained to settle time
and place of meeting. Bagshot Heath and
the evening of October 5th were fixed.
The incidents of the rencontre were truly
characteristic, and even grotesque. Mr.
Wilkes employed the whole of the night previous at Medmenham—it is to be presumed
celebrating the orgies of that place—fit preparation for the issue he was about to face!
He had suggested that the whole party, the
two principals, with Colonel Berkeley, and the
adjutant of the Bucks Militia, should sup
together at ' Tilbury's Inn,' then retire to
bed, and fight on the following day. He was
much disappointed at finding his adversary
was not inclined to deal with the matter in
this truly Medmenham spirit.

' I found Lord Talbot in an agony of
passion. He said that I had injured, that I
had insulted him, that he was not used to be

injured, or insulted : what did I mean ? Did
I, or did I not, write *The North Briton* ? He
would know; he insisted on a direct answer :
here were his pistols. I replied, that he
would soon use them, that I desired to know
by what right his lordship catechised me
about a paper which did not bear my name ?
That I should never resolve him that question
till he made out the right of putting it, and
that if I could have entertained any other idea
I was too well bred to have given his lordship
and Colonel Berkeley the trouble of coming to
Bagshot. I observed that I was a private
English gentleman, perfectly free and independent, which I held to be a character of the
highest dignity ; that I obeyed with pleasure
a gracious sovereign, but would never submit
to the arbitrary dictates of a fellow subject, a
lord steward of his household, my superior
indeed in rank, fortune, and abilities, but my
equal only in honour, courage, and liberty.
His lordship insisted on finishing the affair
immediately. I told him that I should very
soon be ready, that I did not mean to quit
him, but would absolutely first settle some

7—2

important business relative to the education of
an only daughter, whom I tenderly loved,
that it would take up a very little time, and I
would immediately after decide the affair in
any way he chose, for I had brought both
swords and pistols. I rung the bell for pen,
ink, and paper, desiring his lordship to conceal
his pistols, that they might not be seen by
the waiter. He soon after became half frantic,
and made use of a thousand indecent expressions, that I should be hanged, damned, etc.
I said : " That I was not to be frightened, nor
in the least affected by such violence; that
God had given me a firmness and spirit equal
to his lordship's, or any man's; that cool
courage should always mark me, and that it
would be seen how well bottomed I was."

'After the waiter had brought pen, ink, and
paper, I proposed that the door of the room
might be locked, and not opened until our
business was decided. Lord Talbot, on this
proposition, became quite outrageous, declared
that this was mere butchery, and that I was a
wretch, who sought his life. I reminded him
that I came there on a point of honour, to

give his lordship satisfaction, that I mentioned the circumstance of locking the door only to prevent all possibility of interruption. Lord Talbot then asked me if I would deny the paper? I answered, that I neither would own, nor deny it; if I survived, I would afterwards declare, not before. Soon after he grew a little cooler, and in a soothing tone of voice said : " I have never, I believe, offended Mr. Wilkes : why has he attacked me ? He must be sorry to see me unhappy." I asked upon what grounds his lordship imputed the paper to me ? that Mr. Wilkes would justify any paper to which he had put his name, and would equally assert the privilege of not giving any answer whatever about a paper to which he had not ; that this was my un-doubted right, which I was ready to seal with my blood. He then said he admired me exceedingly, really loved me, but I was an unaccountable animal—such parts ! But would I kill him, who had never offended me ? etc.

' We had, after this, a good deal of conver-sation about the Buckinghamshire Militia, and the day his lordship came to see us on Wycombe Heath, before I was colonel. He soon after flamed out again, and said to me : "You are a murderer, you want to kill me, but I am sure that I shall kill you, I know I shall, by God. If you will fight, if you kill me, I hope you will be hanged. I know you will." Berkeley and Harris were shocked. I asked if I was first to be killed, and afterwards hanged ; that I knew his lordship fought me with the King's pardon in his pocket, and I fought him with a halter about my neck ; that I would fight him for all that, and if he fell, I should not tarry here a moment for the tender mercies of such a Ministry, but would directly proceed to the next stage, where my *valet de chambre* waited for me, and from thence I would make the best of my way to France, for men of honour were sure of protection in that kingdom. He seemed much affected by this. He then told me that I was an unbeliever, and wished to be killed. I could not help smiling at this, and observed that we did not meet at Bagshot to settle articles of faith, but points of

honour; that, indeed, I had no fear of dying,
but I enjoyed life as much as any man in it;
that I was as little subject to be gloomy, or
even peevish, as any Englishman whatever;
that I valued life, and the fair enjoyments of
it so much, I would never quit it by my own
consent, except on a call of honour.

' I then wrote a letter to your lordship,
respecting the education of Miss Wilkes, and
gave you my poor thanks for the steady
friendship with which you have so many years
honoured me. Colonel Berkeley took the
care of the letter, and I have since desired
him to send it to Stowe, for the sentiments of
the heart at such a moment are beyond all
politics, and indeed everything else, but such
virtue as Lord Temple's.

' When I had sealed my letter, I told Lord
Talbot that I was entirely at his service, and
I again desired that we might decide the affair
in the room, because there could not be a possibility of interruption; but he was quite
inexorable. He then asked me how many
times we should fire? · I said that I left it to
his choice; I had brought a flask of powder,

and a bag of bullets. Our seconds then
.charged the pistols which my lord had
brought. We then left the inn, and walked
to a garden at some distance from the house.
It was near seven, and the moon shone very
bright. We stood about eight yards distant,
and agreed not to turn round before we fired,
but to continue facing each other. Harris
gave the word. Both our fires were in very
exact time, but neither took effect. I walked
up immediately to Lord Talbot, and told him
that now I avowed the paper. His lordship
paid me the highest encomiums on my courage,
and said *he would declare everywhere that I
was the noblest fellow God had ever made.*
He then desired that we might now be good
friends, and retire to the inn to drink a bottle
of claret together, which we did with great
good humour and much laughter.'

This dramatic account is given in a letter to
Lord Temple. Wilkes had ever a rather sentimental and affectionate turn in his nature.
The letter he entrusted to Colonel Berkeley
was for his dear friend, Lord Temple, 'to be
delivered in case he fell.'

'October 5, seven at evening.

' My Lord,

' I am here just going to decide a point of honour with Lord Talbot. I have only to thank your lordship for all your favours to me, and to entreat you to desire Lord Temple to superintend the education of a daughter whom I love beyond the world. I am, my lord, your obliged and affectionate humble servant.'

After the affair had terminated so bloodlessly, the Colonel offered it back to Wilkes; ' but was desired to enclose it to Lord Temple, as a proof of regard and affection he bore him, at a moment which might have been very nearly his last.' All this was rather melodramatic, and in reserving so important a disposition to the very last moment, and then leaving it in uncertainty, he showed his usual reckless spirit.

Lord Temple acknowledged his friend's regard.

' My Dear Colonel,

' How eagerly do I long to embrace you ! What words can express the satisfac-

tion your last letter gave me in every particular.   Firmness, coolness, and a manly
politics make up the whole of this transaction
in great part.'

He then asks him to come to Stowe.

'We will talk over the whole at large.
The little woman is full of delight, as she
interests herself so warmly in your honour
and your welfare.'

Wilkes received great praise and gained
much celebrity for his behaviour in the encounter.   He had met in the field the champion
of the court, in defence of his paper.   He was
now before the kingdom.   Nothing was talked
of but his conduct in the affair.   As he wrote
to Churchill, 'Berkeley has told so much that
I am surfeited with caresses.   A sweet girl
whom I have sighed for unsuccessfully these
four months, now tells me she will trust her
honour to a man who takes so much care of
his own.'

His regiment acclaimed him.   The camp,
he wrote to Lord Temple, approved of his
conduct.   'The whole camp,' he wrote to

his friend, ' censured Lord Talbot for firing one pistol only. Both seconds declared that Lord Talbot, having asked me how many rounds we should fire, my answer was, " Just as many as your lordship pleases !" I am caressed more than I can tell.' This seems rather to verge on ' vapouring.'*

By a curious accident, Wilkes was now drawn into a controversy with a schoolboy, Lord ¦Bute's son ! There was something un- dignified in such a discussion, but faction and party spirit were raging. He met the lad in a shop at Winchester, and it was reported addressed him in this style :

* Yet Mr. Wilkes seems scarcely to deserve these rapturous encomiums. Lord Talbot could not well have asked for another shot, as his opponent, after the first discharge, walked up to him and avowed the paper. Lord Talbot, who seems to have been an impulsive man, would not, on reflection, have considered him one of the ' noblest of God's creatures,' as Wilkes had acknow- ledged the paper only after having tried to kill his lordship. As it happened, he was much disgusted and angered at finding a minute account of the transaction —given in Wilkes' letter to Lord Temple—published in the papers. He thought of bringing Lord Temple to account ; but it was the act of Wilkes himself, who was determined that the whole kingdom should ring with his exploits.

' Young gentleman, your father will have his head cut off '—' *Sir !*'—' He will lose his head in less than six months '—' *For what, sir ? —I never heard that he has done anything amiss; he has a great many friends—such as . . .— . . . and . . . — and . . . — and the right honourable George . . .*' — ' Ay ! He is your father's great puppy dog—but depend upon it your father will lose his head, or the mob shall tear him to pieces.' The youth upon this burst into tears with indignation, and turning short as he rushed out of the shop, ' You are a squinting scoundrel,' says he, ' for offering to talk to me in this manner.'

Much indignation was expressed at this conduct, and Wilkes indiscreetly tried to justify himself by appealing to the public, and to Dr. Burton, the schoolmaster. In an article in his own journal, probably written by Churchill, he stated that the whole story was a fabrication. At the same time he took the undignified course of assailing the schoolboy. ' The youth has very frequently in the bookseller's shop abused me in the grossest terms. He knew so little of me, as to be afraid, if I

heard of his behaviour, that I should complain to you; and he dreaded the punishment
he thought must follow. To save himself he
has invented this curious tale, the falsity of
which in every particular he knows better
than anybody.'

In literary scufflings of this kind, most of
the 'brawlers,' from their obscurity, pass into
oblivion after the occasion. But it was the
fate of some of these persons, after being
soundly belaboured by Wilkes and Churchill
in their journal, to receive immortality from
the stinging lines of Churchill. Such was
Arthur Murphy, a needy adventurer from
Ireland, who seems to have been the chief
writer in *The Auditor*, a task to which he
brought little but the hireling's zeal. It is
amusing to read the never-flagging spirit
with which his absurdities were exposed:
how he was scoffed at and jibed. Churchill
had already gibbeted him in a line declaring
that 'Dulness had marked him for a Mayor!'
But harder still was the fate of Hogarth,
whose satirical caricatures of various politi-
cians of the day, as we have seen, exposed him

to retaliation, and subjected him to a cruel attack in *The North Briton.* But the painter took a proper mode of revenging himself on both. When Wilkes was brought up for trial, Hogarth concealed himself behind a pillar in the court, and there made a sketch of his former friend—the well-known ' counterfeit presentment '—a leering, impudent face, with the expression of a satyr, a stick upon his shoulder, upon which was stuck a cap of Liberty.* In the following year Churchill had ready his ' bloody ' retaliation — his ' epistle ' to Hogarth—in which he assailed the painter with gross and cruel severity, ridiculing his infirmities and age. The painter retaliated with his portrait of Churchill as a Russian Bear, arrayed in torn clerical bands and ruffles, ' with a pot of porter that has just visited his jaws hugged in his right, with a knotted club of " Lies " and *North Britons* clutched in his left ;' to which, in a later edition, he added

---

* This caricature must have been as profitable to the artist as it was satisfactory to his hostile feelings. Some four thousand copies were sold.

a scoffing caricature of Pitt, Temple and
Wilkes. The inscription described him as
' regaling himself after having killed the
monster caricature *that so galled his virtuous
friend, the Heaven-born Wilkes.*' This was a
melancholy and discreditable squabble; but
there was something unique in the contest,
each carrying it on with the weapons he was
most skilled in—the journalist with his news-
sheet, the poet with his verses, the artist
with his pencil. This, too, was the opening
fight of Wilkes's long series of battles and
scuffles *contra mundum*, against both friends
and foes.

How the favourite could have endured the
unceasing tide of libellous abuse seems extraordinary. There was one paper in the series so
bitter, so ironical, and even witty, that it is
not possible to read it without admiration
for the gifts of the writer. This was a
' Dedication ' to a supposed republication
of the ' Tragedy of Mortimer,' and which
filled the fifth number, published on July 3rd.
There was much truth in the note which Wilkes
added with his usual cynicism : ' No. 45 had

indeed wonderful luck ; but the elder one deserved still more to have been taken notice of, and perhaps laid the foundation of the younger brother's fortune.' There was justice, too, in the complaint here implied that Ministers tolerated worse things than what they afterwards prosecuted, being thus *agents provocateurs.**

* The reader will be glad to find here the most effective portions of this striking piece :

' MY LORD,
        ' Many and various motives have concurred to give a peculiar propriety to the fond wish I had formed of making this humble offering at the shrine of Bute. I have felt an honest indignation at all the invidious, unjust, and odious applications of the story of Roger Mortimer. I absolutely disclaim the most distant allusion, and I purposely dedicate this play to your lordship, because history does not furnish a more striking contrast, than there is between the two Ministers, in the reigns of Edward III. and of George III.
        ' Edward III. was held in the most absolute slavery by his mother and her Minister. The first nobles of England were excluded from the King's councils, and the minion disposed of all places of profit and trust. The King's uncles did not retain the shadow of power and authority. They were treated with insult, and the whole royal family became not only depressed, but forced to depend upon the caprice of an insolent

favourite. The young King had been victorious over
the Scots, then a fierce, savage, and perfidious people, in
that reign our cruel enemies, happily in this our dearest
friends. On every favourable opportunity, either by the
distractions in the public councils of this kingdom during
a minority, or by the absence of the national troops,
they had ravaged England with fire and sword. Edward
might have compelled them to accept of any terms, so
glorious and decisive was the success of his arms, but
Roger Mortimer, from personal motives of power and
ambition, hastily concluded an ignominious peace, by
which he sacrificed the triumphs of a prosperous war,
and the justest claims of conquest.

'It is with the highest rapture, my lord, I now look
back to that disgraceful era, because I feel the striking
contrast it makes with the halcyon days of George III.
This excellent prince is held in no kind of captivity. All
his nobles have free access to him. The throne is not now
besieged. Court favour, not confined to one partial
stream, flows in a variety of different channels, enriching
this whole country. There is now the most perfect
union among all the branches of the royal family. No
Court minion now finds it necessary, for the preservation
of his own omnipotence, by the vilest insinuations to
divide either the royal, or any noble families. The
King's uncle is now treated with that marked distinction
which his singular merit is entitled to, both from the
nation and the throne, established by his valour in extinguishing a foul rebellion, which burst upon us from
its native North, and almost overspread the land. No
favourite now has trampled upon the most respectable
of the English nobility, and driven them from their
sovereign's councils.

'The present internal policy of this kingdom, my
lord, is equally to be admired., Our gracious sovereign
maturely examines all matters of national importance,
and no unfair or partial representation of any business,
or of any of his subjects, is suffered to be made to him,
nor can any character be assassinated in the dark by an
unconstitutional Prime Minister. The important promise you made us, that we should frequently see our
sovereign, like his great predecessor, William III., pre-
siding in person at the British Treasury, has been fulfilled to the advantage and glory of these times, and to
the perfecting of that scheme of economy so earnestly
recommended from the Throne, and so ably carried into
execution by yourself and *your* Chancellor of the Exchequer,* as well as so minutely by the Lord Steward of
the Household.† Your whole Council of State too is
composed of men of the first abilities—the Duke of
Bedford; the Earls of Halifax, Egremont, and Gower;
the Lords Henley, Mansfield, and Ligonier; Mr. George
Grenville, and Mr. Fox. The business of this great empire
is not, however, trusted to them; the most arduous and
complicated parts are not only digested and prepared,
but finally revised and settled, by Gilbert Elliot, Alex

* 'Sir Francis Dashwood, now Lord Le Despenser,
who, from puzzling all his life at tavern bills, was called
by Lord Bute to administer the finances of a kingdom
above a hundred millions in debt, and styled by him, in
the royal manner, my Chancellor.'
† 'Earl Talbot, who thought a civil list of £800,000
a year insufficient to keep up the hospitality of a private
noblemen's kitchen, in the King of England's palace.'

ander Wedderburn, Esqrs., Sir Henry Erskine, Bart., and the Home.

'Another reason why I choose your lordship for the subject of this dedication is, that you are said by former dedicators to cultivate with success the polite arts. How sparing and penurious is this praise! Such literary economy is really odious. They ought to have gone further, and to have shown how liberally you are pleased to reward all men of genius. Malloch and the Home have been nobly provided for. Let Churchill, or Armstrong, write like them ; your lordship's classical taste will relish their works, and patronise the authors. You, my lord, are said to be not only a patron but a judge, and Malloch adds that he wishes, for the honour of our country, that this praise were not almost exclusively your own.

'Almost all the sciences, my lord, have at length made so great a progress in England, that we are become the objects of jealousy to the rest of Europe ; but under your auspices Botany and Tragedy have now reached the utmost height of perfection. Not only the System of Power, but the Vegetable System likewise has been completed by the joint labours of your lordship and the great Dr. Hill. Tragedy, under Malloch and the Home, has with us rivalled the Greek model, and united the different merits of the great moderns. The fire of Shakespeare, and the correctness of Racine, have met in your two countrymen. One other exotic, too, I must not forget : Arthur Murphy, gent. He has the additional merit of acting, no less than of writing, so as to touch, in the most exquisite manner, all the fine feelings of the human frame. I have scarcely ever felt myself more forcibly affected, than by this excellent but

poor, neglected player, except a few years ago at the
Duchess of Queensbury's, where your lordship so frequently exhibited. In one part, which was remarkably
humane and amiable, you were so great that the general
exclamation was, here you did not act. In another part
you were no less perfect. I mean in the famous scene of
Hamlet, where you pour fatal poison into the ear of a
good, unsuspecting king. If the great names of Murphy
and Bute, as players, *pensantur eâdem trutinâ,* it is no
flattery to say that you, my lord, were not only superior,
but even unrivalled by him, as well as by all, who have
ever appeared on the great stage of the world. I should
have added, my lord, that the play, of which I now
make the humble offering, is a tragedy, the most grave
and moral of all poems. With a happy propriety, therefore, it comes inscribed to your lordship, the most grave,
the most moral of all men. A witty comedy I would
never have offered to your lordship, nor indeed to any of
your countrymen. Wit is an *ignis fatuus,* which be-
wilders and leads astray. It is the primrose path which
conducts to folly. Your lordship has never deviated
into it. You have marched on with a solemn dignity,
keeping ever the true tragic step, and on the greatest
occasions, give us a complete play. It is the warmest
wish of my heart that the Earl of Bute may speedily
complete the story of " Roger Mortimer." I hope that
your lordship will graciously condescend to undertake
this arduous task, to which parts like yours are peculiarly
adapted. To you everything will be easy. The fifth
act of this play will find those great talents still in full
vigour, even after you have run so wonderful a career.
If more important concerns, either of business or amusement, engage you too much, I beg, my lord, that you

will please royally to *command* Mr. Murphy, as Mr. Macpherson says you *commanded* him, to publish the prose-poems of Fingal and Temora.

' I will no longer intrude on your lordship. The Cocoa-tree and your countrymen may be impatient to settle with you, the army, and the finances of this kingdom. I have only to add my congratulations on the peculiar fame you have acquired, so adequate to the wonderful acts of your Administration. You are in full possession of that fame at the head of Tories and Scotsmen; but alas! my lord, the history of mankind shows how fantastic as well as transitory is fame. Although Mr. Pitt is still adored at the head of Whigs and Englishmen, he, too, will experience that

 ' "The greatest can but blaze and pass away."

  ' I am, my lord,
   ' With a zeal and respect equal to your virtues,
    ' Your lordship's very humble Servant.
' *March* 15, 1763.'

We find a striking touch here of Wilkes' reckless indifference to decent consistency. When the paper was written, no terms of panegyric could be too high for Mr. Pitt, then his friend and patron; yet, after he had quarrelled with him, he did not scruple to add this grossly offensive note, expressive of his dislike and hostility.

' Of all political adventurers Mr. Pitt has been the most successful, according to the venal ideas of modern statesmen. Pulteney sold the people only for a barren title. The mercenary Pitt disposed of his popularity like an exchange-broker. Besides the same title with

the other apostate, Pitt secured from the Crown a large
family pension, and the lucrative sinecure of the Privy
Seal, which he held for a few years. His retreat into the
House of Lords was a political demise. He passed away,
but is not yet quite forgotten. His treachery to the
cause of the people, still loads his memory with curses.

. 'He raised himself to the greatest offices of the state
by the rare talent of command in a popular assembly.
He was, indeed, born an orator, and from nature
possessed every outward requisite to bespeak respect and
even awe. A manly figure, with the eagle-face of the
famous Condé, fixed your attention, and almost commanded reverence, the moment he appeared, and the
keen lightnings of his eye spoke the haughty, fiery soul,
before his lips had pronounced a syllable. His tongue
dropped venom. There was a kind of fascination in his
look, when he eyed anyone askance. Nothing could
withstand the force of that contagion. The fluent
Murray has faltered, and even Fox shrunk back appalled
from an adversary fraught with fire unquenchable, if I
may borrow the expression of our great Milton. He
always cultivated the art of speaking with the most in-
tense care and application. He has passed his life in the
culling of words, the arrangement of phrases, and choice
of metaphors, yet his theatrical manner did more than
all, for his speeches could not be read. There was
neither sound reasoning, nor accuracy of expression, in
them. He had not the power of argument, nor the
correctness of language, so striking in the great Roman
orator, but he had the *verba ardentia*, the bold, glowing
words. This merit was confined to his speeches; for his
writings were always cold, lifeless, and incorrect, totally
void of elegance and energy, sometimes even offending

against the plainest rules of construction. In the pursuit of eloquence he was indefatigable. He dedicated all his powers and faculties, and he sacrificed every pleasure of social life, even in youth, to the single point of talking well.

> ' "Multa tulit fecitque puer; sudavit et alget;
> Abstinuit venere et vino,"

to a greater degree than almost any man of this age.

' He acknowledged, that when he was young, he always came late into company, and left it early. He affected at first a sovereign contempt of money, and, when he was Paymaster, made a parade of two or three very public acts of disinterestedness. When he had effectually duped his credulous friends, as well as a timid Ministry, and obtained enormous legacies, pensions, and sinecure places, the mask dropped off. Private interest afterwards appeared to be the only idol to which he sacrificed. The old Duke of Newcastle used to say, "That Mr. Pitt's talents would not have got him forty pounds a year in any country but this."

' At his entrance into Parliament, he attacked Sir Robert Walpole with indecent acrimony, and continued the persecution to the last moment of that Minister's life. He afterwards paid servile and fulsome compliments to his memory, not from conviction, as appeared from many other particulars, but to get over a few Walpolians. He had no fixed principle, but that of his own advancement. He declared for and against continental connections, for and against German wars, for and against Hanoverian subsidies, etc., etc., still preserving an unblushing, unembarrassed countenance, and was the most perfect contradiction of a man to himself which the world ever saw. If his speeches in Parliament had been faithfully published to the English, soon after they were delivered, as those of Demosthenes and Cicero were to the Greeks and Romans, he would have been very early detected, and utterly cast off by his countrymen.

'He is said to be still living at Hayes, in Kent.'

CHAPTER VI.

THE 'GENERAL WARRANT.'

By the end of March the position of the
Ministry seemed to grow desperate, and *The
North Briton* more daring. Yet it is difficult
to say, as we look through the last few
numbers, that the bounds of legitimate
political criticism had been passed. Sir
Francis Dashwood and his odious Cyder
Bill were attacked, and his peculiar expressions ridiculed in such style as, ' He
was not for an extension of the Excise Laws,
but for an *enlargement* of them;' and what
caused still more amusement, his declaration
that ' all the *whole total* was, anything for
peace and quietness;' also the odd reference
to previous Chancellors of the Exchequer,
who, he said, ' *were not ashamed to know something of their business.*' Public attention has

always naturally settled on 'No. 45' of the paper, but No. 44, with date of April 2, was remarkable in its way. It contained one more venomous onslaught on the unlucky Premier —a final 'kick,' and a short and brutal summary of his career. 'The mean arts,' he said, 'by which the present Minister acquired his power, the long and dark scenes of dissimulation which he ran through for the sake of greatness, with the open and insolent outrages he hath committed against men much better than himself, the little capacity which he has shown for business; the inglorious peace which he hath infamously patched up; his gross partiality to his own beggarly countrymen; his virulence against all who will not slavishly comply with his destructive measures; his associating with a man justly odious to every party, and who, having been false to all, ought to be trusted by none; 'these things laid together have rendered the Minister justly suspected by the people, and have, if possible, made the name of Stuart more odious and contemptible than it was before.'

He sounded the note of his approaching fall, holding up to him the fate of Strafford —'How soon this desired change may be brought to bear we cannot pretend to ascertain, but it cannot be far distant.' He then utters a curious prophecy, and mentions a sign by which all shall know the fall of Ministers is at hand. This was :—' Mr. Fox, whose steadiness to his own interest, with his remarkable talents of penetration, will induce him to quit his post when he can keep it no longer, and to leave his friends in the lurch. When we see him, therefore, flying from the storm, accepting of a peerage, or relying on the Government of an ally, we may safely conclude that a change is at hand.'

Within ten days Mr. Fox resigned, became Lord Holland, and went abroad.

But more remarkable still, the editor was able in the republished edition of his *North Briton* to add this triumphant note in capitals to this number :

' JOHN, EARL OF BUTE, RESIGNED ON THE FRIDAY FOLLOWING.'*

* A little chronological summary made it perfectly

We are now come to the eve of that great struggle for English liberty, fought out in a most spirited and intrepid way by our hero. It cannot be contended that there were any ' pure ' or holy motives at work, or that there was not some vanity and much self-interest involved. All the turmoil and talk *The North Briton* occasioned only excited him the more, and made him long for the moment when issue could be directly joined with the hated Government. No one was more fortunate and more favoured in this respect, for it fell out that after letting opportunities go by when they could have had him on the hip, and perhaps crushed him with ease, they selected the most unfavourable one, and dealt their blow in a fashion that was as ineffective

clear how large a share *The North Briton* had in driving him out, and extinguishing the hireling journals.

' John, Earl of Bute, was made First Commissioner of the Treasury, May 29, 1762. On the same day the first number of the *Briton* was published. The first number of the *Auditor* was published June 10, 1762. The last number of the *Auditor* was published February 8, 1763. The last number of the *Briton* was published February 12, 1763. Lord Bute resigned April 8, 1763.'

as it was illegal. It will be seen, that from the beginning to the end of his political course the same good fortune attended his efforts, and that he had the art or sagacity to bring about the combination of circumstances which was most favourable to his plans, and of which he took the best advantage.

When the new Government was formed, Mr. Grenville, who was appointed Prime Minister, was not able immediately to secure his re-election, owing to the fact that he had quarrelled with his brother, Lord Temple, to whom the borough which he represented belonged. He was obliged to submit to the mortification of asking for his sanction; and his secretary, who brought the application, carried also a copy of the King's Speech, which was to be delivered on the following day, viz., on the 18th. Mr. Pitt was at the moment closeted with Lord Temple, and both were much disgusted with the tone of the document, Mr. Pitt being particularly indignant at the passage relating to the King of Prussia.

It chanced that Wilkes, who had just

arrived from Paris, came to call on Lord Temple, and joined in the general reprobation of the speech. Being thus stimulated, he went home and set down a sketch of the conversation he had just listened to, from which he wrote the famous article ' No. 45.'

Churchill, who had seen the proof of ' No. 45,' was strongly opposed to its publication. But it was a special feature in Wilkes' character never to yield to a friend's advice, but stubbornly to take his own course. Friends to whom he was under the most serious obligation naturally expected some deference to their wishes, when they pressed a point, and were disgusted and cooled at such obstinacy. In this way he lost Lord Temple and many others.

A few days later, on April 23rd, ' No. 45 ' appeared. In this, the passages relating to the Peace were severely dealt with, but we shall quote the portions which were selected by the Ministers for prosecution :

I. ' The King's Speech has always been considered by the Legislature, and by the

public at large, as the speech of the Minister.
It has regularly, at the beginning of every
session of Parliament, been referred by both
Houses to the consideration of a committee,
and has been generally canvassed with the
utmost freedom, when the Minister of the
Crown has been obnoxious to the nation.
The Ministers of this free country, conscious
of the undoubted privileges of so spirited a
people, and with the terrors of Parliament
before their eyes, have ever been cautious,
no less with regard to the matter, than to the
expression, of speeches, which they have
advised the sovereign to make from the
throne, at the opening of each session.
They well know that an honest House of
Parliament, true to their trust, could not fail
to detect the fallacious arts, or to remonstrate
against the daring acts of violence, committed by any Minister. The speech at the
close of the session has ever been considered
as the most secure method of promulgating
the favourite court creed among the vulgar;
because the Parliament, which is the constitutional guardian of the liberties of the

people, has in this case no opportunity of remonstrating, or of impeaching any wicked servant of the Crown. This week has given the public the most abandoned instance of Ministerial effrontery ever attempted to be imposed on mankind. The Minister's speech of last Tuesday is not to be paralleled in the annals of this country. I am in doubt whether the imposition is greater on the sovereign or on the nation. Every friend of his country must lament that a prince of so many great and amiable qualities, whom England truly reveres, can be brought to give the sanction of his sacred name to the most odious measures, and to the most unjustifiable public declarations, from a throne ever renowned for truth, honour, and unsullied virtue.'

II. 'The Minister cannot forbear, even in the King's Speech, insulting us with a dull repetition of the word *economy*. I did not expect so soon to have seen that word again, after it had been so lately exploded, and more than once, by a most numerous audience, hissed off the stage of our English theatres.

It is held in derision by the *voice of the people*, and every tongue loudly proclaims the universal contempt in which these empty professions are held by this nation. Let the public be informed of a single instance of *economy*, except indeed in the household.'

III. 'In vain will such a minister, or the foul dregs of his power, the tools of corruption and despotism, preach up in the speech that spirit of concord, and that obedience to the laws, which is essential to good order. They have sent the spirit of discord through the land, and I will prophesy that it will never be extinguished but by the extinction of their power. Is the spirit of concord to go hand in hand with the peace and excise through this nation? Is it to be expected between an insolent exciseman, and a peer, gentleman, freeholder, or farmer, whose private houses are now made liable to be entered and searched at pleasure? Gloucestershire, Herefordshire, and in general all the cider counties, are not surely the several counties which are alluded to in the speech. The spirit of concord hath not gone forth among them; but the spirit of liberty has, and a noble opposition has been given to the wicked instrument of oppression. A nation as sensible as the English will see that a spirit of concord, when they are oppressed, means a tame submission to injury, and that a spirit of liberty ought then to arise ; and I am sure ever will, in proportion to the weight of the grievance they feel. Every legal attempt of a contrary tendency to the spirit of concord will be deemed a justifiable resistance, warranted by the spirit of the English constitution.

—   ‘ A despotic minister will always endeavour to dazzle his prince with high-flown ideas of the prerogative and honour of the crown, which the minister will make a parade of firmly maintaining. I wish as much as any man in the kingdom to see the honour of the crown maintained in a manner truly becoming royalty. I lament to see it sunk even to prostitution. What a shame was it to see the security of this country, in point of military force, complimented away, contrary to the opinion of royalty itself, and sacrificed to the prejudices and to the ignorance of a set of

people, the most unfit from every consideration to be consulted on a matter relative to
the security of the House of Hanover !'

The ground for the action in reference to this
paper was that it was an attack on the King
personally ; though the speech was always
known to be the work of his Ministers. We
might nowadays smile at so forced a construction, as ministers are made responsible, and
treated very unceremoniously in debates on
such compositions. Wilkes, in some notes
later added to this famous paper, quoted
statements from the journals of the House, in
which it was laid down that the so-called
' King's Speech ' might be held to be the
composition of his Ministry. But in fairness,
it must be said that Wilkes' attack passed
beyond these limits. It represented the King
as hoodwinked and enslaved to his advisers ;
as too feeble to resist, their opinions being
violently imposed upon him. To hold him
up as such a cipher was offensive in the
highest degree. The attack was no doubt taken
in connection with the gross and scurrilous
libels that had gone before, where he was repre-

sented under the image of King Edward subject
to the degraded domination of a Mortimer.

Mr. Grenville, the new Premier, was made
of different stuff from his predecessor.
He felt that these assaults would only
increase in virulence, and he determined to
strike without a moment's delay. The two
Secretaries of State were Lords Egremont
and Halifax. The article appeared on the
23rd : on the 25th the law officers, Sir
Fletcher Norton and Mr. Charles Yorke,
were applied to for their opinion ; and on the
following day, before it was received, the
warrant was made out and dated. On the
27th the law officer declared his opinion that
the paper was ' a most infamous and seditious
libel, tending to inflame the minds and alienate
the affections of the people from his Majesty,
and to incite them to traitorous insurrections
against his Government.' And on this it was
determined to proceed to action, which proved
to be of the most violent and high-handed
character. As in all such instances of over-
zeal, it was to involve them in a most unlucky and annoying contest, which, however,

was to have the most important constitutional
consequences. On the 29th the warrant* was
placed in the hands of four of his Majesty's
messengers in ordinary. The moving spirit
seemed to have been Mr. Philip Carteret Webb,

---

* The document was in these terms :

> 'George Montagu Dunk, Earl of Halifax, Vis-
> count Sunbury, and Baron Halifax, one of the

L. S. lords of his Majesty's Most Honourable Privy
Council, Lieutenant-General of his Majesty's Forces, and
Principal Secretary of State. These are in his Majesty's
name to authorise and require you (taking a constable to
your assistance) to make strict and diligent search for the
authors, printers, and publishers of a seditious and treasonable paper entitled *The North Briton*, Number XLV., Saturday, April 23, 1763, printed by G. Kearsly in Ludgate-
street, and them or any of them having found, to apprehend and seize, together with their papers, and to
bring in safe custody before me, to be examined concerning the premises, and further dealt with according
to law. And in due execution thereof all mayors,
sheriffs, justices of the peace, constables, and all other
his Majesty's officers civil and military, and loving subjects whom it may concern, are to be aiding and assisting
to you as there shall be occasion. And for so doing this
shall be your warrant. Given at St. James's the twenty-
sixth day of April, in the third year of his Majesty's
reign.   ' DUNK HALIFAX.'

> ' To Nathan Carrington, John Money, James
> Watson, and Robert Blackmore, four of
> his Majesty's messengers in ordinary.'

Solicitor to the Treasury, to whom Wilkes was destined to bring many a *mauvais quart d'heure.* [*]

It was little suspected that this contemptible little bit of paper or parchment was to engender such confusion and strife as the country had not known for a century. And yet it became known later that one of the secretaries had opposed this irregular proceeding, and pressed that Wilkes' name should be inserted in the warrant. But he was overruled by the ' permanent clerks ' in the office and by the lawyers, who insisted that there were precedents. They were right, but these exceptional acts had been applied in time of war, and to aliens—a serious difference. It will be seen that no person is

---

* This opponent of Wilkes' justified his behaviour in a pamphlet : ' Some Observations on the Late Determination for Discharging Mr. Wilkes from his Commitment to the Tower of London. 1763. By P. Carteret Webb.' A copy was in Wilkes' catalogue, and a note says it was printed by P. C. Webb, but never published. This gentleman was a distinguished antiquary ; born 1700 ; M.P. for Haslemere in 1754, and again in 1761. He had been Secretary of Bankrupts. He lived till 1770.

named in this warrant, except the printer.
Neither was there any information on oath
from which knowledge of ' author, publisher,
or printer,' could be furnished. It amounted,
in fact, to a direction to the messenger to
seize on anyone whom he believed or fancied
to be the author, printer, etc. So arbitrary
a proceeding was quite in the style of a
lettre de cachet, and was carried out in the
true spirit, as Lord Camden said, of the
Spanish Inquisition.

The proceedings that followed were all in
keeping. The messengers first broke into the
house of David Leach, a well-known printer,
after midnight. He was dragged out of bed,
his papers were seized, his servants, journeymen, etc., apprehended, and all were carried
to prison, where they were detained several
days. The messenger said he had heard that
Wilkes was seen going into the house. It
was at once found that the unfortunate printer
had nothing to do with *The North Briton*, and
he was released. Yet this outrage was only
the direct consequence of so ' general ' a
warrant, where nobody was named.

On the same morning they seized on
Kearsly, the real printer and publisher,
together with all his servants, printers, books,
accounts, etc. He was taken before the
two secretaries and interrogated: another
un-English proceeding. Kearsly told all he
knew—that one Balfe was the printer, that
Wilkes had given orders for the printing, and
that Churchill received the profits. He was
pressed as to the author, but on this ' he
could say nothing,' or would not, for he
was familiar with Wilkes's handwriting.
Having obtained this information, the printer,
Balfe, and his men were next seized on—
the whole number of persons arrested already
amounting to forty-eight! He also was put
to the question by the secretaries in presence
of Mr. Philip Carteret Webb, Solicitor to the
Treasury, who managed all these arbitrary
proceedings. Another legal functionary,
Lovell Stanhope, ' law clerk to the Secretary
of State,' assisted. Nothing about the author
could be extracted from him,* on which

* Lawyers held that the warrant, such as it was, was
exhausted by its first exercise, and that then a fresh

these two officials announced authoritatively that Kearsly's statement as to Wilkes giving orders for the printing, was sufficient to criminate him. It was determined, therefore, to arrest him, also, under the warrant, now made to do duty for the fourth time. It was said that there were some scruples as to the legality of this too abundant use of a single document, but Mr. Webb declared that another document was unnecessary; and as to naming Wilkes, he added, with an emphasis, '*it was better not.*' In this he was certainly right, for Wilkes could not be described as either publisher, printer, or author of the paper, as yet at least.

one should have been issued. On the other hand, Sir George Yonge says that the holders of it were sent to Carrington to learn from him 'whom they were to suspect and what persons they should take up. He gave them his opinion that Leach was the printer, and that *he had been told* that Wilkes had been seen to go in there.' Sir G. Yonge adds that a second warrant was issued to take Balfe and Kearsly, upon the information of the latter, by a verbal information given to the messengers, so that Wilkes was actually arrested without any order at all !

More violence was now determined on. The messengers were directed to go to Wilkes' house at midnight, arrest him, and seize all his papers. As to this, however, they prudently hesitated, and hung about the house till the morning. Wilkes himself tells us all that followed in his own spirited style; and it will be noted what a pleasant mixture of humour, insolence, and vivacity is displayed through the whole account.

'On my return to the city early in the morning, I met at the end of Great George Street one of the king's messengers. He told me that he had a warrant to apprehend me, which he must execute immediately, and that I must attend him to Lord Halifax's. I desired to see the warrant. He said it was against the authors, printers, and publishers of *The North Briton*, No. 45, and that his verbal orders were to arrest Mr. Wilkes. I told him the warrant did not respect me. I advised him to be very civil, and to use no violence in the street, for if he attempted force I would put him to death in the instant, but if he would come quietly to my house I would convince him of the illegality of the warrant, and the injustice of the orders he had received. He chose to accompany me home, and then produced the general warrant. I declared that such a warrant was absolutely illegal and void in itself, that it was a ridiculous warrant against the whole English nation, and I asked why he would serve it on me, rather than on the Lord Chancellor, on either of the secretaries, on Lord Bute, or Lord Cork, my next door neighbour. The answer was, I am to arrest Mr. Wilkes. About an hour afterwards two other messengers arrived, and several of their assistants. They all endeavoured in vain to persuade me to accompany them to Lord Halifax's. I had likewise many civil messages from his lordship to desire my attendance. My only answer was that I had not the honour of visiting his lordship, and this first application was rather rude and ungentlemanlike.

'While some of the messengers and their assistants were with me, Mr. Churchill came into the room. I had heard that their verbal

orders were likewise to apprehend him, but
I suspected they did not know his person,
and by presence of mind I had the happiness
of saving my friend.   As soon as Mr.
Churchill entered the room, I accosted him :
" Good morrow, Mr. Thomson. How does
Mrs. Thomson do to-day ?   Does she dine
in the country ?"   Mr. Churchill thanked me,
said she then waited for him, that he only
came for a moment to ask me how I did,
and almost directly took his leave.   He
went home immediately, secured all his
papers, and retired into the country. The
messengers could never get intelligence where
he was. The following week he came to
town, and was present both the days of hearing at the Court of Common Pleas.

   ' A constable came afterwards with several
assistants to the messengers. I repeatedly
insisted on their all leaving me, and declared
I would not suffer any one of them to continue
in the room against my consent, for I knew
and would support the rights of an Englishman in the sanctuary of his own house. I
was then threatened with immediate violence,

and a regiment of the guards, if necessary.
I soon found all resistance would be vain.
The constable demanded my sword, and insisted on my immediately attending the
messengers to Lord Halifax's. I replied that
if they were not assassins they should first
give me their names in writing. They
complied with this, and thirteen set their
hands to the paper. I then got into my
own chair, and proceeded to Lord Halifax's,
guarded by the messengers and their assistants.'

Not less amusing is the account of the
scene with the two secretaries :

' I was conducted into a great apartment
fronting the park, where Lord Halifax and
Lord Egremont, the two Secretaries of State,
were sitting at a table covered with paper,
pens, and ink. Lord Egremont received me
with a supercilious, insolent air ; Lord
Halifax with great politeness. I was desired to take the chair near their lordships,
which I did. Lord Halifax then began that
he was really concerned that he had been
necessitated to proceed in that manner against

me, that it was exceedingly to be regretted
that a gentleman of my rank and abilities
could engage against the King and his
Majesty's Government. I replied that his
lordship could not be more mistaken, for the
King had not a subject more zealously attached to his person and Government than
myself; that I had all my life been a warm
friend of the House of Brunswick and the
Protestant Succession; that while I made
the truest professions of duty to the King,
I was equally free to declare in the same
moment that I believed no prince had ever
the misfortune . of being served by such
ignorant, insolent, and despotic Ministers,
of which my being there was a fresh, glaring
proof, for I was brought before their lordships by force, under a general warrant,
which named nobody, in violation of the
laws of my country, and of the privileges
of Parliament; that I begged both their
lordships to remember my present declaration, that on the very first day of the ensuing
session of Parliament I would stand up in
my place and impeach them for the outrage

they had committed in my person against
the liberties of the people. Lord Halifax
answered that nothing had been done but by
the advice of the best lawyers, and that it
was now his duty to examine me. He had
in his hand a long list of questions, regularly
numbered. He began, " Mr. Wilkes, do you
know Mr. Kearsly ? when did you see him ?"
etc., etc. I replied that I suspected there
was a vain hope my answer would tend rather
to what his lordship wished to know, that he
seemed to be lost in a dark and intricate
path, and really wanted much light to guide
him through it, but that I could assure his
lordship not a single ray should come from
me. Lord Halifax returned to the charge,
" Mr. Wilkes, do you know Mr. Kearsly ?"
etc., etc. I said that this was a curiosity
on his lordship's part which, however laudable
in the secretary, I did not find myself disposed to gratify, and that at the end of my
examination all the quires of paper on their
lordships' table should be as milk-white as
at the beginning. Lord Halifax then desired
to remind me of my being their prisoner, and

of their right to examine me. I answered that I should imagine their lordships' time was too precious to be trifled away in that manner; that they might have seen before I would never say one word they desired to know; and I added, " Indeed, my lords, I am not made of such slight, flimsy stuff;" then, turning to Lord Egremont, I said, " Could you employ tortures, I would never utter a word unbecoming my honour, or affecting the sacred confidence of any friend. God has given me firmness and fidelity. You trifle away your time most egregiously, my lords." Lord Halifax then advised me to weigh well the consequences of my conduct and the advantages to myself of a generous, frank confession. I lamented the prostitution of the word *generous*, to what I should consider as an act of the utmost treachery, cowardice, and wickedness. His lordship then asked me if I chose to be a prisoner in my own house, at the Tower, or in Newgate, for he was disposed to oblige me. I gave his lordship my thanks, but I desired to remark that I never received an obligation but from

a friend ; that I demanded justice and my
immediate liberty as an Englishman who
had not offended the laws of his country ; that,
as to the rest, it was beneath my attention—
the odious idea of restraint was the same
odious idea everywhere ; that I would go
where I pleased, and if I was restrained by
a superior force, I must yield to the violence,
but would never give colour to it by a
shameful compromise ; that everything was
indifferent to me in comparison of my honour
and my liberty ; that I made my appeal to
the laws, and had already by my friends
applied to the Court of Common Pleas for
the Habeas Corpus, which the Chief Justice
had actually ordered to be issued, and that I
hoped to owe my discharge solely to my
innocence, and to the vigour of the law in a
free country. Lord Halifax then told me
that I should be sent to the Tower, where I
should be treated in a manner suitable to my
rank, and that he hoped the messengers had
behaved well to me. I acknowledged that
they had behaved with humanity and even
civility to me, notwithstanding the ruffian

orders given them by his lordship's colleague. I then again turned to Lord Egremont, and said, " Your lordship's verbal orders were to drag me out of my bed at midnight. The first man who had entered my bedchamber by force, I should have laid dead on the spot. Probably I should have fallen in the skirmish with the others. I thank God, not your lordship, that such a scene of blood has been avoided. Your lordship is very ready to issue orders, which you have neither the courage to sign nor, I believe, to justify." No reply was made to this. The conversation dropped. Lord Halifax retired into another apartment. Lord Egremont continued sullen and silent about a quarter of an hour. I then made a few remarks on some capital pictures which were in the room, and his lordship left me alone.

' I was afterwards conducted into another apartment. I found there several of my friends in argument with the most infamous of all the tools of that Administration, Mr. Philip Carteret Webb. He confirmed to me that I was to be carried to the Tower, and

wished to know if I had any favours to ask.
I replied that I was used to confer, not to
receive favours; that I was superior to the
receiving any even from his masters; that
all I would say to him was if my *valet de
chambre* was allowed to attend me in the
Tower, I should be shaved and have a clean
shirt; if he was not, I should have a long
beard and dirty linen. Mr. Webb said that
orders would be given for his admission at the
Tower.'

Such was this amazing proceeding, which
seems as if directed by the Star Chamber.
After the interview the Ministers must have
had some misgiving as to the step they had
so rashly taken, and as to the spirit of the
man that was encountered. Wilkes instantly
determined to obtain a writ of *habeas corpus*
to frustrate these unlawful proceedings. His
friend Almon, the Radical publisher and
writer, shall now take up the narrative.

He arrived just after the irruption of the
messengers. Mr. Wilkes took him to the
other end of the room, and there informed
him, in a low tone of voice, that the men

were the King's messengers, who had arrested
him by a warrant in which he was not named;
and begged of him to step immediately to
Lord Temple, and acquaint his lordship of
the affair.   The messengers, not knowing
that the editor was one of Mr. Wilkes'
intimate friends, permitted him quietly to
leave the house; for which they were afterwards severely reprimanded.   Lord Temple
desired the editor to go, with all possible
despatch, to Mr. Arthur Beardmore, his lordship's attorney in the City, and request him to
apply immediately to the Court of Common
Pleas for a writ of *habeas corpus* to bring
Mr. Wilkes before the court.

'This information was treated with the utmost contempt; but the Secretaries of State,
after some consultation, perhaps to evade the
writ of *habeas corpus*, shifted the custody of
Mr. Wilkes from the messengers who had
taken him, into the hands of other messengers; and in this manner was the custody of
Mr. Wilkes changed no less than four times
in half a day.'*

First he was in the hands of Robert Blackmore and

Every moment the complications and em·
barrassments of the original illegal act seemed
to increase. In consequence, the answer of the
two messengers, Blackmore and Watson, to the
writ, was ' that they had him not in their
custody.'

' When the messengers had taken Mr.
Wilkes to Lord Halifax's, they returned to
his dwelling, and seized all his papers of
every kind whatever. They broke open
every closet, bureau, and drawer in the
house ; Wood and Webb looking on. At
this time Earl Temple, Mr. Townsend
(afterwards Lord Sydney), Mr. Welsh, Mr.
Hopkins, Mr. Cotes, and other gentlemen,
arrived. Mr. Wood asked Earl Temple if he
would see Mr. Wilkes' papers sealed up ; but
his lordship replied "that it was too barbarous
an act for any human eye to witness ;" and

James Watson, who had apprehended him under the
general warrant ; he was carried by them to the Secretary
of State's office, where he was in the custody of the Earls
of Halifax and Egremont ; they transferred him to
George Collins and Thomas Ardran ; and finally, these
last delivered him to the Deputy-Lieutenant of the
Tower, to be kept a close prisoner.

all the other gentlemen present likewise refused. The papers were thrown promiscuously on the floor, and when collected from every part of the house, they were thrust into a sack, with his will (which was sealed and endorsed) and his private pocket-book, which was then carried to Lord Halifax's.'

The town now learned with astonishment that a member of Parliament had been seized on violently, and was at that moment in the Tower of London. The prisoner did not lose his gaiety, begging to be placed in the room in which Sir W. Wyndham, Lord Egremont's father, had been confined for treason. If that were refused, let them not put him in a room which a Scot had lately occupied, ' as he did not wish to catch the national disorder.'

Lord Temple and the Duke of Grafton came to call on him, but were not admitted. On which, the next step of the Ministers was to have Lord Temple dismissed from the Lord-Lieutenancy of the county, and struck out of the Privy Council—a truly tyrannic proceeding. He was consoled by some

pretty lines addressed to him by his Coun-
tess. These proceedings seem to have
alarmed the Duke of Grafton, to whom he
had written after his release. It was clearly
an attempt to join the Duke in his interests.
The latter asked Lord Temple to put the
matter on its proper footing. He had no
intention to commit himself to Wilkes'
principles.

Both offered to join in bail to any amount
—it was said for so large a sum as £100,000.
No one was allowed to see him.*

Next morning, magistrates of the Court
ordered a return to be made to their writ, and
finding the return made not sufficient, viz.,
that he was not in custody, directed another
order to the Constable of the Tower. In
consequence, he was brought up next day
before the Court of Common Pleas, when he
thus addressed the judges :

---

* The order issued by the Governor, Major Rainford,
to his warders, was of incredible harshness. They
were to keep Wilkes a close prisoner ; not to leave him
alone for a single moment night or day ; no one was to
be admitted to see him, and a list was to be kept of the
names of all the persons who applied to see him.

'I feel myself happy to be at last brought before a Court, and before judges, whose characteristic is the love of liberty. I have many humble thanks to return for the immediate order you were pleased to issue, to give me an opportunity of laying my grievances before you. They are of a kind hitherto unparalleled in this free country, and I trust the consequences will teach Ministers of Scottish and arbitrary principles that the liberty of an English subject is not to be sported away with impunity, in this cruel and despotic manner.

'I am accused of being the author of *The North Briton*, No. 45. I shall only remark upon that paper that it takes all load of accusation from the sacred name of a prince, whose family I love and honour as the glorious defenders of the cause of liberty, and whose personal qualities are so amiable, great, and respectable, that he is deservedly the idol of his people. It is the peculiar fashion and crime of these times, and of those who hold high ministerial offices in Government, to throw every odious charge from themselves upon majesty. The author of this paper, whoever he may be, has, upon constitutional principles, done directly the reverse, and is therefore in me, the supposed author, meant to be persecuted accordingly. The particular cruelties of my treatment, worse than if I had been a Scottish rebel, this Court will hear, and I dare say, from your justice, in due time redress.

'I may perhaps still have the means left me to show that I have been superior to every temptation or corruption. They may indeed have flattered themselves, that when they found corruption could not prevail, persecution might intimidate. I will show myself superior to both. My papers have been seized, perhaps with a hope the better to deprive me of that proof of their meanness, and corrupt prodigality, which it may possibly, in a proper place, be yet in my power to give.'

It will be noted how studiously he dwelt on his loyalty and devotion to the Crown. All the Bar declined the *risk* of taking up his case, but he found an intrepid advocate and friend in Serjeant Glynn, who also spoke, dealing with the legal points of the case, and arguing that the warrant was illegal. The Court reserved judgment, and Wilkes was conducted back to his prison, attended by a crowd of distinguished persons, and saluted with shouts from the mob. These were the first sounds of that particular form of music in which he was now to take such delight. By-and-by he was to be saluted with the more welcome note of ' Wilkes and Liberty !'

He demanded a copy of the warrant on which he had been committed, and it was found that it now took the shape of ' being an author and publisher of a most infamous and seditious libel.' It was noted that the word ' treasonable ' of the original warrant had been dropped, ' infamous ' being sub-stituted.

Indeed, from this time, he was to be for half-a-dozen years one of the most celebrated persons, not in England alone, but in Europe. His name was on everyone's lips, for good or for evil. Mr. Walpole thus sketched him at this moment.

' This hero is as bad a fellow as ever hero
was, abominable in private life, dull in Parliament; but, they say, very entertaining in a
room, certainly no bad writer, besides having
had the honour of contributing a great deal to
Lord Bute's fall.'

He was now permitted to see his friends.
Twice he was allowed to write a letter, but a
warder stood over him, and then carried what
he wrote to the Governor. He wrote a
characteristic one to his daughter, his favourite
' Polly,' which, however, was not forwarded.

' I am only accused of writing the last
North Briton; yet my sword has been taken
from me, all my papers have been stolen by
ruffians, and I have been forcibly brought
here. I have not yet seen my accusers, nor
have I heard who they are. My friends are
refused admittance to me; Lord Temple and
my brother could not be allowed to see me
yesterday. As an Englishman, I must lament
that my liberty is thus wickedly taken away:
yet I am not unhappy; for my honour is
clear, my health good, and my spirit unshaken—I believe, indeed, invincible. The

most pleasing thoughts I have, are of you ;
the most agreeable news I can hear, will be
of the continuance of your health.   I beg you
not to write a word of public business, or of
my public situation.   Can you get me made
membre du parlement de Paris? for that of
Westminster is losing all its privileges.   Continue to love me ; and believe me.'

Lord Temple, meanwhile, had received
orders to dismiss him from the militia, his
Majesty ' deeming it improper that he should
continue to be colonel.'   Lord Temple did as
he was directed, very delicately conveying to
him ' that he was to please to observe that he
no longer continued colonel of the militia.   I
cannot,' he added, ' at the same time help
expressing the concern I feel in the loss of
an officer, by his deportment in command,
endeared to the whole corps.'

On the following day, May 6th, he was
again brought to the Court, when he indulged
himself in another speech of spirit and good
effect.   After complaining of the harsh treatment he had received, he went on to say : ' I
will no longer delay your justice.   The nation

is impatient to hear, nor can be safe or happy
till that is obtained. If the same persecution
is after all to carry me before another Court,
I hope I shall find that the genuine spirit of
Magna Charta, that glorious inheritance, that
distinguishing characteristic of Englishmen.
is as religiously revered there, as I know it is
here, by the great personages before whom I
have now the happiness to stand ; and (as in
the ever-memorable case of the imprisoned
bishops) an independent jury of free-born
Englishmen that will persist to determine
my fate, as in conscience bound, upon constitutional principles, by a verdict of guilty or
not guilty. I ask no more at the hands of
my countrymen.'

The Chief Justice, Pratt, afterwards Lord
Camden, then gave judgment, first dealing
with the warrant, which he justified. And,
indeed, on the general merits of the case, he
justified the action of the Crown. A Secretary
of State's warrant he should consider through
the whole business as nothing more than the
warrant of a common justice of the peace ;
and thought no magistrate had a right *ex*

officio to apprehend any person without stating
the particular crime of which he was accused :
still there were many precedents where a
nice combination of circumstances gave so
strong a suspicion of facts, that though the
magistrate could not be justified *ex officio*, he
was nevertheless supported in the commitment even without receiving any particular
information for the foundation of his charge.
The word 'charge' was in general greatly mis-
understood ; and did not mean the accusation
brought against any person taken up, but his
commitment by the magistrate before whom
he might be brought.   Upon the whole of
this point he was of opinion that Mr. Wilkes's
commitment was not illegal.

' With respect to the second head—requiring a specification of the particular passages
in the paper which were deemed a libel—he
held that the insertion of these passages, so
far as they related to the point in question,
was not at all necessary : for even supposing
the whole of the forty-fifth number to have
been inserted in the body of the warrant, yet
it by no means came under his lordship's
cognizance at that time ; for the matter in

consideration then was, not the nature of the
offence, but the legality of the commitment—
the nature of the offence not resting in the
bosom of a judge, without the assistance of a
jury, and not being a proper subject of inquiry
until regularly brought on to be tried in the
customary way of proceeding.

'Then, as to the last point—that of privilege as a member of Parliament—that there
were but three cases which could possibly
affect the privilege of a member of Parliament,
and these were treason, felony, and the peace.
"The peace," as it is written in the institutes
of the law, signifies a breach of the peace.
When the seven bishops were sent to the
Tower, the plea that was used when the
spiritual lords contended for their privilege,
was, that they had endeavoured to disturb the
peace.* Then, turning to his brethren on
each side (the other judges were Bathurst and
Gould), said : " that the privilege of Parliament must be held inviolable and sacred :
there were but three cases in which that

---

* This point, it will be seen, was raised in a more
important way on the later argument of the case, and
was a criminal one.

privilege was forfeited, and it only remained to examine how far Mr. Wilkes' privilege was endangered. Mr. Wilkes was accused of writing a libel; a libel, in the sense of the law, was a high misdemeanour, but did not come within the description of treason, felony, or breach of the peace ; at most it had but a tendency to disturb the peace, and consequently could not be sufficient to destroy the privilege of Parliament." '

The Court unanimously held, therefore, that, on this point, he must be discharged.

It is clear that this judgment was not law, and that a sort of generous construction was extended to the acts of Government. In a matter concerning the liberty of the subject it is usual to construe everything strictly, and it will be seen later that this tolerant view was held to be wrong. Wilkes had now an opportunity for yet another harangue.

' Great as my joy must naturally be,' he said, ' at a decision which this Court, with a true spirit of liberty, has been pleased to make concerning the unwarrantable seizure of my person, and all the other consequential grievances, allow me to assure you, that I feel far less sensibly on my account, than I do for the public. The sufferings of an individual are a trifling object, when compared with the whole; and I should blush to feel for myself in comparison with considerations of a nature so transcendently superior.

'I will not trouble you with my poor thanks; thanks are due to you from the whole English nation, and from all the subjects of the English crown. They will be paid you; together with every testimony of zeal and affection to the learned serjeant (Glynn) who has so ably and so constitutionally pleaded my cause, and in mine (with pleasure I say it) the cause of liberty. Every testimony of my gratitude is justly due to you; and I take leave of this court with a veneration and respect which no time can obliterate, nor can the most grateful heart sufficiently express.'

The result of this Ministerial violence was disastrous enough, and, as it will be seen, Wilkes later recovered £4,000 damages from the Secretary of State. This was the greatest of his many successful struggles, for every low pettifogging art was employed to protract the proceedings. The reader will see, from the following, what legal ingenuity was exerted :

The original writ was issued on June 1st, and was returnable on June 19th, 1763. The Earl then ' cast an essoign ' (whatever that means), which was adjourned to November 18th. Thus, having availed himself of his privilege, a ' distringas ' was taken out for May 9th, 1764, returnable on May 27th. To this the Earl did not appear. Another ' distringas ' was then taken out on May 30th, returnable June 18th. Issues were made up, but the Earl still did not appear. A ' pluries distringas ' was taken out on 22nd June, returnable July 8th. In November Wilkes was outlawed, and *then* the Earl appeared without any delay, when he was, of course, discharged from the suit, as Wilkes had no standing in the court. This monstrous and oppressive use of the law in favour of a Government officer seems incredible.

When he had finished this address, the audience broke out into shouts of applause. He waited for some time in a room adjoining the court, in the hope that the crowd would disperse; at last, finding that it only increased, he left the place by a private door, but was recognised by an enormous crowd who were waiting for him, and who attended him home. That night there were bonfires and illuminations.

Such was this victory, which completely altered the tone of his life. Such shouts, attending him home, are inexpressibly sweet to the demagogue, who is certain to confuse the crowd with the nation. He was formally started on his course as a 'Demagogue.' He had been persecuted, imprisoned, and had triumphed, all within a few days. His hopes had been realized; what he contrived had come about. The blunders of his opponents had given him the victory and encouraged him to try and tempt them into committing yet more blunders, which would bring him fresh profit and fame.

A few days after his release, he was served with a subpœna to answer an information in the King's Bench, so persevering were his opponents; but of this, he took no notice.

There was something of the *scapin* in Wilkes, as will be seen from his next step. So soon as he reached home, he sat down and wrote the following amusing letter to the Secretaries of State.

'My Lords,

'On my return here from Westminster Hall, where I have been discharged from my commitment to the Tower under your lordships' warrant, I find that my house has been robbed, and am informed that the stolen goods are in the possession of one or both of your lordships. I therefore insist that you do forthwith return them to your humble servant,

'John Wilkes.'

This statement was strictly true, and it was afterwards proved to a jury, that these noblemen had broken into his house and robbed him of his property. Not content with this, he resolutely repaired next morning to the Police Court in Bow Street, and demanded a warrant 'to search the houses of Lords Egremont and Halifax, for goods stolen out of his house, which, as he had received information, were

detained at the said houses, or one of them.'
There was a happy insolence in this pushing
home the logical consequences of their act.
But the magistrates declined to take his view.

With a curious lack of dignity or of
humour, the two lords answered him, quite
au sérieux :

'Sir,—In answer to your letter of yesterday, in which you take upon you to make
use of the indecent and scurrilous expressions
of your having "found your house had been
robbed, and that the stolen goods are in our
possession ;" we acquaint you that your papers
were seized in consequence of the heavy
charge brought against you, for being the
author of an infamous and seditious libel,
tending to inflame the minds, and alienate
the affections of the people from his Majesty,
and excite them to traitorous insurrections
against the Government : for which libel, notwithstanding your discharge from your commitment to the Tower, his Majesty has
ordered you to be prosecuted by his Attorney-
General.

'We are at a loss to guess what you mean by stolen goods : but such of your papers as do not lead to a proof of your guilt, shall be restored to you ; such as are necessary for that purpose, it was our duty to deliver over to those whose business it is to collect the evidence, and manage the prosecution against you.

'We are, your humble servants,

'EGREMONT.

· 'DUNK HALIFAX.'

The indiscretion, not to say stupidity, of this argument is extraordinary.   On a mere suspicion that he had published a libel, his papers are plundered in the hope of collecting some evidence to help to make out the charge.

He returned this crushing reply :

'Little did I expect, when I was requiring from your lordships what an Englishman has a right to, his property taken from him, and said to be in your lordships' possession, that I should have received in answer, from persons in your high station, the expressions of *indecent* and *scurrilous* applied to my legal

demand. The respect I bear to his Majesty,
whose servants it seems you still are, pre-
vents my returning you an answer in the
same Billingsgate language. If I considered
you only in your private capacities, I should
treat you both according to your deserts : but
where is the wonder that men who have
attacked the sacred liberty of the subject, and
have issued an illegal warrant to seize his
property, should proceed to such libellous
expressions ? You say, " that such of my
papers shall be restored to me, as do not lead
to a proof of my guilt." I owe this to your
apprehension of an action, not to your love of
justice ; and in that light, if I can believe
your lordships' assurances, the whole will be
returned to me. I fear neither your prosecution, nor your persecution ; and I will assert
the security of my own house, the liberty of
my person, and every right of the people, not
so much for my own sake, as for the sake of
every one of my English fellow-subjects.'

In compositions of this kind Wilkes had
a style of his own, full of impudence or insolence combined with wit.

CHAPTER VII.

CHARLES CHURCHILL.

NOTWITHSTANDING all this enthusiasm, there were admirers of Wilkes who began to feel alarm at certain signs of almost revolutionary violence which were now displayed by the popular hero. Thus the Duke of Grafton, who had shown his sympathy by a personal visit to the Tower, now shrank from further committing himself. He wrote to Lord Temple that a letter from Wilkes had come to him that morning while he was out riding. 'As it was now too late to send him my answer in time, I flatter myself you will add this to many other obligations, and tell him how I stand circumstanced the first time you see or meet him. In short, my lord, I went —as I think every acquaintance is almost bound to do—to see Mr. Wilkes in his con-

finement, to hear from himself his own story
and defence, and to show that no influence
ought to stop the means of a man's justifying
himself from an accusation, though it should
be of a most heinous nature. But when I
look upon myself as called on to bail, though
it had been from a person in the world who
had the most right to have asked that sort of
favour from me, I must have trod very warily
on ground that seemed to come in any way
under the denomination of an insult to the
Crown.'—It was a rule laid down by him,
and which he would most religiously observe,
that while opposing the Minister, nothing
should even be carried on by him with the
shadow of offence against his Majesty's person
or family.—'This consistency of my character
will, I hope, therefore, be my excuse to him.'
The same motive operated also on Lord
Villiers, who accompanied the Duke on his
visit.

This was significant enough, and Wilkes,
had he seen this letter, might have anticipated the treatment he was later to receive
from the Duke.

In October, 1763, we find him grumbling at his treatment by his admirers. ' Lord Temple will see how little that same public which bore me so triumphantly can be trusted to.' This trust he meant should be of a pecuniary kind. ' I am proud '—and he repeats an old form of complaint—' to be under obligations to Lord Temple, yet they are so great that I am uneasy under them.' Notwithstanding, he proposed to trespass further on his friend's generosity. He wished to raise £3,000 by selling his estate, or a portion of it, and ' it was no reflection on the patriot Wilkes, in the cause of friendship and the public, to have .£200 a year less, but it will hurt him to owe even to a tailor. To speak my sentiments freely, I wish to part with other lands to Lord Temple. I regret nothing that is past; I exult when I look back to the testimony your lordship has borne me; it is the glory of my life. £400 I was bond for to Mr. Stow, and I must pay it in a very few days.' There is something disagreeable, it must be confessed, in this *mélange* of flattery, gratitude, and loaning. Lord Temple at once sent him a note for £500.

With these serious anxieties pressing on him, the mercurial Wilkes went over to Paris to enjoy himself, and to see his daughter. But here fresh annoyances awaited him, from adventurers in as sorry a plight as he was himself.

'On the morning of August 15, 1763, he was walking to Notre Dame, in company with Lord Palmerston, to see the *fonction* of the day, when he was stopped by a person, who asked if his name was Wilkes, after which he said, " Mr. Wilkes wrote *The North Briton,* and must fight him." Mr. Wilkes desired to know what evidence the gentleman had for so round an assertion ; that a squabble in the streets was unbecoming a gentleman, and an indecent affront to the laws of the country; that he lived at the Hôtel de Saxe, and wished him a good day. This person, in the afternoon, called at the Hôtel de Saxe, and left a card. The next morning he returned about six. He said his name was Forbes, a captain in the French regiment of Ogilby, which had been broken, or, as it is there called, reformed. Mr. Wilkes regretted that he had not left on his card where he lived, to have prevented him that second trouble of coming to the Hôtel de Saxe, and desired to know his commands. He said that Mr. Wilkes must fight him, because he had written against Scotland. Mr. Wilkes asked what he had written, and wished to see the papers objected to, or to know what they were. Mr. Forbes replied, " You have written against my country. Your name is Wilkes ; do you not write ?" Mr. Wilkes said that he did now and then write receipts for tenants, and sometimes on post nights ; but would give no account to Mr. Forbes, nor to any man. Mr. Forbes then asked him if he would fight him that day. Mr. Wilkes told him that he would fight him upon his honour ; but he believed he could not indulge him that day, for he had a previous account to settle with Lord Egremont, and went into the circumstances of that affair. Mr. Wilkes added that it was very unfit Captain Forbes and he should talk over so critical a business alone; therefore desired him to return the same day at noon, and to bring one gentleman for a second along with him; and Mr. Wilkes' friend and second would likewise attend. Mr. Wilkes declared he would leave every particular of time, place, etc., to their two friends, and would abide by their determination. Captain Forbes promised that he would bring his second; but came alone at twelve at noon, and found Monsieur Goy and Wilkes. Captain Forbes insisted on Mr. Wilkes fighting him that day, and directly. Mr. Wilkes reminded him of his promise in the morning to return with a second. Mr. Forbes said that Mr. Wilkes knew enough; that his friend was near, and that he would fetch him. He accordingly went away; in a quarter of an hour he returned again alone, and said he would bring no friend; but Mr. Wilkes should soon hear from him. Mr. Wilkes asked how he could know that the person he was conversing with was a gentleman, or was Captain Forbes, having never seen him till the day before; and observed that his coming in such a manner, and re-

fusing to bring a second, had more the air of
an assassin than of a gentleman.   Mr. Forbes
said that he was well known to the Prince of
Soubize, and then went away.'

There was but one opinion as to Wilkes'
behaviour—that he had behaved with folly
in treating this swashbuckler *au sérieux*.

If he accepted such provocation, he was for
the future at the mercy of any swaggering
adventurer who might hope to recommend
himself to the favour of the Government by
fastening a quarrel on their opponent, and
possibly disposing of him.

After this, Forbes unaccountably disap-
peared from the scene, and Wilkes discovered
that he was concealed at a house of a country-
man, the Hon. Mr. Murray, who, it was assumed, was his adviser and second.   The
adventure presently attracted the attention of
the Court of Marshals, who put both Murray
and Wilkes under guard.   They were then
summoned before Marshal Noailles, the
President, and, on giving their *parole*—Mr.
Murray engaging for Forbes — that they
would not offend against the law, were

allowed to go free. 'The Marshal asked Wilkes what was his quarrel with Captain Forbes, and the other answered, "*Monseigneur, je n'ai ni l'honneur ni l'envie de connoitre Monsieur Forbes.*" Mr. Wilkes then, before several French gentlemen, after Marshal Noailles was retired, begged Mr. Macdonald, who was an intimate friend of Mr. Forbes, to assure him, that as soon as the affair with Lord Egremont was settled, if he was alive, he would indulge Captain Forbes, should he choose to fight him; and that it would be Captain Forbes's own fault if he did not; for Mr. Wilkes would meet him for that purpose anywhere in Europe, Asia, Africa, or America, except the dominions of France.'

Meanwhile, by a strange coincidence, the obstacles which had prevented Wilkes giving the Scot satisfaction were suddenly removed by the death of Lord Egremont, whom he was thus prevented from calling to account. He felt bound, then, to satisfy his new opponent, who still kept in retirement.

After some three weeks' vain search for the Scotch captain, the pugnacious Wilkes addressed the following curious letter to Murray :

' SIR,

'I have waited with no small impatience, and I believe you will agree with me, that, before this, *Captain Forbes* ought to have sent for me. You know everything which has passed between us, and the wild, extravagant wish he formed of fighting me, on no pretence, nor provocation. I am no prize-fighter ; yet I told him that I would indulge him, and as soon as I could.

'I stated the circumstances of the insolence and inhumanity of Lord Egremont, and my resolution of calling his lordship to account. I had likewise then fixed the hour of his losing the seals as the period I should call his lordship to that account ; and I am sure that I would have left Paris, or any other place, immediately on receiving news so interesting to myself, so welcome to the nation.

'Lord Egremont, to my great regret—greater, I believe, than that of any other person—has prevented my proceeding farther, and, as a Frenchman would say, *il m'a joué un vilain tour.*

'I am now, therefore, most entirely at Captain Forbes's service, and shall wait his commands. I do not know where he is, for he has not appeared at Paris since Tuesday, the 16th of August. As your house has been his asylum, I am necessitated to beg you, sir, to acquaint Captain Forbes that I will be at Menin, the first town in Austrian Flanders, on the confines of France, the 21st of this month, and that Mr. Goy will do me the honour of accompanying me; but he only. I shall request my letters to be sent there, and the moment of my arrival I shall go to the post-house.

'No person, but Monsieur Goy, is acquainted with any part of this transaction; he is so obliging as to take charge of this letter.

'Give me leave to acknowledge the personal civilities you have been pleased to confer on me at Paris, and to assure you, etc.'

During the progress of this incident he kept

his friend Churchill *au courant* with his proceedings.

He wrote, in reference to the unexpected death of Lord Egremont :

' What a scoundrel trick has he played me ! I had formed a fond wish to send him to the devil ; but he is gone without my passport.'

He then repeated his rather vaunting declaration that he had long determined to challenge Lord Egremont, so soon as he had ceased to be Secretary of State ; and he appealed to his declaration made in the Tower, to Major Ramsden, to that effect.

' I desire you to blot out of your book of maxims, "De mortuis," etc. : it is a vile, levelling principle, which makes Cato and Catiline the same men. You and I will be as distinguished when we have put off this mortal coil.

' Do not think I hold myself obliged to fight every dirty Scot ; but I choose to show what I can do with such a fellow as Forbes. If I live to return to England, I will, under your auspices, be the first, at least the boldest, political writer England has produced.

'My time here has not been lost. I am like a river—the farther it runs from its source, the greater, the richer, it becomes. I shall hail the fogs of November; for no man can be more impatient than I am for the winter, which will be infinitely interesting to us all, and to me above all entertaining, if, indeed, you keep your word, and give us the poems you promise. *Culloden* is an excellent idea, and soothes our natural pride. I have a rod steeping for Hogarth. You are read and admired here. My intimate friend Goy has almost got you by heart. I have promised the *beaux esprits* of Paris that you will keep Christmas among them. I wish you could come over now, and strengthen in the true Protestant faith that great pillar Wilkes, who is assailed on every hand. But I am determined to import into England all the religion I exported.'*

In this we see a tone of elation, and even hope. He was, in truth, of a mercurial temper, always at its highest when engrossed by some present action.

* Wilkes MSS., B. Mus.

His friend, however, took a more serious
view of his position. He totally disapproved
of the Forbes business, and even more of
the vaunt as to Lord Egremont, which was
in bad taste, considering the recent death of
that personage. He set out his view in a
long and weighty letter :

'In the first place, I think that your reputation stands upon a fairer ground—by reputation I mean, not the character coming from
one virtue, but from the assemblage of many
—in the reports now received than in your
own account.' He doubted if his behaviour
did much honour to his discretion, and here,
he said, he had the world on his side. When
it was rumoured that he had been killed, not
a man he met but condemned him for having
accepted such a challenge. His account now
sent exculpated him in point of courage,
'where even your foes did not doubt you, but
condemns you in point of prudence, where
even your friends suspected you. If valour
was all you desired a reputation of, my Lord
Talbot would have granted you a certificate.

But we required something more—some instance of judgment ; and I own, for my own
part, it would have given me the greatest
pleasure to have found that the life which
I valued almost equally with my own was
not to be sacrificed to false principles of
honour.'

After some admirable remarks on duty, he
goes on :

'The first part of your conduct is most
noble ; but I think that, in mentioning your
design with relation to Lord Egremont, your
engaging to fight Forbes, and your renewing
that engagement with Macdonald, are points
on which you were infinitely to blame ; and
you seem in those parts to live in romance,
rather than under the direction of that
well-tempered, cool, distinguishing reason
in which no man is more happy than yourself. Why reveal your designs with relation
to Lord Egremont, and make it plain to the
world what you ought to have kept to yourself—a resolution of calling him to such an
account as must stamp the act premeditated
and planned long before ? . . . The cause of

liberty is in your hands. Your county demands that life . . . It is with me a question
whether there may ever be another Wilkes.
You have pledged yourself, and cannot in
honour recede ; and your name will go down
to posterity with tenfold honour if you adhere
to that sacred engagement.

' Another thing I cannot help mentioning,
which gives all honourable Englishmen uneasiness—I mean your stay in Paris. The
very going to France is to the public eye an
unpopular measure, and your staying there
beyond the appointed time gives me great
pain. Changes are much talked of, and
must soon take place ; nor can I think but
that George Street will be infinitely more
elegible than Paris. Lord Temple wishes
much to see you, nor is he by any means
singular in this respect.'

To encourage him to come he tells him
various items of political news—Pitt had been
with the King ; Lord Bute with Pitt, etc. *

This letter of wholesome counsel was
entrusted to a friend, but it did not reach

Wilkes's hands till long after. There was some mystery about the affair.*

Churchill must have been hurt to find his advice so disregarded; for the impetuous Wilkes had set off for an obscure town on the frontier, giving his opponent a rendezvous, but without waiting to hear whether he was willing to repair to the meeting. The next news that Churchill had of his friend was from Menin, an Austrian town. It will be noted in what a reckless strain it is couched :

' This is not the affair of the Horatii and Curatii ; but, however, I think Forbes a pitiful fellow, except indeed it should be Murray's fault.' (He found no letter there from either.) ' I shall stay here to-night, and to-morrow, if I hear nothing from Forbes, shall return to Lille. I have seen one of the most charming of our countrywomen at Lille, who has made me amends for leaving Paris. I hasten back to her ; if honour

* It was found thus endorsed: ' This letter Mr. Wilkes never received, but it was given to him after his return by Mr. Cotes, who could not recollect the reason why it was not sent.'

permits me, love calls. Those stars have been for us two polar ones through life, and I am sure will continue so.

'I saw Garrick by chance on the road to Paris. He was travelling on, as I thought, in the stupid matrimonial way, not the least superior to the humdrum blockheads you meet through life at every stage—to speak as a traveller. I talked with him only half an hour, but his plans seemed to me very absurd.'

This sketch, though not intended as complimentary, is what the great actor would have thought the highest praise, and the contemptuous opinion of the two debauchees would have been to him a matter of supreme indifference.

He waited one day, and, as was to be expected, no one arrived; then set off 'to Dunkerque, to Calais, to London, and to Churchill.' Within a few weeks he was engaged in another affair of honour, which had disagreeable results. Thus within a year the fire-eating Colonel had 'on hand' no less than four of these rencounters, and cer-

tainly ' graduated with honour ' in that mode
of argument.

Churchill, who could gravely advise and
reprove his friend in weighty words for failing
to govern his conduct by prudence, himself
sadly lacked such guidance. In one of his
letters, when writing to his friend of the
chastisement with which he intended to punish
Hogarth, he says :

' I intended an elegy on him, supposing
him dead ; but —— (Betsy) tells me he will
be really dead before it comes out that I
have already killed him, etc. How sweet is
flattery from the woman we love ; and how
weak is our boasted strength when opposed
to beauty and good sense with good-nature !
Those who value themselves on the dignity of
man may form such a supposition ; but I
would rather bear that slavery (and it is the
only slavery I would tamely bear) than enjoy
the empire of mankind.'

It would be difficult to suppose that this
placid and philosophical language, and almost
pastoral tone, was used in reference to one of
the most discreditable scandals of the time,

and which was being talked of over the town.* The story was this : He had become acquainted with the daughter of a stone-cutter in Westminster, and persuaded her to leave her father's house and live with him. The family vowed vengeance, and all voices were raised against the depraved parson, who was, besides, a husband. Indifferent to this howl, he withdrew to Aylesbury, to Wilkes's house, a little, it would appear, to the disquiet of his friend.†

* The compound of tumultuous passions and placid purpose which characterized this extraordinary being is better shown by an appeal made by him at this very time to Garrick for pecuniary aid :

'MY DEAR MR. GARRICK,

'Half drunk—half mad—and quite stripped of all my money, I should be much obliged if you would enclose and send by the bearer five pieces, by way of adding to favours already received by

'Yours sincerely

'CHARLES CHURCHILL.'

† Mr. Forster quotes a passage from Southey's 'Life of Cowper,' in which it is stated that after a fortnight both felt compunction, and on the entreaty of friends the girl was taken back by her family. It was said, however, that her sister's continued taunts and reproaches goaded her into quitting the house, when she finally remained with Churchill.

Wilkes had other reasons for anxiety, even as to the safety of his friend's person, and thus wrote to warn him, on Nov. 3rd :

'Great George Street,
'Nov. 3.

'Written in great anxiety, for it presents to me a scene I own I dread of what is likely to happen. I fear much a warrant, signed by the pale Mansfield, beginning the "*thing against Charles Churchill*, clerk." Then a picture of the said Charles handing into court his Betsy, who will be ordered back to an angry papa, locked up, etc.; and this you can't prevent. The family are in the greatest distress ; and you are universally condemned for having made a worthy family unhappy. I except Cotes, your brother, and myself. It is known that you are at Aylesbury; therefore I submit to your PRUDENCE, if you choose to continue there. You may command me, my house, servants, etc. I wish you would love yourself half as well as I love you ! I dread Mansfield's warrant. Think of the great card we all have to play !

When you can so nobly assist us in our great parts, ought you to run away to sport in dalliance ? I fear not for your person, though I hear many schemes against your life, if you persevere. The father, brother, and a servant went with pistols charged to Kingston Garden, in consequence of an anonymous letter, to have assassinated you. Are you not more private in my place near London than in any country town ? Do not give to dull Bishops and others such advantages against you.'

It is almost amusing, if it were not melancholy, to find the two rakes thus lecturing one another. The answer is almost appalling from its settled desperate purpose, and the horrible confession of faith in the underlined passage :

'I am infinitely obliged to you for your letter, and those offers of service which were no more than I expected, from my knowledge of you. Your advice, and the illness of Mrs. Carr, more than the fears of assassination, brought me to town. Assassination! a pretty word, fit for boys and men to laugh at. I never yet played for so deep a stake. But if called on, I think I dare set my life on a cast, as the rash young man her brother shall find, if he puts me to the proof. *My life I hold for purposes of pleasure ; those forbid, it is not worth my care.* Mansfield I laugh at and despise. I long to see you and assure you that I deserve the name of friend, which you honour me with. I will rather seek danger than shun it.'

Nothing so serious as Wilkes anticipated came of this adventure. Churchill was left to reap the usual fruits of such escapades, and to find himself burdened for life with one who probably proved to be less of a divinity than his disturbed fancy had pictured her.

CHAPTER VIII.

THE 'ESSAY ON WOMAN.'

THUS baffled and discredited, we might have expected that the Ministers would have been inclined to leave Wilkes, as it is called, severely alone. The lesson had been a painful one. Lord Egremont, indeed, died within a few weeks, which led to a general reconstruction, and, to the astonishment of most people, the debauched Lord Sandwich was appointed to fill his place. He had been, as we have seen, the partner of Wilkes's pleasures, who might hope for toleration, if not for indulgence, from such an ally. But this was 'the worst Ministry England ever had,' and the head of this worst Ministry went nigh to shipwrecking the country, being accountable for both the disastrous American war, and for the no less unlucky contest with Wilkes.

One would think that their recent defeat would have warned them not to molest Wilkes further; but dull, stupid Ministers, like the Bourbon race, learn nothing, and forget nothing. In the raid on Wilkes's property, there had been carried off all his private papers; and in looking through them, the officials came on a few printed leaves that astonished and shocked, and at the same time pleased, them. The discovery was reported to the highest authorities, who now thought they had Wilkes on the hip ; but it was pointed out by legal advisers that as the evidence had been ill-gotten, unlawfully too, no use could be made of it.

This was the famous ' Essay on Woman,' of which it may be said that it was the most scandalous of such productions, horrible and monstrous in its language; while its author, whoever he was, better deserved whipping at the cart's tail than many of lower infamy. Explanatory notes in the same vein were added, purporting to be written by the Bishop of Gloucester. Here now was a *pièce de conviction* to support a prosecution for indecency and blasphemy ; for at the end there were some fearfully profane parodies on the Church Hymns. But in this view a copy must be secured in a legal way.

A printer named Farmer, being in company with one of Wilkes's men, was given by him some butter, which was wrapped up in a sheet of the production in question. He showed it to some of his fellows at Faden's, the office where he worked, when the foreman, hearing of it, bade him secure the rest if he could, giving him money for the purpose. He found great difficulty, and made several attempts to tamper with the printers, notably one Curry, who worked in Wilkes's house, for the Patriot indulged in that most costly of literary luxuries—a private press. This faithless workman, who had a grudge against Wilkes, engaged to secure the other sheets ; for the first portion had been only a stray trial sheet picked up off the floor. The treacherous printer at last contrived to put together a copy, which was then placed in the hands of Kidgell, 'a dirty dog of a parson,' a disreputable fellow who was chaplain to Lord

March. The world wondered when it learnt that so prime a *roué* kept a chaplain. This cleric at first thought of publishing his prize for his own profit ; as obviously no printer would venture on this, he took counsel with his pious patron. ' My Lord March,' the chaplain tells us in his account of the transaction, ' was extremely offended ' at what was shown to him, and promised his assistance in discountenancing so shameful an undertaking. In a few days he informed his chaplain that ' proper means would be taken for the discovery and punishment of so avowed an enemy to society.'

A precious trio then sat in committee to settle measures for bringing the guilty writer to justice. One was the Bishop of Gloucester, a violent prelate, long supposed to be unorthodox or unsound in his doctrine ; Lord Sandwich, an abandoned, scandalous liver, and Lord March—' Old Q.' later—whose iniquities it would be idle even to hint at. The next step in the plot was to call in Mr. Carteret Webb, one of the Secretaries to the Treasury, who took charge of Curry, the printer, kept him at his house with a weekly allowance, and, as it was later urged, a promise of a place worth £100 a year.

Curry later claimed the fulfilment of these promises, but was put off with general assurances that ' he had done a good act,' and ' that they hoped merit would be rewarded.'*

Having thus secured what they wanted, the Government now proceeded to fortify their case by all those meaner arts which are in favour with oppressive rulers abroad. The Secretary did not disdain to issue instructions to his witnesses to make up a consistent tale among themselves.†

* The printer seems to have been intimidated into surrendering the papers ; for threats of a prosecution for felony were used, either by Wilkes' friends or by the Government. We have a glimpse of Churchill in this business, to whom the printer applied for advice, and who gave him ' a short answer,' and characteristically assured him that ' as to what the people in power could do, they might be damned.' This short answer showed that his treachery was suspected ; and when he was refused admission to Wilkes, from whom he no doubt wanted a price for secrecy, he went in a passion to Faden, and for five guineas gave up the papers.

† Thus he wrote : ' Before Mr. Curry goes, desire him to put down in writing what passed between Mr. Faden and you, and between Churchill and Carnegie ; and what

We find Lord Sandwich writing to Grenville, in November, 1763, 'You know we have had Wilkes regularly watched ever since his return from France,' and he encloses a report from the spies, who day after day hung about his door, and tracked him from place to place.*

Indefensible as this was, it must be further

Churchill said of Murphy previous to his giving up the papers; and *to state the particular slights, ill-usage, and affronts* he received from Wilkes before and after his going to France, and what passed on " the d————d :" *I mean by way of justification of Mr. Curry, that you may all concur in one story.*'—' English Liberty,' p. 255.

* A regular report of the detectives was enclosed : ' Oct. 31.—Mr. Wilkes went out at half-past ten. Mr. Leach, the printer, came, and staid an hour and a half. Nov. 2.—Mr. Churchill came, and staid an hour and a half. Nov. 5.—Mr. Wilkes went out this morning at half-past ten to Mr. Karr's at Vauxhall, where was Mr. Churchill. One of my Lord Temple's post-boys came and delivered a parcel to Mr. Wilkes' footman. N.B.—The printers are very busy composing in the two-pair-of-stairs room all this evening.'—'Grenville Diaries.' It is amusing to find from these reports that the writer of the ' Essay on Woman ' was, after all, as pharisaical as his enemies, for on the Sunday morning Mr. Wilkes is reported to have gone to St. Margaret's Church at half-past ten, 'and stayed till the service was over ' !

13—2

remembered that these inquisitorial acts were directed against what was as private a matter as though it were a manuscript. The scandalous essay was not published, nor intended to be published. About a dozen copies were printed, presents, no doubt, for the twelve Monks of Medmenham.

Up to a few years ago there was much curiosity as to this mysterious book. No one had ever seen or described a copy. In one of Wilkes' publications a line or two is given.

It seems that Kearsley, the printer, just before the seizure, had made up a selection of pages, which were printed as a sort of specimen, and of this fragment a single copy is all that is in existence.* The late Mr.

---

* The title of the tract runs :

'AN ESSAY ON WOMAN,
    By Pego Borewell, Esq. ;

With Notes by Rogerus C——. And a Commentary by
    the Rev. Dr. Warburton. Inscribed to
        Miss Fanny Murray.'

A quotation from Homer follows, and at the bottom an allusion to Dr. Stone, the Primate, and Lord G. Sackville. The whole consists of 94 lines. There is a space left on the title for a copper-plate vignette of an indecent description, and wanting in Mr. Dyce's copy. In

Dyce, by some wonderful chance, succeeded in securing this copy—no doubt the one perloined by Parson Kidgell.

Something, though not much, turns on the question of authorship; for it was contended, to show with what harshness Wilkes was treated, that he was not the actual writer. Sir C. Wentworth Dilke, Wilkes' advocate *in omnibus*, relies on the indictment, in which he was charged with merely printing and publishing.

One of Wilkes' printers, Jennings, however, found on the floor a proof in which were four words of his writing. It would be difficult to prove the act of composition; but there is a passage in one of Wilkes'

---

favour of Wilkes it should be mentioned that the fragment is made up of a few disjointed pages selected from different portions of the original, which it seems likely was never printed in its entirety, as he tells the Aylesbury electors : 'Not quite a fourth part of the volume had been printed at my own private press. The work had been discontinued for several months. Of that fourth part only twelve copies were worked off, and I never gave one of those copies to my friends.'—Letter, Oct. 22, 1764.

addresses to his Aylesbury electors (the letter
of October, 1764) which might favour the
theory of his being the author :

‘ The most vile blasphemies were forged,
and published as part of a work which in
reality contained nothing but fair ridicule on
some doctrines *I could not believe,* mock
panegyric, flowing from mere envy, which
sickened at the *superior parts and abilities,* as
well as *wondrous deeds* of a man *I could not
love,* a few portraits drawn from warm life,
with the too high colouring of a youthful fancy,
and two or three descriptions.’

This, though not quite free from ambiguity,
seems to imply that he was the writer.   It
has been always stated that he was assisted
by Thomas Potter, and Wilkes probably
wrote the notes.   But we cannot find that he
formally repudiated the authorship.   Further,
Mr. Curry, the printer, deposed that Wilkes
had told him that ‘ it had taken him a great
deal of pains and trouble to compose.’   On the
other hand, it was stated that—‘ It is a circumstance of almost universal notoriety that the
“ Essay on Woman ” is a parody on Mr.

Pope's " Essay on Man," wrote about fifteen
years ago by Mr. Potter, son of the late great
Archbishop of Canterbury, and that it has
been publicly and often read many years ago
at the Beefsteak Club, by the very Lord
who moved against it in the House of Peers.'*

This curious statement, it will be seen,
was merely suggested as a topic for counsel to
cross-examine upon, and does not go beyond
the assertion of 'notoriety.' If it be true
that Lord Sandwich behaved as stated, a
more flagrant instance of impudent, shameless hypocrisy has never been chronicled. In
Mr. Dyce's copy he has written the following inscription : ' My late venerable friend,
William Maltby, was intimately acquainted
with Wilkes, and assured me Wilkes said to
him, " I am not the author of the 'Essay on
Woman ;' it was written by Potter." ' Wilkes'
share, therefore, would have been simply the
adoption and printing.†

* From the 'case' for counsel ; MS. Brit. Mus.
† Kidgell issued an account of the essay :
' A genuine and succinct narrative of a scandalous,
  obscene, and exceedingly profane libel, entitled
　　AN ESSAY ON WOMAN,

Unluckily for Wilkes, there is some direct evidence against him. On the seizure of papers at Kearsley the printer's, under the general warrant, some letters of Wilkes' were found, one of which ran : ' I am impatient for my " Essay on Woman." Let it be on very good paper ; two proofs.' And again : ' You are to send by the bearer the MS. of the essay.' Dr. Birch, who writes an account of the investigation to Lord Royston, accepting this as a convincing proof, says : ' His letters, which discovered the piece, had been seized at Kearsley, the bookseller's.' It was stated, too, ' that when he delivered the copy to be printed, he enjoined the men in the most solemn manner not to rob him of a sheet of it, for he had not the least intention of publishing it.' It was stated also

And also of other poetical pieces containing
The most atrocious blasphemies submitted to the
candour of the public,
By the Rev. Mr. Kidgell, A.M., Rector of Herne in
Surrey, Preacher of Berkeley Chapel, and Chaplain to the
Rt. Hon. the Earl of March and Ruglen, 1763.
To " the violated laws, the abused liberty, and the in-
sulted religion of our country," this authentic
narrative is inscribed.'

that the whole of the MS. was in Wilkes'
handwriting. Unhappily, too, the presump-
tion is that it was Wilkes' own, from the
character of the work, which was but too
congenial to his nature and ideas.

When thus enjoying the sweets of popularity,
already, as we have seen, considering the
public under heavy obligations to ' the
Patriot Wilkes,' he little dreamed what
a plot was being hatched against him, nor
the quarter from which it was to come. He
had supped at a tavern with Lord Sandwich,
where they had enjoyed much loose talking
together. Yet at the moment it was
Sandwich who had actually arranged the
second plot which Ministers had contrived
against him !

On July 26th he quitted London for Paris,
where his daughter was, and with whom he
always affectionately longed to be   His gratitude to Lord Temple at this moment knew no
bounds. ' As to my own little concerns, I
shall sacrifice all revenge, all interest, all
plans of *dédommagement* against Lords Egremont and Halifax, the moment your lordship

wishes, whom I leave the most absolute and entire master of my conduct. I will serve under your lordship, and no other man. My obligations to your lordship are indelibly engraven on a grateful heart.' At Dover he was well received by the sailors, ' no enemies to " Wilkes' and Liberty." ' He met the Duke of Rutland coming from Paris, who told him that the King of France had asked many questions about him. He returned on September 27th, when he learned that his friend disapproved of his behaviour, at ' which he was truly unhappy ; for Lord Temple had given him the noblest proofs of his partiality.' The truth, no doubt, was that Wilkes, while professing loudly that he would be guided by his friend, insisted on taking his own course.

Parliament was to meet on November 15th, and during his absence the plot was concocted. Wilkes styled Carteret Webb, the Treasury Secretary, ' a mean, dirty fellow,' but he might have applied the term to all concerned in the business.* Nothing indeed

* This will be evident from Curry the printer's deposition, made when repentant, some five years later :

could match the zeal 'and unscrupulousness shown by all the parties who joined in the shameful confederation.

'Michael Curry, printer, maketh oath and saith, that in May, 1763, he was hired by John Wilkes, Esq., at the rate of twenty-five shillings per week ; that he lived in the house of the said Mr. Wilkes, and was boarded and regularly lodged there ; that he was employed by the said Mr. Wilkes in several things about his private press ; that the said Mr. Wilkes employed this deponent to compose and print part of a poem entitled " An Essay on Woman ; " that the said Mr. Wilkes gave this deponent the strictest charge to keep it secret, and to suffer no person whatever to see the said poem ; that the said Mr. Wilkes ordered this deponent to work off only twelve copies—which were all to be delivered, and were actually given, to the said Mr. Wilkes himself ; but that without the knowledge of the said Mr. Wilkes this deponent worked off another copy for himself. That from the carelessness of this deponent four pages (only) of the said poem came into the hands of one Jennings, who likewise worked at the said Mr. Wilkes's ; that by the means of this Jennings it was shown to Mr. Farmer, Mr. Faden, and the reverend Mr. Kidgell ; that the next day this deponent waited on Mr. Churchill ; that this deponent asked him if any harm could come to Mr. Wilkes or this deponent for the " Essay on Woman ; " that Mr. Churchill said there could not, but for anything the people in power could do, they might be damned ; that, however, he would write to Mr. Wilkes, who was

Having once set their hand to the business of destroying their enemy, having carried him

---

then in France.' After relating the various laborious attempts to tamper with him, he goes on : 'Several other meetings were had between the said Faden and this deponent; that the same offers were repeated—and ten, twenty, a hundred guineas, or any sum, would be given as a security that the copy should be returned ; that there was a strong report that Mr. Wilkes intended to prosecute this deponent for felony, in having stolen a copy of the "Essay on Woman ;" that this deponent applied to see Mr. Wilkes on his return from France, and was refused by his servant; that soon after the applications to this deponent were renewed by the said Faden and the said Hassell ; that he was desired to name any sum ; that he might depend on being supported from any injury he might apprehend, and firmly rely on being protected by those in power ; that otherwise he might be prosecuted for having printed the copy ; that afterwards the reports of this deponent's being to be prosecuted by Mr. Wilkes for felony gaining ground, this deponent in a passion went to the said Globe tavern, sent for the said Faden, and gave him the copy, saying he hoped that he should be taken care of, as he found he was not safe either in keeping or destroying the copy ; that the said Faden then gave him five guineas as a security to return him the copy, and promised him protection. That this deponent went with the said Faden on the same evening to the house of Philip Carteret Webb, Esq., Solicitor to the Treasury, in Great Queen Street, where was the Reverend Mr.

to gaol under a *lettre de cachet*, hunted him
through the kingdom, set spies on him, not

Kidgell ; that the said Webb bid this deponent be easy,
for that he should be provided for ; that this deponent
afterwards for several weeks lodged and boarded in the
said Webb's house ; that this deponent was often told by
the said Webb that Government would take care of him
if he would give evidence on the trials against Mr.
Wilkes—that he must remain staunch, and directions as
to what this deponent should say on the trials were
given him by the said Webb ; that a few days before
the meeting of the Parliament, the said Webb bid the
said Faden take this deponent out of town ; that accordingly the said Faden and this deponent went first to
Hounslow, then to Hampton Court, and afterwards to
Knightsbridge, till the morning the House sat, when they
went to the Horn tavern in Westminster, where were
the said Webb and the said Kidgell, and from thence to
give evidence before the House of Lords. That the said
Webb a few days afterwards carried this deponent to
the Earl of Sandwich, who was then Secretary of State :
that his lordship said to this deponent, " You have saved
the nation, and you may depend on anything that is in
my power ;" that this deponent said he was without
money, to which his lordship replied he must not hear
that ; that the said Webb added, " You had no occasion
to mention that ;" that at the bottom of his lordship's
stairs the said Webb ordered this deponent to go to Mr.
Carrington, one of the King's messengers ; that this deponent accordingly went to the said Carrington's, who
gave him a guinea and a half, for which this deponent

daring now to break into his house, as they
had done before in search of papers, they had
chosen the safer course of corrupting his
own servants to steal them.   Having got
their evidence, they were now in a difficulty
as to how to use it   Some of the Ministers,
notably the Chancellor, had scruples as to
such ' dirty work.'*   But on November 5th,

gave a receipt in these words, " For subsistence, for
which I shall be accountable," or to that effect; that the
same payment of a guinea and a half was continued for
about twenty-five weeks by the said Carrington.'

* The crop of actions, legal punishments, and penalties
that grew out of Wilkes' original act was astonishing.
Fifteen journeymen printers took action against the
Secretary's messengers, and recovered from £120 to
£150 a-piece; two booksellers, Fell and Wilson, obtained £600 damages; Beardmore, who, it will be recollected, was arrested for his connection with the *Monitor,*
was encouraged by Wilkes to proceed at law, and recovered £1,000 damages; the Rev. Dr. Entick, who
wrote in the same paper, received £300; Kearsley, publisher of No. 45, became bankrupt.   Foote, who was one of
the creditors, put the claimants in good-humour by saying
the usual practice was that authors were in debt to the
publishers, but this was an instance of the reverse case.
Wood, the under-secretary, the cause of all this confusion,
had to resign his office.   Wilkes even contrived to involve his friend and publisher, Almon, in his own perils.
During his exile in France he sent him a paragraph,

Lord Sandwich was glad to tell Mr. Grenville that 'he had set everything right with the Chancellor.' In a most curious letter he shows how the plot was arranged beforehand :

'I was with him last night. He objected to the impropriety of bringing it before the House merely as a blasphemous and impious work ; but that if it was brought as a complaint on account of the improper mention of the name of a peer, he had no sort of objection to it, and he thought the House would certainly take it up upon that, and the other point likewise.

which seems to have had little point : 'Although the Earl of Hertford was the English ambassador at Paris, and David Hume was his secretary, yet his Scottish chaplain, the Reverend James Trail, administered to the English subjects in spirituals there.' No man upon earth would suspect that this silly thing could possibly become a subject of complaint in the House of Lords : yet, upon the motion of the Earl of Marchmont, it was resolved that this paragraph was a breach of privilege ; and Almon was fined one hundred pounds besides fees, amounting to about sixty pounds more. We heard lately of 'mending or ending' the House of Lords—Mr. Morley's phrase, applied with but small justification—but such a spectacle of tyrannical sensitiveness more than justified such summary process.

'I then asked him if Bishop Warburton authorized me to complain in his behalf. He answered, " By all means."

'I was this morning with the Bishop (of Gloucester), and have shown him the papers. He comes heartily into the affair, says he will not only authorize me to complain in his name of this outrage, but will take any part in it himself that shall be judged proper by the King's Government. I shall tell him we have nothing to do but to settle the modes of bring it on in detail. I shall hope for your advice and assistance.'

Thus with an extraordinary infatuation did these persons concoct their plot. The Kidgells and other instruments contrived the dirty work of bribing, stealing, etc., while the Peer and Bishop arranged the more showy parts of the business. Never was plot so fruitful in annoyance and disaster.

CHAPTER IX.

On November 15th, the first day of the meeting of Parliament, an exciting scene took place in the House of Lords. Before the King's Speech was read, Lord Sandwich rose, with the 'Essay' in his hand, and affecting to be deeply shocked, denounced the whole as a blasphemous, obscene, and abominable libel. Wilkes, he said, 'had violated the most sacred ties of religion as well as decency.'

Wilkes' old friend and 'co-drinker,' Dashwood, was present, and no doubt also affected to be shocked; but in private he said that ' he had never before heard the devil preach.' At his request the House was treated with a recitation of the most horrible passages, when Lord Littleton interposed, and in much distress entreated that their ears might not be shocked with such utterances. Then the Bishop of Gloucester rose in much excitement, and laying his hand upon his heart, assured the House with a solemnity that must have amused, that he had *not* written any of the notes, calling God to witness to the truth of his statement. In a feeble strain of absurdity he added, that 'no one, in his opinion, but the devil concocted the contents of such a production.' But he added, after a pause, 'I beg the devil's pardon, for I do not think even him, capable of so infamous a production.'

Finally, the matter having been discussed, it was resolved that 'a printed paper entitled " An Essay on Woman," with the notes; and another printed paper entitled " The Veni Creator paraphrased," highly reflecting upon a member of this House, is a manifest breach of the privilege thereof, and is a most scandalous, obscene, and impious libel; a gross profanation of many parts of the Holy Scriptures, and a most wicked and blasphemous attempt to ridicule and vilify the person of our blessed Saviour.'

An address was then voted to his Majesty, praying him to give directions for the prosecution of the author, as yet undiscovered.

The astonishment and amusement of the public at this pharisaical display may be conceived. Everyone was struck by the ludicrous incongruity of men like Sandwich and Warburton exhibiting themselves as purists. At the theatre the allusion that 'Jemmy Twitcher should peach does surprise me,' produced a roar, and Sandwich at once became known as 'Jemmy Twitcher.' Warburton chiding blasphemy and heresy, seemed as absurd, though we need not accept Churchill's awful sketch of one who

> 'Lived with men infamous and vile,
> Trucked his salvation for a smile ;
> To catch their humour, caught her plan,
> *And laughed at God* to laugh with man.'

But Lord Chesterfield more happily expressed the prevailing feeling when he spoke of Wilkes as 'the intrepid defender of our rights and liberties ;' adding 'it was no less a mercy that God had raised up the Earl of

14—2

Sandwich to vindicate true religion and morality.'

But another more exciting scene in Wilkes' presence was to take place on this memorable day. A Bill for preventing clandestine outlawries being the first proceeding, an amendment was introduced opening the thorny question of privilege in connection with his case. Mr. Grenville and Wilkes had both important communications to make to the House on the subject. The former had a message from his Majesty, inviting the House to deal with Wilkes' case; the latter complained of the breach of privilege as a violation of the House's right. Mr. Grenville said that the King having information that Mr. Wilkes was the author of a most seditious and dangerous libel, had caused him to be apprehended and secured, but he had been discharged on the ground of privilege; that having been called upon to answer process in the King's Bench, he had stood out and declined to appear. His Majesty, therefore, 'not wishing public justice to be eluded,' ordered the whole to be laid before the House.

A humble answer was formally voted, and the House at once proceeded to consider the case. It was now moved by Lord North ' that the paper was a false, scandalous and seditious libel, containing expressions of the most unexampled insolence and contumely towards his Majesty, and the grossest asper- sions upon both Houses of Parliament, the most audacious defiance of the authority of the whole Legislature, and most manifestly tend- ing to alienate the affections of the people from his Majesty, to withdraw them from their obediences to the laws of the realm, and to excite them to traitorous insurrection against his Majesty's Government.' This exaggerated statement seems almost ridiculous, and suggests the ' not having the fear of God, but moved by,' etc., in an indictment for stealing a bit of ribbon. Ministers were eager to sub- stantiate the original proceedings in which they had met so disastrous a defeat. This was so much felt that it was proposed to leave out, at least, the last few words as to the exciting insurrection. Mr. Pitt was particularly vehe- ment on this point, and maintained the chief

burden of the debate. He urged, too, the
Mawworm character of the proceedings,
suggesting that ' they should search the Bishop
of Gloucester's study for heresy.' The
motion was carried that ' the paper be burned
by the hands of the common hangman.'

Wilkes during these proceedings had several
times stood up to state his own complaint.
He began by setting out the treatment he
had received, and the decision of the court
in his favour. Notwithstanding which he
had been served with a subpœna for the same
charge. 'I lost no time,' he went on, ' in
consulting the best books, as well as the
greatest living authorities ; and, from the
best judgment I could find, I thought this
was a violation of the privilege of Parliament,
which I will neither desert nor betray, and
therefore I have not yet put in an appearance.' He concluded by assuring the House
that if they maintained their privilege he was
not only *ready,* ' but eagerly desirous,' to
waive it, and put himself up before a jury of
his countrymen. A motion was then proposed of an extraordinarily partial kind,

devised to cover the case : ' That Parliament does not extend privilege to the case of writing and publishing seditious libels ; nor ought it to be allowed to obstruct the ordinary course of the laws, in the speedy and effectual prosecution of so heinous and dangerous an offence.'

After several adjournments it was finally decided on November 24th, when a debate of an exciting character took place, during which Mr. Rigby and ' Jemmy ' Grenville exchanged such hot words that they had to be bound over to the peace before the Speaker. The debate was, however, most remarkable for the speech of Mr. Pitt, ' who was so severely afflicted with the gout that he had to be attended to his seat ;' notwithstanding which he spoke with extraordinary animation, making the whole a constitutional question. He protested against this surrender of a privilege of the House. No man ' could condemn the *North Briton* more than he did ; but he would come at the author fairly—not by an open breach of the constitution, and a contempt of all restraint. Such a sacrifice

placed all the members in terror of imprisonment.'

After vindication in this strain of the
rights of the House, he came to the paper
itself; and Wilkes must have been confounded
to hear the new language in which his former
patron—whose praise he had sung in nearly
all the numbers of his seditious paper, and to
whom he had vowed fealty and perpetual
service—entirely cast him off and denounced
him. He said that he condemned the whole
series of *North Britons* as ' illiberal, unman-
nerly, detestable! The King's subjects were
one people. Whoever divided them was
guilty of sedition. *The author did not deserve
to be ranked among the human species; he was
the blasphemer of his God, and the libeller of
his King!* He had no connection with him;
he had no connection with any such writer.
He neither associated nor communicated with
any such. It was true that he had friendship
and warm ties. He had obligations, and
great ones; but no friendship and no obligations could induce him to approve what he
firmly condemned. It might be supposed he

alluded to his noble relative Lord Temple.
He was proud to call him his relative. He
was his friend, his bosom friend, whose
fidelity was as unshaken as his virtue. They
went into office together, they came out
together; they had lived together, and would
die together! He knew nothing of any connection with the writer of the libel. If there
subsisted any, he was totally unacquainted
with it.'

This was an extraordinary declaration; for
it was matter of notoriety that Lord Temple
was on the most intimate terms with Wilkes,
and Pitt's own relation with him was far
more close than these hysterical disclaimers
warranted. He was too unwell to wait, and
departed before the division.

It was no wonder that Wilkes could not
forgive this gross attack, in which there
seems something unchivalrous, as everyone's
hand was now lifted against Wilkes.*

A conference was now ordered with the
House of Lords.

* See the savage note on the character of Pitt in the
North Briton, which Wilkes later, in his anger, added to
his text.

This debate and the one that followed seemed to let loose all the angry passions, and resulted in one nearly fatal duel. It all but led to another. Mr. Samuel Martin had been Secretary to the Treasury under Lord Bute, and was of a warm temper. Rising now, he looked steadily at Wilkes, and declared, to the astonishment of his hearers, that he took the opportunity of saying, ' whosoever the writer of that paper was, in that work he was *mean enough to stab another man's reputation. He was a coward and a malignant scoundrel !* which words he repeated, that they should be heard.'

Such an insult could not pass unnoticed. The provocation shows how unfair is Macaulay's statement that Wilkes *picked* this quarrel with Martin.

It was presently known that the cause of his outburst was a grossly offensive passage in the *North Briton* (No. 40), in which Martin was described as ' the most treacherous, base, selfish, mean, abject, low-lived, and dirty fellow that ever *wriggled* himself into a secretaryship.' In No. 37 he was as offen-

sively described as ' a very apt tool of Ministerial persecution, with a spirit worthy of a
Portuguese Inquisitor looking for carrion,' etc.

Wilkes, it was noticed, listened to Martin's
attack with complacency. The debate continued, and the House finally resolved that
' No. 45 was a false, scandalous, and
seditious libel,' and ordered it to be burned
by the common hangman. Wilkes had ' put
on the paper ' his own complaint that the
privileges of the House had been violated
in his person. In moderate language he
gave a short account of how he had been
treated, and concluded by declaring that if
the House sustained the privilege he would
engage to go before a jury and stand by their
decision. As this opened a delicate question,
the discussion was adjourned. The original
resolution was submitted to the Upper House,
and their co-operation was invited.

One would have thought Wilkes had
enough on his hands. But he could not
pass by Martin's public insult. On the next
day the latter received this cartel, original
enough in its style :

'You complained yesterday before five hundred gentlemen that you had been stabbed in the dark by the *North Briton*, but I have reason to believe that you was not so much in the dark as you affected and chose to be. Was the complaint made before so many gentlemen on purpose that they might interpose? To cut off every pretence of your ignorance as to the author, I whisper in your ear that every passage of the *North Briton*, in which you have been named, or even alluded to, was written by your humble servant,

'JOHN WILKES.'

The reply was prompt. Mr. Martin wrote that as he had described the anonymous writer to be a 'cowardly, malignant, infamous scoundrel,' he now, in knowledge of the writer, 'must take the liberty to repeat that you are a malignant, infamous scoundrel, and that I desire to give you an opportunity of showing me whether that epithet of cowardly was rightly applied or not. I desire that you may meet me in Hyde Park immediately with a brace of pistols each, to determine our differences.' Reading which, the choleric Sir Lucius O'Trigger seems scarcely an exaggeration. It will be seen that seconds were dispensed with by the angry combatants.

The incidents of this singular duel—in so public a place, too—were thus recorded by Wilkes:

'When they met in Hyde Park they walked together a little while to avoid some company which seemed coming up to them. When they were alone, the first fire was from Mr. Martin's pistol, which missed Mr. Wilkes. The pistol in Mr. Wilkes' hand only flashed in the pan. They then each took one of Mr. Wilkes' pair of pistols. Mr. Wilkes missed; and the ball of Mr. Martin's pistol lodged in Mr. Wilkes' belly. He bled immediately very much. Mr. Martin came up, and desired to give him all the assistance in his power. Mr. Wilkes replied that Mr. Martin had behaved like a man of honour; that he was killed; and insisted on Mr. Martin's making his immediate escape, adding that no person should know from him (Mr. Wilkes) how the affair happened. Upon this they parted. Wilkes was carried home.'·

But a curious incident in the case, one not known, is that Wilkes would have been killed by the bullet but for a fortunate accident. He had been hit in the delicate region of the groin, but the ball first struck two of his metal buttons, and had thus spent its force. One more instance of the luck that so invariably attended him.*

During the progress of his recovery he was glad to indulge in his favourite Scapin-like raillery of his foes, which is amusing enough, though it rather impaired his dignity as a serious performer. The House justly suspect-

---

* An ardent admirer placed the coat and waistcoat buttons in a silver box, on which was this comic inscription :

'These two simple yet invaluable
BUTTONS
Preserved the Life of my Beloved and Honest Friend
JOHN WILKES,
In a duel fought with Mr. Martin
On the Sixteenth of November, 1763,
Where true courage and humanity distinguished him
in a manner scarcely known in
former ages ;'

with more of the same high-flown panegyric.

ing that he was exaggerating his injuries, to
put off the evil day as long as possible, ordered
two physicians to report upon him. He was
already in the hands of Dr. Brocklesby, and
there was something curiously despotic in
this direction, which suggests the practice of
the French manager of a Government theatre,
who, on the illness of a performer, is entitled
to require that a report should be made.
From this serious wound it was long before
he recovered.*

His wound was really serious. As his physicians described it to the House of Lords

---

* Notwithstanding his handsome testimony to his adversary's behaviour, he had reason to suspect him of
some unworthy conduct. One of his charges was
that Martin had been seen practising at a target of late,
which was confirmed by his neighbours in the country.
Another was that he had lain by for two years under
the affront offered. Finally, though Mr. Wilkes had
sent him back his letter, lest, if found, it should compromise him, he had not restored Wilkes' letter, which
occasioned somebody to remark 'that in all probability
it was kept in order to be made use of as a proof of Mr.
Wilkes being concerned in the *North Briton.*' In fact,
the letter was not given up till nearly a month later, viz.,
on December 10th. But these suspicions were scarcely
well founded.—*English Liberty*, p. 96.

on December 14th, fever had supervened. There was much suppuration, and they had to use the knife freely. He was, in fact, for a time in great danger. Notwithstanding the reckless patriot, instead of keeping himself quiet, opened his doors to all his friends, who poured in and surrounded his bed. As Walpole heard, 'while he himself was all spirits and riot, and sat up in his bed to correct the next *North Briton*. His *bon-mots* were all over the town, but too gross, I think, to repeat—the chief are at the expense of poor Lord George Sackville. Indeed, the tide ran violently for him.'

Wilkes now addressed letters to the House, begging the question might be put off till his recovery. But the Commons proceeded, on the 23rd of November, to pass a resolution that 'the privilege of Parliament did not extend to the case of writing and publishing seditious libels, nor ought to be allowed to obstruct the ordinary course of the laws in the speedy and effectual prosecution of so heinous and dangerous an offence;' thus, in their loyal ardour, actually curtailing their own privileges. After a conference with the House of Lords, the question was debated there, and Wilkes' cause ardently urged by Lord Temple. Indeed, the defence was ' led and managed by him, and he showed himself a zealous defender of the privileges of Parliament.' He drew up a forcible protest, signed by seventeen peers. After a further conference held on December 1st, the two Houses, now in the greatest harmony, joined in ordering that the obnoxious paper should be burnt at the Royal Exchange on the Saturday following, and that the Sheriffs ' do attend and cause the same to be burnt there accordingly ;' after which both Houses joined harmoniously in an address, the terms of which his Majesty must have found more than satisfactory. They felt it their ' indispensable duty ' to express their surprise and indignation that neither the public nor private virtue of the King, and the gracious expression of his tender care and affection, thus ' infamously traduced,' should have protected him from so insolent and unexampled an indignity. Moreover, ' the same audacious hand which had dared thus

grossly to affront his Majesty had violated other
sacred regards.'

No wonder the King was gratified, and
spoke of the 'very affectionate zeal' of his
Parliament, and assured them 'he would
not fail in carrying the law into execution
against such delinquents.' After having indulged this loyal feeling, the House of Commons ordered Wilkes to attend within a week.

The next step, accordingly, was the foolish
and antiquated ceremony of the burning ' by
the hands of the common hangman.' This,
however, led to a serious riot. On December
3rd, when the hangman arrived with the wood,
he was awaited by an immense mob, who
greeted him with a storm of hisses, hustling
him so that he could not get up to the place
fixed. An intrepid alderman, Harley, a
relation of Lord Oxford's, showed much
spirit and resolution; making his way through
the crowd, he read the order. As the mob
would not allow the fagots to be lighted, he
had the paper burnt on a torch. It was
noticed that there were a number of well-
dressed persons in the windows of the coffee-

houses and elsewhere encouraging the mob.* It was noticed that the Lord Mayor, though at the Mansion House, well knowing what was going forward, sent no help. He was believed to sympathize with Wilkes. The cry of the mob was ' Wilkes and Liberty!' The windows of Harley's coach were broken by a fagot hurled at it by one of the mob, and he himself was struck and severely hurt; but, nothing daunted, he proceeded with his task.

The invalid, however, could laugh heartily at this childish exhibition, and presently contrived to furnish the town with a new adventure to talk of. After the duel, and burning, etc., was to come an attempt at assassination!

Nothing could have been more favourable

---

* It shows the almost fanatical spirit of the House, all through this incident, that they should have considered the sheriff's display of courage worthy of a formal vote of thanks; and the Speaker, as he performed his function, dwelt on the ' high insult lately offered to the House,' and the ' spirit of licentiousness— forerunner of the greatest tyranny and despotism.' The merits of the sheriff were merely glanced at. Harley in his reply, lamented that he had not been able to execute their wishes ' in a manner more suitable to the dignity of Parliament.'

to him than this diversion. The story went
that on the evening of December 6th, a man
came to his house, who, as his dialect was
Scotch, was refused admittance. Next morning Mr. Wilkes received a warning to be on
his guard. This man's name was found to
be Dunn, a Scot, and he had been heard
to declare that 'he and ten others were
determined to cut off Mr. Wilkes, be the
consequence what it would.' Mr. Wilkes
took no notice of the matter until the morning of the 8th, when the same person arrived
and left a letter, asking for an interview, as he
had something of importance to communicate.
Wilkes wrote a polite answer, inviting him
to his house at seven o'clock. In the meantime he sent and gathered a number of
his friends, gentlemen of distinction, about
him. The man came, and was shown into
the parlour, and informed that he should be
introduced to Wilkes ; but on going out, two
gentlemen seized him and threw him on his
back. On searching him a new penknife was
found in his pocket, which he owned he had
bought at Chatham about a fortnight since.

In this state of affairs, Wilkes, chiefly

prompted by his friend, Mr. George Onslow, swore an information 'that he went in peril of his life.'

This matter was brought before the House of Commons, and it was found that the man was insane. Nor did this close his adventures during this crisis.

He was near being drawn into another difficulty, which only the restraint and indifference of his opponent prevented taking the shape of a new duel. When it was thought he was likely to be deprived of his seat, it was mentioned in a local paper that a Sir William Lee, of his own county, had been looking after the borough in the interest of a friend, on which an Aylesbury paper commented with severity, saying it was 'ungenerous and ungentlemanlike' to dispose of a member's seat, before it was known that he would be expelled. The Baronet wrote to the paper that 'he was ready to vindicate his conduct to anyone that shall require it.'

The pugnacious Wilkes at once came forward, and wrote him a scoffing letter in his own inimitable style:

' Sir,

      ' Give me leave to congratulate you
on your having commenced author, and the
London Evening Post on the great acquisition
made of such talents as yours for that paper.
I doubt not of your soon distancing all the
other *Ministerial* writers; and though you may
not regularly on Saturday nights have your
pay counted out to you, yet some little snug
sinecure, or a Ministerial mandate to a county,
for what you were very lately so awkwardly
gaping after (though, thank heaven, you were
disappointed), may, in the end, recompense
your labours.

      ' I must, however, recommend to you rather
more temper ; you *start* too furiously.   As a
young man, you are entitled to portion, but
you should have laughed at an idle paragraph
in a newspaper, in which your GREAT name is
not at length.   Did the conscientiousness of
having merited that little satire sting you ?
I have a right to ask you ; for in your curious
letter you say *I have done nothing therein, or
upon any occasion whatever* (bravo ! W. LEE de
scipso) *that I am not ready to vindicate as a*

gentleman to anyone THAT (not who) *shall require it.* Now I will only remark *that, that that* worthy baronet urges is the very pink of chivalry, and is *that that* is very brave. But do you mean to *vindicate* it by your *pen* or your *sword ?*

' But perhaps I mistake you, and you meant to justify it by your *sword.* You have just begun by *inking* your *maiden pen,* and you might possibly mean at the same time to contrive to *flesh your maiden sword.* Pray be explicit, and let me know if you meant to send a challenge to all the world by the *London Evening Post.* Was ever anything so truly noble and great ?

' But I tire you and myself: I shall therefore conclude, with only begging of you, that, instead of beginning any disturbance at Aylesbury, you would keep your own little parish of Hartwell quiet, and be reconciled to a worthy clergyman who never offended you, and whom your good father cherished and honoured.'

Three days after the burning, another

triumph waited the lucky Wilkes. He had lost no time in commencing actions against those who were concerned in breaking into his house. The first of the series, that against the Under Secretary Wood, came on before Lord Camden at the Guildhall, when a verdict was found for Wilkes, with £1,000 damages and full costs.*

Nothing could be more resolute or more truly judicial than the language of this judge, which won him the admiration of the kingdom :

' This warrant is unconstitutional, illegal, and absolutely void ; it is a general warrant, directed to four messengers, to take up any persons without naming or describing them with any certainty, and to apprehend them, together with their papers. If it be good, a Secretary of State can delegate and depute any of the messengers, or any even from the lowest of the people, to take examinations, to

---

* It will be seen how many victims were brought in connection with this business; but in the case of Carteret Webb and Lord Egremont, the 'fell sergeant,' Death, baffled his purpose.

commit, or to release, and do every act which the highest judicial officers the law knows can do or order. There is no order in our law-books that mentions these kinds of warrants, but several that in express words condemn them. Upon the maturest consideration, I am bold to say that this warrant is illegal; but I am far from wishing a matter of this consequence to rest solely on my opinion. I am only one of twelve whose opinions I am desirous should be taken in this matter, and I am very willing to allow myself to be the meanest of the twelve. If these higher jurisdictions should declare my opinion erroneous, I submit, as will become me, and kiss the rod; but I must say I shall always consider it as a rod of iron for the chastisement of the people of Great Britain.'*

* He also pointed out a curious mistake in the action of the law officers, saying that Wilkes could not have raised the question of privilege at all, but for the description of him as Member of Parliament, needlessly introduced into the warrant. In the case of the seven Bishops this description was of the essence, but in Wilkes' case it was not. On this very action against

The judge had presided on the former occasion, but, doubtful then as to the question of general warrants, he had now changed his views.

The House now growing impatient at Wilkes' slow convalescence, began to suspect that he was malingering. They accordingly selected two physicians, Dr. Heberden and Mr. Hawkins, to visit him and report on his state. Wilkes, as usual, seized on the incident, and ridiculed the medical mission in inimitable style :

'The Commons, like true country people, seem to have an overflowing of kindness for me, which is very apt to surfeit ; and yet, like the others, sometimes in the same moment, they fail in a point of good breeding, even to one of their own members. The House desires Dr. Heberden and Mr. Hawkins to come to me, but forgot to desire

---

him he contrived to engraft another. For Webb having sworn that 'he had nothing' in his hand when searching Wilkes' house, he was indicted for perjury, and acquitted.

me to receive them, and I most certainly will not.

' My brother members seem quite wild in their rage. They would force a physician and surgeon upon me when I have one of each already, and they forget that my dear friend and chaplain Churchill has left me for some time. Would it not therefore have looked better if these obliging friends had shown some regard to my spiritual concerns, and had ordered their own chaplain, the very learned brother of the very conscientious merchant, and of the very acute secretary, to attend me ?—or they might perhaps have prevailed on the good Mr. Kidgell.

' This last act of the Commons seems almost to perfect the scene, and quite overwhelms me with gratitude. Yet though I am a young member, I cannot but observe and lament that the ancient established forms of Parliament have in the present case been laid aside, as if order had taken leave of the House with good old Onslow. The course of business has always been that affairs of importance should previously go to a Committee. The affair you have mentioned is of so much real consequence that it should (in my poor opinion) have been referred to two Committees. First, it should have gone to the Committee of Ways and Means, to contrive how the State physician and surgeon can get into my house. Secondly, to the Committee of Supply, to vote the fees due to the gentlemen for their attendance.'

Not forgetting at the same time his politeness, he wrote to Dr. Heberden to excuse himself, saying that 'though he cannot say he wished to see the doctor at present, he hopes that he will be well enough to beg that honour to eat a bit of mutton in Great George Street.*

* It appears that two physicians did actually report on Mr. Wilkes' case to the House. This was owing to his good-nature, as he thought it due to the medical friends who were attending him. So he sent for Dr. Duncan and Mr. Middleton, who had appointments at Court. His lively humour was shown in his speech to these two gentlemen : 'That as he found the House thought it proper he should be watched, he himself thought two Scotchmen most proper for this duty.' The Lords also required physicians to attend, but were content to accept the report of Wilkes' own medical attendants.

Unfortunately there was a perverse folly
and wilfulness in Wilkes' own nature that
was to do more to destroy him than the
hostility of his opponents. He determined
on the step of republishing the *North Briton*
—issued in folio size, after the pattern of the
Spectator and *Tatler*—in a small, convenient
duodecimo. He fancied he could do this in
security by having it printed in his own
house. He was tempted to this step by
the hope of large profits; and the book
was sold at the enormous price of a guinea
for three little duodecimos. This was giving
his foes the very assistance they desired, for
it had been found impossible to prove from
the first seizure of his papers that he had
printed, or published, or written the paper.
But now it became easy to suborn some of
his servants and printers, as was done in the
instance of the ' Essay on Woman.'* In vain
his friends tried to dissuade from this fatal

* There were two processes against him, one in the
House of Commons, the other on the King's Bench, and
in both of these he furnished the proof that was wanting.
This seemed like infatuation ; or he may have thought
that the weakness of the case against him might rob
him of the honour of a fresh prosecution.

step.   Almon, the publisher, was present
when Lord Temple implored him to give up
this scheme, offering to guarantee a sum
equal to the expected profits of the venture ;
but the other was obstinate.   The result
proved that he had made a complete mis-
calculation, the sale of copies being incon-
siderable.

But now events took a new and startling
turn.   On the 7th, when the doctors made
their report to the House, the time of grace
was enlarged for a week, and later this period
was enlarged till after Christmas, and the two
doctors were ordered to report again on
January 19th, 1764.   This was treating him
with all indulgence.   On Christmas Day, it
was known that he had fled the kingdom.
With King, Lords, Commons, bloodthirsty
Scots, duellists, and courts of law all seeking
his ruin, he began to think that he was
scarcely secure in England.

CHAPTER X.

IT seems to have been thought that Wilkes, in the face of the dangers that menaced his liberty and future, had taken a sudden resolution to save himself by flight. But the truth is he had for weeks determined to quit the country. Early in November he had assured his daughter that he would be in Paris, and in December he had renewed this assurance. He set off on Christmas Eve, and on Christmas Day was waited on at Dover before his embarkation by some enthusiastic gentlemen of the town, 'who desired to drink his health in good claret.' His imprudent haste had nearly opened his wound, which 'was a good deal fretted by the vile jolts through the rascally towns of travel, Rochester, Chatham, etc.' 'Friday and

yesterday,' he wrote to his friend Cotes,
' were, I think, the two most unhappy days
I have known.' The passage was rough, and
his sickness inflamed the wound still more, so
that he had to go to bed. On the 29th he
was at Paris, having put up at the Hôtel de
Saxe.

In that gay and witty city he was welcomed
with much interest and curiosity. Almost his
first act was to call on the ambassador, who,
of course, was not at home, but, to his
surprise, returned his visit.* ' I left a card for

* This simple act of courtesy had exercised the ambassador considerably, and he wrote home to explain his
motives :

'Paris, Jan. 4, 1764.
'Soon after his arrival he was at my door. I did not
think proper to admit him, and he left his name. He was
afterwards, as my chaplain tells me, here at chapel, when
there is a general freedom, for divine service, but I did
not see him, being then at Versailles.' On his return,
inquiry was made as to what had been the practice of his
predecessors in relation to Mr. Wilkes ; and he ' found
that the Duke of Bedford had visited him, and invited
him twice to dinner, and Mr. Wilkes had twice left his
name at his door. So I propose doing the same, but I
will show him no further countenance, unless directed to
do so.'

the private secretary, David Hume, who returned my visit likewise; and to-day I met him at Baron Holbach's, where we laughed much. I went last Sunday to the ambassador's chapel, and go again next Sunday to take my leave of a dull preacher there. I am caressed here more than one of my modesty will let me tell you.'

He soon made the most favourable impression by his wit and gaiety—an impression strengthened by his pleasant *mot* in answer to Madame de Pompadour's question, ' How far he considered that an Englishman could safely go in attacking the Royal Family?' ' That, madame, is exactly what I am trying to find out.'

This appearance of Wilkes at chapel was characteristic. One of his particular instructions to his daughter that very year had been ' *not to miss the ambassador's chapel on Sunday.*' One of his earlier visitors had been his antagonist Martin. He had received a friendly warning from Wilkes that he was in a dangerous way, and had prudently withdrawn to the Continent.

The unfortunate patriot, now in exile, bankrupt in reputation, and almost without means, was reduced to a pitiable situation indeed. In a foreign country, cast among strangers, with the most gloomy prospects before him, he might well despair ; and his state of despondency is shown in a letter which he wrote home to his agent :

'I think myself an exile for life ; and I flatter myself, my dear Cotes, with no foolish hopes, not even on the restoration of Mr. Pitt and the Whigs. I never meant to embarrass them about me. I love only Lord Temple. Him I almost adore ; and I grieve that I have been the cause of so much disquietude to the most excellent and most amiable man alive. I am reconciling myself to my fate, and I come apace to it. Nature has given me some philosophy, and the necessity of the case perfects it.

'At first I found an awkwardness, I confess, at being considered as exiled from my native country. It is a prejudice against me, which I must take more pains to get over. The English, too, here will generally be of

the majority ; therefore I shall have no com-
fort from my own countrymen, nor reliance
on them : and as to the French, though they
are a very amiable and entertaining people,
full of little wit, and abounding with pleasing
sallies of fancy, they are incapable of great or
solid actions, or real friendship. I am, however, well diverted here ; though my health
has not hitherto permitted me to go once to a
place of public entertainment, nor even to
sup.

'I am now got from the Hôtel de Saxe,
which was very expensive ; and am with Miss
Wilkes, in the Rue St. Nicaise. I pay 2,400
livres a year for the apartments, and my
servants I give fifteen-pence English a day to
find themselves everything. Miss Wilkes and
I generally dine alone, and we pay half-a-
crown a head for our dinner. When anybody
dines with me, I only order for one more at
the same rate ; by which I shall know certainly my expense. Travelling is the most
expensive of all things, and therefore I am
determined not to stir till I can well afford it.
Then I shall wish to go one year to Rome,

16—2

with Miss Wilkes ; and afterwards to Constantinople, alone, for six months. For that I shall be content to pass my whole time in a dirty seaport on the coast, if I there can do any real good ; and I shall ever be happy to receive your orders. My plan for my daughter's education is the greatest expense to me, and that is a point I cannot dispense with.

'I leave to your discretion to sell whatever you please. Perhaps, in my circumstances, it might be prudent to sell Aylesbury too, and convert my fortune into *rentes viagères* (a kind of annuities here). In time, after the decease of Mrs. Mead and Mr. Sherbrooke, who have no relations but Miss Wilkes, her income would be very considerable ; and she would live with me. Mrs. Mead and Mr. Sherbrooke are both old ; and, as they have no other relation but Miss Wilkes, I therefore suppose they will leave everything to her, independent of me. Yet this is, after all, waiting for dead men's shoes.'

Desponding as the tone of this letter was, we can see the traces of his ' incompressible ' mercurial nature ; and the slightest change of fortune would have restored him his old buoyancy.

In this spirit he was ever looking to an early return to London—counting on some unlikely turn of the wheel. He had actually issued invitations to a dinner to be given on the eve of the meeting of Parliament, and, to the astonishment of many, sent a message by his late adversary, Mr. Martin, that he would not fail to attend. He had assured this gentleman that he had really only gone away for the purpose of seeing his daughter, concluding that he would be shut up in gaol for six months.

From these dreams, however, he was to be presently rudely awakened. More and more rumours reached him as to the peril of an early return, and his courage at last failed him. When the House met on January 19th, 1764, the Speaker read out a letter of excuse from Wilkes, enclosing a certificate from some French physicians, which, the Speaker pointed out, was not authenticated in the proper manner before a notary, nor were their signatures verified.*

Wilkes being thus brought formally before the House of Commons, no time was lost in dealing with him, and that in the severest way. Not a day's grace was given. What really influenced the House was the fact that if he were too ill to attend in his place,

* This deficiency was at once supplied in a second letter from Wilkes, who had the certificate duly verified before the ambassador :

'This day, the 5th of February, 1764, there appeared before me M. de la Rue, and made oath that he was a notary public; that he had signed the above paper; that M. Robineau was also a notary public, and had signed the same. In witness whereof I have hereunto affixed my hand and seal.   'HERTFORD.'

This furnished Wilkes an occasion for one of those sarcastic comments in which he was unrivalled : 'Lord Hertford signs a paper of only two sentences, in our language, and yet we find three palpable blunders in it. " *There* appeared "—*Where?* Where did Lord Hertford see M. de la Rue ? We have no hint where Lord Hertford was on that day. He might be returned to London, and might have signed it as a Justice of the Peace. *There appeared M. de la Rue* is a strong and harsh construction, not very usual. The verb takes the place of its own nominative. It should be, "M. de la Rue appeared before me." Lord Hertford says he has *affixed* his hand and seal. How does a man *affix his hand ?*' This is a lively, fair, and amusing criticism.

he could not have been able to travel all the way to Paris.

It was proposed and carried that Mr. Wilkes, being required to attend and answer the charges of having published the libel, and having refused to see the physicians appointed by the House, and having withdrawn himself into a foreign country, ' was guilty of a contempt of the authority of this House,' and it should proceed to consider the charges against him. This motion was carried by 275 votes to 70. Some printers and publishers were called to prove the charges of writing and publishing; but their evidence seemed weak enough. Miller and Cadell, however, testified that Wilkes had proposed to them to publish his *North Briton;* while his own printer, Curry, proved the actual ' composing ' of the republished *North Briton.* The House sat till daybreak, when it first agreed to a resolution that Wilkes had published ' a false, scandalous and seditious libel, full of insolence and contempt,' etc., towards his Majesty. This was followed by another, expelling him from the House.

Some interest was excited as to the share Mr. Pitt would take in this business. His former patronage of Wilkes was known, and he might at least have been passive or neutral. But the House was astonished to hear him break out with a furious attack upon his late friend and admirer. It is difficult to account for this envenomed burst, unless we look for the reason in his present morbid state—for he was now racked by what Dr. Johnson styled ' the arthritic pangs ' of gout, and had to be led to his seat by sympathizing friends. Yet this was the same Wilkes who had been closeted with him and Lord Temple but a few weeks before, to whose service and panegyrics the *North Briton* had been given up, and to whom, for many years, Wilkes had devoted himself in the most earnest manner.

It may be conceived how such ingratitude affected the demagogue. He was stung to frenzy, and he naturally became the bitter, uncompromising enemy of the man to whom he had been so attached. He stored up his resentment, which some years later found vent in one of his letters to the Duke of Grafton, of which the most bitter portion was the retort on Pitt for the latter's denunciation of the profane parodies which were printed in his 'Essay on Woman.' These, he declared, had been shown to and then praised by Pitt :

'He may remember the compliments he paid me on two certain poems in the year 1754. If I were to take the declarations made by himself and the late Mr. Potter *à la lettre*, they were more charmed with those verses after the ninety-ninth reading than after the first.

'I will now submit if there was not something peculiarly base and perfidious in Mr. Pitt's calling me a *blasphemer of my God* for those very verses at a time when I was absent, and dangerously ill from an affair of honour. The charge, too, he knew was false, for the whole ridicule of those two pieces was confined to certain mysteries, which formerly the *unplaced and unpensioned* Mr. Pitt did not think himself obliged even to affect to believe. He added another charge equally unjust, that I was the *libeller of my King*, though he was sensible that I never wrote a single line disrespectful to the sacred person of my sovereign, but had only attacked the despotism of his Ministers, with the spirit becoming a good subject and zealous friend of his country. The reason of this perfidy was plain. He was then beginning to pay homage to the *Scottish* Idol, and I was the most acceptable sacrifice he could offer at the shrine of Bute.

· Although I declare that the conscious pride of virtue makes me look down with contempt on a man who could be guilty of this baseness, who could in the lobby declare that I must be supported, and in the House, on the same day, desert and revile me, yet I will on every occasion do justice to the Minister. He has served the public in all those points where the good of the nation coincided with his own private views—and in no other.'

This, it must be said, seems likely to be true, when we consider the affectionate intimacy that existed between Potter, who was said to be joint author of the ' Essay,' and the Minister. No denial of this charge was ever made.*

* The verses thus exhibited were not the ' Essay,' but

Wilkes had forecasted what the decision of the House would be ; and, in an agitated letter to his friend Cotes,* set out all his hopes and fears, and also an explanation of his policy. This letter is given in full, as it furnishes a complete and singular illustration of Wilkes' character, who is willing at the same moment to be bought by the Tories, and, in default of his price being found, threatens them with a renewed war. A happy characteristic of Wilkes is the sentiment as to ' a lucky death ' amiably associated with that of his rich mother-in-law.

' I argue,' he wrote, on the 20th January, ' upon the supposition that I was expelled this morning, at one or two o'clock, after a warm

---

parodies of the hymn 'Veni Creator' and others. It is possible that Pitt may have thought them clever, in their profane way, as parodies, and that this sort of approbation was distorted by report.

* This Cotes was a wine merchant, in St. Martin's Lane, a faithful, useful tool, who gave up or neglected his business to devote himself to the great agitator. After ruining himself in the service, he was repaid, it is said, with ingratitude, and accused of robbing his patron !

debate.   I am, then, no longer a member of
Parliament.   If I return soon, it is possible
that I may be found guilty of the publication
of No. 45 of the *North Briton*, and of the
" Essay on Woman."   I must then go off to
France ; for no man in his senses would stand
Mansfield's sentence upon the publisher of a
paper declared by both Houses of Parliament
scandalous, seditious, etc.   The " Essay on
Woman," too, would be considered as blasphemous ; and Mansfield would, in that case,
avenge on me the old Berwick grudge.   Am
I then to run the risk of this ?

'But I am to wait the event of these two
trials.   I have in my own case experienced
the fickleness of the people.   *I was almost
adored one week ; the next neglected, abused, and
despised.*   With all the fine things said and
wrote of me, have not the public to this
moment left me in the lurch, *as to the expense
of so great a variety of lawsuits?*   I will serve
them to the last moment of my life ; but I
will make use of the understanding God has
given me, and will owe neither my security
nor indemnity to them.   Can I trust likewise

a rascally court, who bribed my own servants
to steal out of my house ? Which of the
Opposition, likewise, can call on me, and
expect my services ? I hold no obligation to
any of them, but to Lord Temple, who is
really a superior being.

' Does any one point suffer by my absence ?
I have not heard that it does. I believe both
parties will rejoice at my being here. Too
many personalities, likewise, have been mixed
with my business ; and the King himself
has taken too great, not to say too indecent, a
share in it to recede. Can it be thought, too,
that the Princess Dowager can ever forgive
what she supposes I have done ? What, then,
am I to expect if I return to England ? Persecution from my enemies ; coldness and
neglect from friends, except such noble ones
as you and a few more. I go on to some
other things.

' My private finances are much hurt by
three elections ; one at Berwick and two at
Aylesbury. Shall I return to Great George
Street, and live at so expensive a house ?
Forbid it real economy, and forbid it pride, to

go to another unless for some great national point of liberty! Perhaps, in the womb of fate, some important public or private event is to turn up. *A lucky death often sets all right.* Mrs. Mead and Mr. Sherbrooke are both old, and have no relation but Miss Wilkes.

'If Government means peace or friendship with me, and to save their honour (wounded to the quick by Webb's affair), I then breathe no longer hostility. *And, between ourselves, if they would send me ambassador to Constantinople, it is all I should wish.* I think, however, the King can never be brought to this (as to me, I mean), *though the Ministry would wish it.*

'If I stay at Paris, I will not be forgot in England; for I will feed the papers, from time to time, with gall and vinegar against the Administration. I cannot express to you how much I am courted here, nor how pleased our inveterate enemies are with the *North Briton.* Goy felt the pulse of the French Ministers about my coming here, and Churchill's, upon the former report. The answer was sent from the Duke de Praslin, by the King's orders, to Monsieur St. Foy. *premier commis des affaires étrangères,* in these words : " Les deux illustres J. W. et C. C. peuvent venir en France et à Paris aussi souvent, et pour autant de tems, qu'ils le jugeront à propos," etc.

'I am offered the liberty of printing here whatever I choose.'

The House of Commons was now embarked on a struggle which was to be protracted for many years. The minority was not inclined to accept this severe treatment of Wilkes without protest ; and there were plenty of constitutionalists who were eager to raise the question once more.

On February 14th, 1764, his complaint of violation of privilege against Webb and Wood came on. The House disposed of it in the same trenchant style, without giving any reasons, or even asserting the innocence of these functionaries. The Opposition, however, raised the whole question of General Warrants, and a discussion of a spirited kind followed, in which much knowledge of law and constitutional history was exhibited. The

Ministers admitted the general illegality of what they had done.

As the Constitutionalists invited the House to pronounce that such warrants were not legal, the Ministers reasonably opposed this view, and declared it was assuming judicial functions and interfering with those of the courts of law. Norton, who was a lawyer of repute, declared, in coarse language, what was the true view: that the courts would no more recognise such a declaratory resolution than they would 'the utterances of a drunken porter' in the streets. But though the question was awkwardly raised, it was really the first rude conflict between the House and its privileges, and the law of the land, later to come into yet more violent conflict. With much difficulty Government carried an adjournment over some months, which virtually put on the shelf this disagreeable and awkward question.

More extraordinary, for the time, was the length to which the debates were protracted— one lasting from three in the afternoon until seven in the morning. 'Patriotesses' like the Duchess of Richmond sat through the whole fray. Mr. Pitt, as usual, racked with his gout, attended, and sat up with the rest; but his manner and utterance were languid, and showed complete exhaustion. Walpole, who was present all through, in his liveliest vein describes this excited and protracted sitting. 'A company of colliers,' he says, ' emerging from damps and darkness, could not have appeared more ghastly and dirty than we did. We spent two hours in corrections of and additions to the question of pronouncing the warrant illegal, till the Ministry had contracted it to fit scarce anything but the individual case of Wilkes.'

Nothing can be more just than this account of the Ministerial quibblings and metaphysical treatment of the resolution, wishing to appear to adopt something general, and yet confine the application to Wilkes' case. The Opposition was only beaten by 14, though Government ' bought two single votes that day with two peerages, Sir R. Bamfylde and Sir Charles Tynte.' Voters were brought down in flannel and blankets, until the floor of the House

looked, as the witty Horace Walpole said,
'·like the pool of Bethesda.'

While this contest was raging, Wilkes'
recovery, according to his own account, was
slow, and he seldom ventured abroad. But his
great process was coming to maturity, and
the information which had been laid against
him came before the Court of King's Bench
on February 21st. The case was tried by
Lord Mansfield, his personal enemy, as he
considered him, owing to some transaction
during the Berwick election. On the eve of
the trial an alteration of the record was insisted on by the Chief Justice himself; the
word ' purport ' being changed into ' tenor,'
a change which, it was contended afterwards,
prejudiced the defendant's case.* His friend,
Serjeant Glynn, defended him, but without
success. There were two cases before the
Court : one of the *North Briton*, the other

* Other exceptions were taken, and the case ultimately
reached the House of Lords, where they were argued
and held to be trivial. Wilkes' solicitor stated that he
had objected strongly, and contended that ' if the
alteration had not been made, the information must have
been quashed.'

of the 'Essay on Woman,' and in both he was found guilty, sentence being deferred for the time, owing to his absence. Wilkes affected to treat this matter lightly, but it was hard to bear up against such an accumulation of misfortunes.

His attorney, Philips, wrote to him this account of the business, thus attempting to console him :

'I cannot inform you more of the circumstances of your trials, than that the printing and publishing were clearly proved, but nothing admitted ; and the *law* was so happily explained away, that the jury were left only to judge of the *fact.*

'The "Essay on Woman" being under different circumstances, a different management was necessary. The mere fact of printing was manifest ; but how did the publishing appear ?—delivering a paper to a printer to be printed is a legal *publication,* nor were the counsel even permitted to controvert this curious law.

'The alteration of the records was an alarming circumstance. A summons is

17—2

served on my brother, returnable before
Lord Mansfield the very day before the
trials. I consult counsel, who advise me to
attend. I oppose the amendment with all
my might ; my remonstrances are despised ;
the amendment is made ; counsel stare ;
yet think it advisable to attend the trials.
The Crown Office people produce a magazine
of precedents in support of the practice.
Where is the remedy ? The point cannot be
debated, unless you are personally present.
Who dare advise you to take so dangerous a
step ?

'We had a violent struggle to get the new
Bill against Webb received by the Court of
King's Bench. But we are victorious at last ;
and the cause will be tried in a fortnight.'*

Within a reasonable time he was summoned
to come up and receive sentence, but did not
appear.

On November 1st, 1764, the unfortunate
patriot was outlawed. In anticipation of

---

* This Philips seems to have worked hard for his
client, who was, however, suspicious of him, and seemed
to think that he had 'sold' him.

this stroke he had transferred his property to his daughter. All his remaining actions at law became, as it were, void, an outlaw not having power to sue in the Courts. One scandalous result was that Lord Halifax, who had so long ridiculed the processes of the Court, *now* promptly entered an appearance, knowing that the unlucky plaintiff had not power to hurt him.

Still, the indomitable Wilkes, wounded, expelled, defeated, hunted, convicted, soon rallied again, and could write home many a gay and reckless letter, as in time past, to his friend and faithful henchman, Cotes :

' Lord Hertford gave yesterday a grand dinner to all the English here except *one*, and to the true Irish Whigs ; nor, like a good courtier, did he omit the new converts, the Scots. My lot is particular, and droll enough. I am the single Englishman not invited by the ambassador of my country, on the only day I can at Paris show my attachment to my sovereign, as if I was disaffected to the present establishment ; and yet I am frequently and grossly abused, because I am known to hate the other family, by a ridiculous fellow at Bouillon. This scribbler is one Rousseau ; who, by a wretched journal, does all he can, twice a month, to degrade a name made illustrious by one of the best French poets and by the great philosopher, though in these times no longer the citizen of Geneva. He lays at my door the *North Britons* against the Stuarts, and their dear friends in the north of our island.

' You may believe me when I assure you, it was not the slightest mortification to me that I did not receive an invitation to the Hôtel de Brancas (Lord Hertford's). When I was asked how it could happen that so staunch a Whig as Mr. Wilkes was not invited on the 4th of June, I laughed, like the old Roman. I had rather you should ask why I was *not* invited, than why I was invited. Perhaps it should have been asked, why some others *were* invited. The list of the company (of the *Macs* and *Sawneys* not in the French service) would divert you. To say the truth, I passed the day much more to my satisfaction, than I should have done in a set of mixed or suspicious company ; a fulsome, dull dinner ; two hours of mighty grave conversation, to be purchased (in all civility) by six more of Pharaoh—which I detest, as well as every other kind of gaming.

' As to the ambassador, I have never had the least connection with him ; nor indeed wish it—nor, at this time, with his Scottish chaplain.* An ambassador generally owes his very nomination to Ministerial influence, and is almost of course (though this does not extend through his family) under the direction of the Ministers ; or perhaps, as to the present case, in all propriety we ought to say, of the *Minister*, who, behind and between the curtains, still governs our island. I have never been presented at Court, because an Englishman should be presented by the English Ambassador, and I will not ask any favour of Lord Hertford in the present state of public affairs ; though, as a private nobleman, I should be ambitious to merit, and

* Dr. James Traill, afterwards Bishop of Down and Connor.

most fortunate to obtain, his friendship, as well as Lord Beauchamp's*—from their real sterling sense, great intrinsic worth, and (what sets off the whole) their amiable manners.

'I have the protection of the laws, which I never offend; and I am at Paris like any other foreigner who has no favour to ask, nor need seek any other security.

'The eloge which the noblest of poets† gives me, that I neither

' ". . . court the smile, nor dread the frown, of kings,"

is as exact truth here, as you know it to have been while I was at home. The small circle in which I now walk will, however, bear testimony to the just tribute of gratitude I pay to the humane virtues of a prince under whose mild and gentle government I have met with that protection which an innocent man had a right to expect, but could not find, in his own country, under his own sovereign.'

But, gay as this tone was, his affairs were in a desperate way. He was repeatedly

---

* Now Marquis of Hertford. † Churchill.

pressing for money. He had lived extravagantly at the Hôtel de Saxe, but now
moved to the Rue St. Niçaise, where he could
be with his dear daughter in more economical
fashion. His agent seems to have managed
his affairs in an uncertain disorderly fashion ;
at one time assuring him that after sale, etc.,
he would have a handsome income ; at
another, that his affairs were desperate. The
exile, however, soon established a connection with the bankers, and 'drew' hand-
somely on his friend at home, careless as to
how these drafts were to be met. All testi-
monies are agreed as to the companionable
gifts of this gifted man. The judge who
had just tried his case, Lord Mansfield, declared that 'he was the pleasantest companion, the politest gentleman, and the best
scholar he ever knew.' Johnson gave his
testimony almost in the same words, adding
that he was less appreciated from the unbounded praise that was showered on him.
'Full of wit,' said another of his friends,
'easy in his conversation, elegant in his
manners, and happy in a retentive memory,

his company was a perpetual treat to his friends.' It may be imagined, therefore, that the Parisians were not slow to appreciate such an addition to their society. He became the friend of the D'Holbachs, Diderots, and other wits and *savans*. He contrived to secure for his daughter the acquaintance of *très grandes dames*, such as the Duchesse de la Vallière, which became a lifelong friendship. He soon mastered French sufficiently to speak it with elegance and grace, and could utter pleasant turns and *bon - mots* in that un-familiar language. A happy specimen of his easy good-humour is supplied by a little scene which he recounted to Boswell, and who, in his turn, reports it not less happily.

A young man of fashion, who was about to give her *congé* to the lady of his affections, had asked him to a farewell supper. The host was in distress about the lady and her feelings, and proposed to make her a present of 200 louis d'ors as a *solatium*. Mr. Wilkes ' observed the behaviour of mademoiselle, who sighed indeed very piteously, and assumed every pathetic air of grief —but eat no less than three French

pigeons, which are as large as English part-
ridges, besides other things.' Wilkes then
whispered the gentleman : ' We often say in
England, *excessive sorrow is exceeding dry*, but I
never heard *excessive sorrow is exceeding hungry*.
Perhaps one hundred will do.' The other
took the hint.

CHAPTER XI.

DEATH OF CHURCHILL.

BUT now Fortune, which had hitherto dealt him such rude buffetings, offered him some amends, which came to him in a shape that he was likely enough to relish. All the printers and others who had been violently dragged to prison had been encouraged to seek redress from juries of their country. On July 6th the first of the actions brought against the Government, or their messengers and agents, was tried. Hassell, one of the printers, recovered £300. On the following day another obtained £200; on which no less than twelve other actions of the same kind were compromised.

To continue the history of these penalties for a single blunder, on December 10, Leach, the master printer, recovered £400, which

was only one of his suits, after which his
counsel declared that, as they had the happiness of seeing vindicated, asserted, and
maintained, all the great and constitutional
points of liberty, they were willing to accept
nominal damages and costs in the next five
causes. But the real interest lay in Wilkes'
actions against the greater 'fish,' the two
Secretaries of State and their assistants. So
serious were the issues to these personages
that it seems as though they wished to crush
him entirely, before he could be able even to
begin his actions. These, however, did not
exhaust the series, which were protracted
and spread over intervals so as to excite the
popular interest. It will be recollected that
Lord Bute had directed some violent proceedings against the supposed writer of the *Monitor*,
and Beardmore, a lawyer—who had been kept
in gaol a fortnight, and whose papers, with
those of his clients, had been ransacked—now
commenced actions not only against the messengers, but against Lord Halifax himself,
who had directed the outrage. In his charge
the Chief Justice, Lord Camden, who all

through was conspicuous for his constitutional and manly vindication of liberty, now laid it down that ' the seizure of Beardmore's person and papers was illegal.' He warned the Secretaries of State that they should be 'careful to see with their own eyes, and hear with their own ears.' At the same time he recommended moderation in the matter of damages. The jury gave £1,000 against the agents, when Beardmore offered to forego further action if Lord Halifax would accept a trial there and then ; but this fair offer was declined.*

---

* In one of these actions, in which by direction of the Chief Justice a verdict was entered for the plaintiff, the legal questions were raised on a Bill of Exceptions which was argued on appeal before the Court of King's Bench. It was here that the absurdity of the warrant was so admirably argued by Dunning. As he said, you might as well issue a warrant ' to take up *the murderer*, or *the robber*. And it was obvious that such a loose direction did not *warrant* the agent at all : it made him the judge of the whole matter, instead of the person who gave him the warrant. This is the case in 'a nutshell.' (See 3 Burrowes's Reports, p. 1760.) The Court, after argument, seemed to intimate that they were against the Crown, and, having adjourned the Court, on the next meeting the Attorney-General submitted to its judgment on a side issue. In a pamphlet which caused a great sensa-

But this was not enough. Lord Egremont was now beyond the reach of punishment,* but a discreditable spectacle was exhibited by Lord Halifax's attempts to baffle his opponent. This shameful course shows how power was in the hands of the Court and of those influential at Court. The Secretary, half favoured by the judges, half by the cleverness of counsel, was enabled, as we have seen, literally to set Wilkes at defiance.

But nothing is more remarkable in this long struggle with Wilkes than the curious blindness of Ministers, who only seemed eager to prove that, like the Bourbons, they could learn nothing, and forget nothing. No defeat seemed to furnish them any lesson of experience. They even sought for meaner victims when they could not reach the principal.

In February, 1765, there was witnessed a

tion, Dunning argued the whole case with much effect. Such was the result of one unlucky act of some stupid Ministers, and which extended over many years, entailing confusion, annoyance, and general social disturbance.

* A short time before his death he was heard to remark, 'Well, I have but three more turtle dinners to come, and if I survive them I shall be immortal.'

painful spectacle.   Williams, a printer, who
was concerned in the publishing of ' No. 45,'
was brought to be exposed in the pillory,
according to his sentence.   But instead of its
proving a disgrace and degradation, it turned
out an effective demonstration against Ministers.   It will hardly be credited that the
Ministers condescended to such trifling as to
select a hackney-coach that bore the number
' 45,' to bring the prisoner to the place of
exposure !   The mob set up four ladders in a
square, from which were hung ' jack-boots,'
of which the tops were cut off.   At the close
a gentleman went round and made a collection
to the handsome amount of £200, which was
presented to the victim.

During all this turmoil we have lost sight
of Churchill, who, since the exciting day
when he escaped arrest, through the adroit
warning of Wilkes, does not appear to have
met his friend.   But he had never ceased
working in his cause.   Some of his most
powerful satires had been issued ; and it is
evidence of their warm friendship that the
inspiration of these had been something con-

nected with the subject of Wilkes' wrongs. In 'The Duellist,' which had been prompted by the encounter with Martin, he had fallen on Wilkes' enemies, and therefore his own— on Sandwich, Warburton, and even the under-strapper, Carteret Webb.

His own course, in the interval, had been no less troubled, and even stormy. Wilkes was eagerly looking forward to a promised visit from him at Paris, and with infinite delight dwelt on the impression his gifted friend would make on sympathetic and appreciative Frenchmen. But Churchill was negligent and engrossed. ' No line from Churchill,' his friend had often reproachfully to write. Wilkes was anxious, and suffered much from the reports spread there about the anger of Lords and Bishops, who were furious at their treatment in ' The Duellist.' He made him a singular proposal, which was to get a collection of letters from ' old Hanbery ' (Williams), bring them over, and print them there ; for Wilkes had obtained an authorization from the French Government to print anything he pleased. 'A single letter of Fox's, about the Princess

Dowager, is worth £10,000 ; ' referring probably to a very familiar scandal. But Churchill was not likely to lend himself to these arts. ' Sterne and I,' adds Wilkes, ' often talk of you.'

At last he yielded to these affectionate entreaties, and, towards the end of October, went over to Boulogne, where Wilkes met him. But a week after his arrival, on October 29th, he was seized with a fever, and died there on November 4th. Wilkes attended him with much devotion, sitting up with him day and night, and was overwhelmed with grief at the catastrophe. Such was the sudden end of that singular, reckless life. Had he lived as long as Wilkes, it is unlikely that their friendship would have endured ; for his manly, independent spirit could not have approved or endured the descent into the demagogue's unworthy practices.*

---

* Robert Lloyd, another of the jovial coterie, was at this time confined to the Fleet Prison, where his friend Churchill, out of his slender means, supplied him with a guinea a week, and also defrayed the charge of a servant. It was said that he died of a broken heart, only a few weeks after the death of his friend. ' Blush, grandeur, blush !' adds the record.

On the other hand, it might be speculated that the poet's standard might have become so lowered by debauchery as to have made him less sensitive. Indeed, such a result might have been helped by a plan which the dissolute pair meditated of an excursion to Italy, each to be accompanied by the lady to whom he was then attached.*

There was a request in Churchill's will that ' his dear friend John Wilkes should collect and publish his works, with the remarks and explanations he had prepared, and any others he may think proper to make.' This pious duty his friend undertook with a fussy anxiety which, in his case, almost invariably augured

* There is a MS. fragment of autobiography, by Wilkes, in the British Museum, which describes his connection with this person, an Italian courtezan, named Coradini, and on whose perfections he dwelt in rapturous terms. After making the tour, which is described in detail without much vivacity or interest, he and the lady parted, when he presented her with large sums of money, though at this time he was sunk in debt and difficulties. The grossness of Wilkes' nature is shown by the reflections he makes in these notes—where he dwells on the happiness of spending the day with his daughter in intellectual enjoyment, and of then devoting the evening to this other companion.

badly for the completion of the task. His grief was displayed extravagantly on this topic. ' My life shall be dedicated to it,' he declared. He had lost his sleep. ' The idea of Churchill is ever before my eyes.' ' A pleasing melancholy will perhaps succeed in time;' but he believed that ' he never would get quite over it.' However, in a few weeks he had set off on his junketing to Italy, where he appears to have enjoyed himself much. The pious duty was never accomplished, and scarcely attempted. He had not the energy for such serious methodical work. He could talk much, indeed, of what he was about to do in such enterprises, which he undertook readily enough and with much enthusiasm. The chief stimulant in such things was probably the hope of getting money. His letters are full of these flourishings in relation to this pious literary executorship, and one would suppose it was some laborious editor working at his toilsome duty. The editing of the poet's works, fitly illustrated, would be a task requiring extraordinary knowledge and industry ; for the spirit of his writing was personal, and every page was full of allusions that now seem obscure.* Yet most of these meagre notes refer to Wilkes *himself* or to those whom he disliked, or furnish occasion for ventilating some favourite views of his own. It was in truth *all* Mr. Wilkes. To give a single instance, on an allusion to Lord Talbot he puts : ' The poet in various passages alludes to a variety of private anecdotes, most of which are told in the following letters from Mr. Wilkes to the Earl Temple ;' and then follows the long account of Wilkes' prowess in the duel, and his vigorous letters to Lord Talbot.

But a far more ambitious scheme which he conceived a few weeks after the death of his friend was a grand and important ' History of England,' ' done with great care,' ' a large quarto *almost finished* ' — words that should be noted. ' My " History of England " has cost me much time and pains. I believe, with you, it will have a great sale ; it is done

---

* It is amusing, therefore, to see the amount of work which this friend actually accomplished. Walpole, to whom he showed what he had done, declared that there was little more than a single note to each poem. The contributions, indeed, do not fill a sheet.

with care. I shall sell the copy of the first
volume, which contains the history of England
from the Revolution to the accession of the
House of Brunswick ; a *large quarto almost
finished.* It is compiled from materials
which no historian has seen : the original
letters of foreign Ministers to Louis XIV.
and a journal to the death of James
II., wrote by himself, which contains a
variety of curious anecdotes. I will have six
hundred pounds for it ; half now, and the
other half on the delivery of the volume in
January next. I do not think there can be
a single word libellous in the first volume ;
though there may be a great many in the
second, which is from the accession of the
House of Brunswick to the present time. I
have thoughts of a country-house near this
place, that I may entirely attend to the perfecting this great work, without any dissipation. This will cost me a good deal,
therefore I must have three hundred pounds
directly ; and I would engage to deliver the
first volume complete in January, on the payment of three hundred pounds more. I shall

take care that my first volume *shall make the nation wild* for the rest of the work. And you may advertise, when you will, " *In the press* " (or any other expression you prefer), " The History of England ; from the Revolution to the End of the fourth Year of King George III. By John Wilkes. In three volumes, quarto." '

It may be conceived that such a history would be only a ' Wilkite ' pamphlet. In three years he announced to. his publisher, Almon, that ' my history advances very much.' He would give it all the preparation ' his poor abilities could reach.' He was eagerly tempting Almon to put down £500 for it, and he contracted to have it complete within nine months. The publisher at last was seduced by this dazzling account into paying £400, on condition that the first volume was to be delivered in three months, and the whole work completed by the opening of the new year. When Wilkes had received the cash, he wrote : ' I lose no time in *finishing* the first volume of my history. I will make it as perfect as I can here, for both our sakes.' It, indeed, seems to have occurred to him for the first time that there might be some difficulty in writing a ' History of England ' *in Paris*, the author being forbidden to enter his native land. A month later it was ' his daily amusement ;' but almost at once he makes an announcement of literary assistance from a Mr. Rice, which he was in daily expectation of receiving ; matter, he says, ' so important and curious, that he wishes me to see it before I finish. It is your interest and mine to have the work as perfect as we can ; and, therefore, I only send you the in· troduction, until I have examined the pieces he is to send. You will, I hope, approve the introduction. I believe it will much please ; because the English here, to whom I have read it, are high in their commendations. I wish to see the proof-sheets : you, who are a good author, know the importance of correcting one's self the proof-sheets—how much a work gains by it, etc.'

Now, as this was written about the time when he was bound by agreement to deliver the first portion, it was clearly a pretext for delay. The truth appears to be that he had written nothing of the great history ; and a bald introduction of, at most, but fifty pages long, which is still to be read, represented the whole of his labours ! And, further, not another line was ever written of the work. This transaction is not very creditable to him, and must be considered as an elaborate deception. How he could bring himself to say, ' My history is nearly finished,' when only the preface was done, is not to be readily explained, save on the theory that the slave of pleasure in want of money is often obliged to part with truth also. We almost seem to be reading of one of the ingenious Brinsley Sheridan's devices.

There was yet another literary work, also of a testamentary kind, which he had undertaken in a fit of enthusiasm. With Sterne he had always been intimate. When Sterne died, his widow and daughter were left almost in penury, his debts amounting to some £1,100. In this distress a subscription was made up for them, and they proposed to issue an

edition of his sermons by subscription.   In
a piteous letter, the daughter, Lydia, applied to
Wilkes for his aid in pushing the subscription.
They must have been gratified at his enthusiastic and generous response.   He would do
everything : further, he would, in concert
with Hall - Stevenson, write a life of the
humourist, to be prefixed to the collection.
He went into details of the whole plan, suggesting that the daughter should ornament
the work with her own drawings.

Months, however, went by, and the widow
and daughter, pressed by their difficulties,
wrote to remind him of his ' kind promise.'
' If you knew, dear sir,' wrote Lydia, ' how
much we are straitened as to our income,
you would not neglect it.'   They reminded
him that he had volunteered a suggestion of the
plan—' would he stimulate Mr. Hall, who
was somewhat lazy ?'   This would enable them
' to join to their admiration of his character
tears of gratitude whenever they should hear
his name, for the peculiar services he had
rendered them.'   Many more months passed
away—nothing was done.   No notice ever was

taken of their requests, which became tedious. In a despairing and reproachful appeal, Lydia again reminded him of his promise: ' Do not, I beseech you, disappoint us. I trust you will write to Hall—*in pity* do!' She then appealed in almost despairing terms to Hall, recalling what he had so gratuitously promised. It would put £400 in their pockets—would he not press Wilkes ? They were, from their necessities, obliged to ask for a positive answer. Would anything be done—yes or no ? As might be expected, the two voluptuaries never performed their promise. Impulsive persons often thought-lessly undertake engagements of this kind. Wilkes, it must be said, had grown into a habit of expecting everything to be done for *him*, and, in most instances, actually found persons to do everything for him—to supply him with money, pay his debts, and take all trouble off his hands. He found it irksome, therefore, to undertake duties for others, par-ticularly such as this was, of a profitless kind, and involving trouble. Miss Sterne, there-fore, performed the task herself.

CHAPTER XII.

WILKES is entitled to the credit of having introduced a peculiar form of political address, not unfamiliar to our own time under the name of ' the manifesto,' and which is peculiarly effective in the hands of a popular and sympathetic agitator. This, in fact, was the only mode open to him of communicating with his admirers. A short time before going to Boulogne to meet Churchill, he had prepared such an address to the public, nominally directed to the Electors of Aylesbury, and dated October 22nd, 1764. In this paper he recounted once more all the hardships of his case, going over the *North Briton* incident, his expulsion, trials, etc. ; the gross partiality of Lord Mansfield, set out with much caustic remark ; and winding up with a claim for gratitude and praise, in consequence of his exertions. From this time forth this was to be his theme, and on the occasion it was thus modestly enforced :*

' I congratulate my free-born countrymen, and am full of gratitude that Heaven inspired me with a firmness and fortitude equal to the conduct of so arduous a business. Under all the wanton cruelties of usurped and abused power, the goodness of the cause supported me ; and I never lost sight of the great object which I had from the first in my view, the preservation of the rights and privileges of every Englishman. I glory in the name, and will never forget the duties resulting from it. Though I am driven into exile from my dear country, I shall never cease to love and reverence its constitution, while it remains free. It will continue my last ambition to approve myself a faithful son of England; and I shall always be ready to give my life a willing sacrifice to my native country, and to

---

* I do not give this and other letters of the kind at length, as the more important portions have been used in the course of the narrative.

what it holds most dear—the security of our invaluable liberties. While I live, I shall enjoy the satisfaction of thinking that I have not lived in vain; that the present age has borne the noblest testimony to me ; *and that my name will pass with honour to posterity, for the upright and disinterested part I have acted, and for my unwearied endeavours to protect and secure the persons, houses, and papers of my fellow-subjects from arbitrary visits and seizures.'*

Oct. 22.

He was so satisfied with the result of this form of address that it became a favourite one with him. He found that he could thus deal more telling and dramatic strokes than when addressing crowds directly. It must be said some of his efforts in this line are admirable for a certain rude humour.

Four days before Churchill's death, and when he was charitably attending his sick-bed, a terrible blow, as we have seen, fell on his head. Not appearing to answer the summons to receive sentence, he was formally

put under ban ! He had had some months'
notice, and prepared himself.

'My affairs,' he wrote (in August) to Cotes,
'draw to a crisis. By the outlawry I shall
be cut off from the body of English subjects.
I believe an outlaw can neither sue nor be
sued ; it therefore becomes me to have all my
private affairs settled as soon as possible.
Let me therefore, my dearest friend, entreat
you to send me immediately the scheme you
propose. I had rather everything was sold
for my life, and the amount sent me to
manage here ; for I can have no legal connection in England very soon. I wish too, for
the sake of your family, that you would send
a general release from me to you before the
outlawry, to confirm all you have done, that
you may have the fullest sanction the law can
give.'

It is not uncharitable to say that much of
the grief which he suffered from Churchill's
death was mingled with his own private
agony at this blow. For weeks afterwards he
was writing in this strain :

'I am better, my dearest Cotes, but cannot

get any continued sleep. The idea of Churchill is ever before my eyes. A pleasing melancholy will perhaps succeed in time, and then I shall be fit for something. As I am, there is not a more useless animal in the world.'

When we think of what his position then was,—disgraced, outlawed, expelled from Parliament, exiled, anticipating the moment that he would be ordered to quit France at the request of his own Government, bankrupt, and without a shilling—shall we not wonder at the prodigious elasticity, the fertility of resource, the daring spirit which prompted him to renewed exertion in the hope of recouping Fortune? *Tout peut se rétablir*, might have been his motto. Who would have been credited had he declared that this wretched, banned outcast would, within a few years, become the idol of the people, be furnished with abundance of money, and end as Lord Mayor of London, City Chamberlain, and member of Parliament, causing all evidence of his disgrace to be reversed and obliterated!

On Christmas Day he started from Paris to make his tour in Italy, visiting all the most interesting cities on his road. He recorded his progress in a series of natural, vivacious, and chatty letters to his daughter ' Polly '— his ' dear girl,' as he always called her—all being seasoned with sensible, shrewd advice and direction. This affection for his Polly was one of the most pleasing and redeeming features in our *roué's* character. Through all his life, and all his difficulties, it never flagged. It continued to the year of his death. For her he seemed to put on quite a new character, and his letters to her are really charming, from his eagerness to please and their lack of affectation.

He visited Turin, where he met Messrs. Needham and Dillon, the former a fast and eccentric Irish gentleman, and one of the earliest admirers of Mrs. Abington. At Milan he was treated with all honour. As he wrote truly to his child :

' Nothing can please or oblige me more than your journals. Give yourself no trouble about all the idle reports spread concerning me. You and I are the best and most natural friends ; and in everything I shall first of all

consult your happiness and your pleasures.
Look forward and remember what I told you.
Did I not prophesy a great deal of what has
happened? Pope is an excellent author for you;
so are Boileau and Racine. You cannot read
them too often; but never, dear girl, tire yourself.' At Florence all the English, Lord Beauchamp and others, came to wait on him. 'I did
not go to the Resident—to save him the *embarras*
of returning a visit to a man so very obnoxious
to the English (or rather Scottish) Ministry
as myself. I have been caressed more than
I can express, during my whole journey; and
by those in every country whose *éloge* does me
real honour.'

At Naples he hired a pleasant house, 'in a
sweet situation, where from morning till night
he was to be found with a pen in his hand.'
His thoughts travelled affectionately to his
daughter, whose drawings were hung up in his
sanctum, with her portrait, in the absence of
the dear original. 'Let us both,' he said,
'continue to love one another more than all
the rest of the world, and that will sweeten
everything, however cross and disagreeable.'

She was in London, at the old house in Red Lion Court, with his mother, who now re-appears on the scene.

In July he set out on his journey home, embarking for Naples and taking Geneva on his way. He gives an agreeable sketch of two visits which he paid, and which are worth recording. One was a visit to the Chartreuse, where, as usual, he recommended himself to his hosts by his *bonhomie* :

'It is about eight leagues from Grenoble, among the most savage rocks and gloomy woods you can imagine. The situation in-spires horror rather than pensiveness. The monks are extremely hospitable, and entertain strangers very well. They speak only on par-ticular days; but a *père coadjuteur* is appointed to receive and to do the honours to strangers, and the *père général* may always talk. They are allowed to drink wine, and the *père général* sent me a present of the best Burgundy I ever tasted. They receive all strangers ; and there are separate apartments for the English, French, Spaniards, etc., with a large hall for each to dine in. The building is immense, and near

it are small houses for all kinds of workmen.
I lay there ; and was as well entertained as it
is possible to be—with the best fish, bread,
butter, cheese, and wine. I ought to have
mentioned first the pious conversation of the
good fathers, which edified me greatly, though
not quite converted—so obstinate a heretic
as my dear Polly knows me to be. Many of
the fathers have lived much in the gay world,
and are indeed truly gentlemen.'

Mr. Wilkes, always *bon enfant*, seems to
have been as much pleased with his hosts as
they were with him, and he wrote the following in the visitors' album :

'I had the happiness of passing the entire
day of July 24, 1765, in this romantic place,
with the good fathers of the Grande Chartreuse;
and I reckon it among the most agreeable of
my life. I was charmed with the hospitality
and politeness I met with, and edified by the
conversation of the *père général* and the *père
coadjuteur*. The savageness of the woods, the
gloom of the rocks, and the perfect solitude,
conspire to make the mind pensive, and to

lull to rest all the turbulent, guilty passions of the soul. I feel much regret at leaving the place and the good fathers, but I carry with me the liveliest sense of their goodness.

'JOHN WILKES, *Anglois.*'

At Geneva he paid his respects to a celebrated man :

'I found my good friend, Lord Abingdon, here ; and we went together to see Voltaire. I was charmed with the reception he gave me, and still more with the fine sense and exquisite wit of his conversation. He put me to the blush by the many compliments he paid me ; and the most generous offers he made me about his printers, etc. I do not know when I have been so highly entertained; but I know, after all, that I had rather be with my dear girl than with the first wits or beauties in the world.'

But while thus enjoying himself, news reached him of a sudden unexpected change in the Ministry, which was likely to be favourable to his interests. The Rockingham party, who had espoused his cause in Opposi-

tion, were coming into office. The Duke of
Grafton, a brother *roué* and a personal friend,
was now one of the Ministers ; though, judg-
ing from the experience of his treatment by
Sandwich and Le Despenser, this was likely
enough to be of evil omen.   He anxiously
hurried home, post-haste.   Embarking on the
Italian coast in a small and crazy vessel, he
was landed in France, and on September 29th,
1765, once more found himself in Paris.

CHAPTER XIII.

EVERYTHING now seemed to promise most favourably. The amiable and popular Premier, Lord Rockingham, the Duke of Grafton aforesaid, and smaller personages such as Mr. Fitzherbert, all would naturally be supposed to promise indemnity for the past. Nor could it be ignored that serious doubts as to the legality of the treatment he had experienced had been aroused.

Charles Townshend, in a pamphlet entitled 'A Defence of the Minority,' had dealt effectively with the whole question of the expulsion, taking Wilkes' side, though not in a style that flattered or pleased the demagogue. His hopes were, therefore, raised to an extraordinary degree, and he encouraged himself to believe that not only full pardon would be obtained for him, but even a suitable pension of, say, £1,000, with possibly the coveted appointment of ambassador to Constantinople ! The ground of these complacent delusions were some indiscreet, good-natured overtures, or suggestions, made to him by subordinate agents of the party, chiefly by Mr. Fitzherbert, and by his own trusty agent, Humphrey Cotes, who seemed to be as sanguine as he was himself.

' I am still,' he wrote to Cotes, on October 15th, 1765, ' in the same idea as to Constantinople : *nothing can so effectually heal all breaches of every kind.* When you consider what passed as to the brother of a certain man not an Englishman, I believe the person you mention may be brought to yield to it. You, who are on the spot, can best judge of this. *There is nothing I so much wish, on every account my busy mind can suggest to me.'*

The passages in italics are amusingly significant, from his air of confidence. Further letters pointed to a pecuniary compensation for his prosecution :

' The idea of an annual sum of one thousand pounds being to be paid to me does not captivate my imagination. You mention that you do not yet learn upon what establishment or fund it is to be granted ; and you desire me to write a letter for you to deliver to *them*, without mentioning or even leaving me to guess *who*.

' *You avoid, my dear friend, the word "pension" with great care :* yet I believe the world would rather consider such a grant only in that light, though I should myself look upon it as paying very poorly all the costs of suit due to me.'

It appears that the foundation for this delusion was no more than some mysterious hints in a letter from his brother Heaton, which had reached him in August when he was at Geneva :

' Heaton asks me several questions ; I know not by what authority, nor on what foundation. *If I am to give my opinion, Constantinople is by far the most eligible.* Perhaps he is only amusing himself and me. I will mar nothing by precipitation. I am ready ; but I wait for another opportunity. *I fear to do harm, and I do not even wish to irritate.'*

'I have,' he goes on, 'a most kind and friendly letter from Mr. Onslow. Yet it is *couched in general expressions*, and all private intelligence is very disadvantageous to the present powers. *Nothing has yet been done.'*

This thought prompted him to reveal his tactics in a naïvely characteristic way. Where persuasion fails, the demagogue often throws out menaces :

'*Nothing has yet been done ;* and I am afraid, in the bargain for the honours of the State, that the good of it was never thought of by the majority of the present gentlemen. I am an insignificant individual ; but I have given much time and attention to these subjects, and I know what ought to be done, and what the nation expects should be done : I have digested my thoughts very carefully, and I intend to give them to the public the first day of the meeting of Parliament. *How the Ministry will like them, I very little care :* every Whig must, I am sure, approve ; and I think I am secure of every friend of my country (not embarked with either party) giving me applause.

'I have never yet heard who the present Ministry are : I believe the Scot is the breath of their nostrils. *It depends, however, on them whether Mr..Wilkes is their friend or their enemy.* If he starts as the latter, he will lash them with scorpion rods—and they are already prepared. *I wish, however, we may be friends :* and I had rather follow the plan I had marked out in my letter from Geneva. In all cases I shall wait to hear your opinion ; and I shall see what that great chapter in the book, the chapter of accidents, produces before the meeting of the House. I desire, however, you would let it be understood by the present Ministry, that if we are not good friends on public grounds, I am their determined, implacable enemy, ready to give the stab where it will wound the most. *I repeat, however, I wish we may be friends in earnest ; and if we are, I will give every assistance that such mean abilities as mine can afford them—and they know how indefatigable I am in every cause I undertake.* I leave you, my dear Cotes, to negotiate all these matters : I know the goodness of your head and of your heart.'

This extraordinary communication seems rather compromising to our patriot's character. It can be seen, indeed, that from the beginning to the end of his course he was consistent in his principles—viz., to look to the personal interests of Wilkes before all things.

Weeks, however, went by, and matters did not advance. Mr. Fitzherbert ceased to write. Brother Heaton wrote, indeed, but his letters ' were too obscure as to the offers made me to be any guide to me.' Walpole, the Paris banker, his friend, was on intimate terms with Mr. Pitt. Wilkes' ardour made him actually deal in compliments to the great commoner :

' I am the only Englishman here who is visited by Mr. Walpole, the banker. He corresponds with Pitt, which is a most unusual grace to him, from the best orator and the worst letter-writer of our age. I grieve at the coldness between Lord Temple and Pitt. I wish that, like most bosom

friendships, it did not end in an inveterate
hatred. There is nothing I desire so earnestly
to hear of as their reconciliation. I beg you
to tell Lord Temple from me how much I am
devoted to him, and that my mean faculties
shall ever be exerted in any manner he wishes,
and will vouchsafe to prescribe.

' Nothing can so effectually do the business
of the favourite as the quarrel of the two
brothers. Pitt's application of the lines from
Virgil, " Extincti te, neque," etc., went to my
heart, and seemed prophetic.

' I begin to think that I am doomed to an
eternal exile, or that I must force my way
home. Suppose I return immediately ? Will
this Ministry dare to let the law take place ?
A pillory in my case would be worse than the
business of the weavers, which so much
alarmed the first persons of the nation. *If
the Ministers do not find employment for me,
I am disposed to find employment for them.*
As the term does not open till the end of
January, Mansfield in no case could pass
sentence before that time, and the spirit of
the people is too high to let me suffer in

a cause of their own. I am much inclined to this step of coming over directly.'

This idea of a secret return now took possession of him.

'Would it be allowed,' he writes, 'if I asked it, to steal over privately, to see Miss Wilkes, to talk with you, Lord Temple, Mr. Fitzherbert, etc.? *Nothing would alarm the present Ministers so much* as the idea of my coming to London; nothing, perhaps, would so much advance my affairs.'

He more and more inclined to be content with a money *solatium :*

'It is time to take up and grow independent; but one thing is necessary for you and me. I have waited to hear from you on the subject of my private affairs, of Fitzherbert's offer, or any other plan. Living here, not in an *hôtel garni* and privately, £1,000 a year would soon make me easy and independent, as well as pay my debts in time.'

The need of constant indulgence in pleasures made money more than ever necessary to him. All this time he had been, as

the latter arrangement of his debts brought
out, deeply pledged to bankers, Jews, jewellers,
and others, who had advanced him very large
sums, no doubt on the credit of his reputation.
He was now, indeed, more than usually
pressed. Assuming that the grant of
£1,000 held out to him by Mr. Fitzherbert
was his now to deal with, he drew on his
banker for a portion. A little later, having
repudiated some condition or undertaking
which he was required to accept, as not
being in the contract, Mr. Fitzherbert declined
to honour his draft. In vain Wilkes protested
that this was ' a supposition ' of the grant
being in an ' honourable way, according to
his former declarations and his letters to
Heaton.'

He was left to meet the difficulty as best he
could, and he found himself in ' great distress,'
and his banker, Foley, ' much out of humour.'

In February, 1766, he wrote, still more
disgusted :

' I am never disposed to be peevish, but
I cannot but more and more lament the cruel
situation in which I am placed. I am entirely

ignorant of what is most necessary for me to know, and scarcely one friendly star left to point out my way. I have not received one shilling, nor Mr. Foley for me. I am in debt here, and you know that the whole of last year and this you have not sent me anything out of the management of my private estates. I have had great professions of friendship from several of the present, or perhaps I ought to say of the late, Ministry ; but they have been no more than professions. My pardon, I believe, has never been asked, nor anything else ; and I find no man hardly enough to run great risks for me. Mr. Fitzherbert and a few more have it not in their power, though I am satisfied it is warmly in their inclination ; and, if they could, they would not hesitate to grant me the £1,000 per annum on the Irish establishment for thirty years, which I wrote you word Walpole proposed.'

At last, early in the following year, Wilkes, grown desperate, took the bold step of going over to London to look after his own interests. There were some indications which showed

that the Ministry were really favourable to
him, and wished to reconcile him; one of
which was that Pratt, the Chief Justice, who
had so favoured his cause, had been promoted
to the House of Lords.

Early in May he set out with much secrecy,
giving out to his friends that he was going to
make a little tour. He was received at Dover
with acclamation by the mob, and went up to
town in a postchaise and four. This so
delighted him, that a friend wrote of his
proceedings, that ' Mr. Wilkes was very well
pleased with what has happened, every hour
giving him new proofs of the wisdom of
the step he took in returning home under
a Ministry which I know he approves, and
believe will support.'

He remained in London about ten weeks,
and seemed to be quite confident as to the
success of his expedition.

' I believe,' he wrote to Mr. Holles, ' that
I shall have my pardon. I plead the first
day of next term. I have entered into no
political engagements, but I have declared to
the friends of the Ministers that " no con-

sideration shall ever induce me, in any
moment of my life, to do anything offensive
or in the least disobliging to Lord Temple," '
whom, however, he avoided meeting, so as
not to compromise him.   Lord Temple was at
this time spoken of as likely to be the chief
spirit of a new Ministry.

On the other hand, Wilkes's friend throws
a curious light on the motive for this reserve.
He would not even see Lord Temple ' because
he was engaged in an interesting negotiation
with the Ministry.'   Lord Temple, it appeared,
was quite satisfied with this reticence, but,
with some foresight, said that ' he was certain Lord Rockingham had not the least
intention of serving Wilkes, and would certainly deceive him.'

And so it was to prove.   Wilkes, after
remaining some weeks, found all his hopes of
a free pardon, pension, etc., quite vain ; and,
as the dangerous first day of term was approaching, he had to set off again to return to
his dreary exile, having failed in his purpose.

It must not, however, be imagined that

Wilkes had been idle, or that the Ministers were wholly indisposed to deal with him. From Mr. Prior we learn what had been going on, and the reasons for the failure ; he had obtained the story from the friends and connections of Edmund Burke. It is amusing to contrast the simple practical character of the transaction with the lofty patriotic colour which Wilkes found it necessary to import into the affair. It seems that Lord Rockingham declined to see him, but young Mr. Edmund Burke, then commencing his career, was deputed to have secret interviews with the *proscrit*. With Mr. Fitzherbert, he met Wilkes in no less than five interviews, when the following conditions, or demands, were put forward and discussed :

1. A free pardon.
2. A sum of money as compensation for the treatment he had received.
3. A pension on the Irish Establishment of £1,500 a year.

It may be conceived that such proposals were found inadmissible, though no doubt the Ministry would have been glad to arrange

with him on reasonable terms.   This is clear
from their tolerance in allowing him to remain
in London unmolested.   Further, they were
at the moment tottering, or falling to pieces.
But the King's rancorous dislike of Wilkes
was the most serious objection.   He was
always obstinate in refusing a pardon, and,
that withheld, it was impossible, of course, to
confer place or pension.

Wilkes had scarcely reached Paris when
another happy turn again improved his
fortunes.   The Rockingham Government had
fallen, and he now learned that the Duke of
Grafton—a *viveur* of his own class, one as
careless of giving public scandal as he himself had ever been—was now First Lord of
the Treasury.   Such a man—a friend too—
who had visited him in his prison, was sure
to be indulgent.   Less fortunately for his
interests, the ' Great Commoner ' had also
come into office, who was not likely to be
so favourably disposed towards him.   On
the other hand, his old friend, Lord Temple,
had been invited to take an important place ;
and the presence of so warm a friend and

ally in the Ministry would, at least, neutralize Mr. Pitt's hostility. Unluckily, at starting, a painful disagreement, if not quarrel, broke out between the brothers-in-law, on the point of the suitable distribution of offices, and Lord Temple withdrew in high dudgeon.

Still, Wilkes had, not unnaturally, nourished the fairest hopes. He was presently to be once more beguiled with a pretence of negotiations. There was something wanton in this treatment, and these insincere attempts, possibly intended to keep him quiet, almost warranted a part of his later violence.

It chanced that Colonel Fitzroy, the Duke of Grafton's brother, was in Paris early in October. He had several interviews with Wilkes, and gave him 'the most encouraging assurances.' This gentleman, as Wilkes told the story, ' in a conversation at the Hotel d'Espagne, did me the honour of assuring me that I should find his brother my real and sincere friend, extremely desirous to concur in doing me justice ; that *he was to tell me this from* your grace, *the Duke of*

Grafton, but that many interesting particulars relative to me could not be communicated by letter, nor by the post. I fondly believed these obliging assurances ; because on a variety of occasions your grace had testified a full approbation of my conduct, had thanked me in the most flattering terms as the person most useful to the common cause in which we were embarked, and had shown an uncommon zeal to serve a man who had suffered so much in the cause of liberty.'*

Of course this was general enough ; but from the First Lord of the Treasury it could only mean one thing, viz., the gratifying, to a certain extent, Wilkes's desires. He, thus encouraged, at once arranged once more to return to England, and again no objection appears to have been raised. He set off on October 22nd, as he says, ' With the gayest and most lively hopes.' He was very ill in crossing, and bought a pig in the picturesque old town of Arras for the sum of ninepence.

* Letter to the Duke of Grafton, December 12th, 1766.

Indeed, he was 'sick almost to death,' and reached London on October 29th.

' As soon as I arriv'd at London, I desir'd my excellent friend, Mr. *Fitzherbert*, to wait on your grace, with every profession of regard on my part, and the resolution I had taken of entirely submitting the mode of the application I should make to the throne for my pardon. I cannot express the anxiety which your grace's answer gave me : *Mr. Wilkes must write to Lord Chatham.* I then beg'd Mr. *Fitzherbert* to state the reasons, which made it impossible for me to follow that advice, from every principle of honour, both public and private. I show'd too the impropriety of supplicating a fellow subject for mercy, the *prerogative* good Kings are the most jealous of, by far the brightest jewel in their crown, and the attribute, by which they may the nearest approach to the Divinity.'

Somewhat nervous at this unexpected message, he now addressed a personal request to the Duke, couched in the most complimentary, if not obsequious terms, begging him to intercede with his Majesty for his pardon:

'*Nov.* 1.

' My LORD,

'It is a very peculiar satisfaction I feel, on my return to my native country, that a nobleman of your grace's superior talents, and inflexible integrity, is at the head of the most important department of State. I have been witness of the general applause, which has been given abroad, to the choice his Majesty has made, and I am happy to find my own countrymen zealous and unanimous in every testimony of their approbation.

' I hope, my lord, that I may congratulate myself, as well as my country, on your grace's being placed in a station of so great power and importance. Though I have been cut off from the body of his Majesty's subjects, by a cruel and unjust proscription, I have never entertained an idea inconsistent with the duty of a good subject. My heart still retains all its former warmth for the dignity of England, and the glory of its

Sovereign. I have not associated with the traitors to our liberties, nor made a single connection with any man who was dangerous, or even suspected by the friend of the Protestant family on the throne. I now hope that the rigour of a long-unmerited exile is past, and that I may be allowed to continue in the land, and among the friends of liberty.

'I wish, my lord, to owe this to the mercy of my Prince. I entreat your grace to lay me with all humility at the King's feet, with the truest assurances that I have never, in any moment of my life, swerved from the duty and allegiance I owe to my Sovereign, and that I implore, and in everything submit to, his Majesty's clemency.

'Your grace's noble manner of thinking, and the obligations I have formerly received, which are still fresh in my mind, will, I hope, give a full propriety to this address ; and I am sure a heart, glowing with the sacred zeal of liberty, must have a favourable reception from the Duke of Grafton. I flatter myself, that my conduct will justify your grace's interceding with a Prince, who is distinguished by a compassionate tenderness and goodness to all his subjects.

'I am, etc.

It has always been admitted that it would have been a wise and gracious act to have accepted this submission. After the preliminaries in Paris, Wilkes had certainly a claim to attention. But, to his anger and astonishment, scarcely any notice was taken of his appeal. He was kept waiting for many days. For the first time it began to dawn on him that he was being played with.

'I am here, my dear girl,' he wrote on November 4th to his Polly, 'in daily expectation of having a final answer from the Duke of Grafton, which will fix the day of my return to you. I wish that I could, before this, have told you the hour when I shall come to see you; but I suppose I may be on the road to Paris before you may hear again of me. Some of the important persons in this business have been out of town; but, I believe, this evening they will be assembled.'

He hoped ' we would settle our affairs on the morrow, or on the next day.'

The truth was the Duke of Grafton dared not act as he might have wished. This is shown by a passage in his private memoirs, of which Walpole made some use in his ' Memoirs of George III.'

Speaking of Wilkes's appeal to him he says : ' That letter I showed to his Majesty, who, as well as I recollect, read it with attention ; but made no observation on it. Lord Chatham, on being consulted, thought the better way for the present was to take no notice of it.' Thus the unhappy Wilkes was kept hanging in suspense, waiting this ' no answer.' After long delay, the only answer he received was the message : ' Mr. Wilkes must write to Lord Chatham. I can do nothing without Lord Chatham.'

' When I found,' he said with scorn, ' that my pardon was to be bought with the sacrifice of my honour, I spurned at the proposal.'

It might seem, however, that there was

scarcely any need of introducing Wilkes's
honour in the matter. A more pressing
reason for this refusal to apply to Mr. Pitt
was the certainty of meeting a refusal.

Again had Mr. Fitzherbert acted as
Wilkes's agent and friend in the matter and
had seen the Duke. All he could tell was
that the ' great man did not seem offended '
at the news of his arrival, which was little
encouragement. In which state he had to
depart—torn with uncertainty and disappointment. As he put it : ' I left my dear native
London with a heart full of grief that my
fairest hopes were blasted ; of humiliation
that I had given an easy faith to the promises
of a Minister and a courtier ; and of astonishment that a nobleman of parts and discern-
ment could continue in an infatuation from
which the conduct of Lord Chatham had
recovered every other man in the nation.'

His friend Almon declares that Wilkes
assured him it was the bitterest disappointment he ever suffered : all the passions
inspired by grief, rage, vexation, and resentment, rankling and corroding in his breast,

his mental state was in the most painful commotion. Naturally in such a breast the first thought was of revenge, and making the man who had so befooled him smart for his behaviour.

The idea occurred to him of addressing to the public a complete exposure of the trick played him, through the medium of a letter to the Duke of Grafton. He would relate the whole story of his wrongs.

We have already quoted the passages relating to Mr. Pitt, whom he now accused of being a '*tool of parties.*'

This long letter was, however, an important political manifesto. It was published in Paris as well as in London (in this latter shape somewhat mutilated, through the publisher's caution), and it made a great sensation. The half-hearted negotiations of the Ministry were there revealed, and did not add to their credit.

The unlucky Duke was by-and-by to suffer from yet another exposure: the bitter onslaught of 'Junius.' Thus he furnished a subject for two of the most caustic pens of his time.

CHAPTER XIV.

'WILKES AND LIBERTY.'

WE are now on the eve of some most stirring scenes and tumultuous proceedings, when we shall see the befooled and despised demagogue, with singular courage, returning once more to London to fight his battle in the streets. He had appealed to Kings, Ministers, old friends and new; he was now to appeal, and with complete success, to the MOB. The moment particularly favoured his plans, for the Ministry was weak and held in contempt, and the spirit of faction was abroad. At the moment, indeed, he was completely forgotten by the crowd; and it is to the credit of his sagacity and his general ability that he should have discerned that he had the gifts for stirring the masses with the most complete effect.

The extraordinary feature in his case is that he had few of the professional gifts which commend to the idolatry of a mob. He was little of a speaker — nay, could scarcely speak at all to a crowd. Neither did he take up the wrongs or oppressions or any particular grievance of the mob. He urged only his own particular woes and hardships. Yet he was destined to enjoy, for a time at least, the most extravagant popularity. This seems a puzzle ; but it may be accounted for by that magnetic or sympathetic force which, at all times, unaccountably—illogically, no doubt—attracts the crowd so irresistibly. There was something even dramatic in his cause—his struggle, at overwhelming odds, with Ministers and Parliaments, and the King himself ; his exile, his defiant spirit—all these elements, if properly ' worked,' were likely to answer admirably for his purpose.

Before long, towards the end of the year 1767, he felt impelled to come once more to London. It is likely enough that the increasing pressure of his debts at Paris was the chief cause. As his friend Almon tells us :

' His situation at Paris had become disagreeable and his affairs desperate ; but his popularity was high, and he determined upon
taking advantage of this popularity at its
flood. He thought it unnecessary to waste
any more time in trifling negotiations either
with Ministers or their opponents ; they were
not his friends in his present state, and their
enmity could not make it worse. Whatever
the danger might be, therefore, he determined
to meet it.'

He had arranged to meet his faithful friend
Cotes at Ostend, to concert their plots
together, and he now undertook a long,
circuitous journey to reach that place. If
nowadays it requires a strong effort of
imagination to realize the amazing difficulties
of travel and the toilsome journeys by post
which persons in those days undertook cheerfully and for even trivial reasons, it is no
less a surprise, when travel is so easy and
most expeditions are completed in a single
stage, to look back to the toilsome progress
by which a nobleman, even as Lord Grey,
living in the extreme north of England, had

to make his way to the Metropolis ; while
the journey from London to Dover, which now
takes two hours, was generally made in two
easy stages.

In his course by the Hague, Rotterdam,
and other Dutch towns, he was much complimented. 'They are thronging round me,' he
wrote to his daughter, 'to see if I am like
any print which they have got.'

It was droll to find him attending the
Ambassadors' Chapel at the Hague, though
he abused the sermon. He, however, affected
mystery, and letters were addressed to him
under an assumed name. He passed as ' Mr.
Fitz-Osborne.'

In due course his friend met him, and they
had many discussions as to the policy to be
pursued. Cotes' opinion was that 'the
making a faint attempt, without probability
of success, would only contribute to the
triumph of his enemies. On the other
hand, a storm might be raised in Westminster
which might have the best effect. In either
case, you must determine soon what part
you will take. Your presence is indispensable.

He at once told me he was looking for Mr. Fitzherbert, and expected something from him. I have been thinking of opening a subscription, under the title of " a subscription in support of liberty, honour, and gratitude." I fancy it will produce something considerable. Let me have your sentiments.'

Early in February Wilkes made up his mind to wait no longer; and once more arrived in London. His first step was of a conciliatory and dutiful character. He had appealed before to the King, through the Ministers. He now addressed his Majesty directly in a letter, dated March 4th, 1768:

' SIRE,

'I beg thus to throw myself at your Majesty's feet, and to supplicate that mercy and clemency which shine with such lustre among your many princely virtues.

' Some former Ministers, whom your Majesty, in condescension to the wishes of your people, has thought proper to remove, employed every wicked and deceitful art to oppress your subject, and to revenge their own personal cause on me, whom they imagined to be the principal author of bringing to the public view their ignorance, insufficiency, and treachery to your Majesty and to the nation.

'I have been the innocent, but unhappy victim of their revenge. I was forced by their injustice and violence into an exile, which I have never ceased for several years to consider as the most cruel oppression, because I no longer could be under the benign protection of your Majesty in the land of liberty.

'With a heart full of zeal for the service of your Majesty and my country, I implore, sire, your clemency. My only hopes of pardon are founded in the great goodness and benevolence of your Majesty; and every day of freedom you may be graciously pleased to permit me the enjoyment of in my dear native land, shall give proofs of my zeal and attachment to your service.

'I am, sire,
'Your Majesty's most obedient
'and dutiful subject,
'JOHN WILKES.'

21—2

Wilkes was so ignorant of the usages of courts as to despatch this appeal by his footman, who handed it in at the palace door! No answer was returned ; though had it been presented in due form, it would not have met a better reception.

It was thought extraordinary that no notice should have been taken of this emissary of disorder, who, it must be remembered, was still under ban, an outlaw, his goods ' confiscate to the State.' * The supineness of the Ministry who allowed him to go about freely—nay, even presently to canvass for votes—seemed like cowardice. Long after, it was revealed through the private correspondence of political persons that it was distracted councils, ignorance, and general timidity, that permitted the firebrand to lay his plans for throwing the Metropolis into confusion and riot. Had the processes of law been promptly

* It must have been mortifying, also, to find that, in his absence, he had completely passed out of the public recollection. His arrival caused not the slightest emotion. Though he was known, her eceived no acclamations beyond those of a few idle boys.

applied, the community might have been saved much confusion and disturbance.*

Within a few days, after his appeal for pardon had been ignored, he conceived the daring scheme of offering himself as a candidate for the City of London. Thus the withholding of that harmless act of grace was accountable for much of the confusion that followed, and the angry passions that were aroused.

He addressed the electors of the City of London—with but poor chances of success. On this momentous occasion he received the valuable aid of another agitator, now rising into notoriety, the well-known Parson Horne. This person, who at first wished to gain notice through Wilkes's aid, and later grew jealous of his superior popularity with the mob, claimed to have done all the rough and necessary work of the election, engaging public-houses, addressing mobs, in a strain of coarse but

* The Solicitor to the Treasury, in his official capacity, served Wilkes with an Exchequer writ, or bill of discovery of his property—stated to be forfeited to the Crown under the outlawry. This writ was served upon him by a clerk, when at dinner with a number of his friends, during the election, on the 19th of March, 1768.

effective eloquence, of which he had a gift. This Horne, it will be seen, was a violent intolerant being, and was presently to show himself the implacable enemy of Wilkes.

All the recorded utterances of Wilkes at this time were studiously moderate. His position was certainly difficult. Just as he had offered his submission to the King in almost abject terms ; so, all his addresses to the electors were rational, becoming, and well argued. Thus to the City of London (on March 10) : ' The chief merit of you, gentlemen, I know to be a sacred love of liberty. I will yield to none of my countrymen in this noble zeal. I may appeal to my whole conduct, both in and out of Parliament, for the demonstration that such principles are deeply rooted in my heart, and that I have steadily pursued the interests of my country, without regard to the powerful enemies I have created, or the manifold dangers in which I must thence necessarily be involved, and that I have fulfilled the duties of a good subject. The two important questions of public liberty, respecting General Warrants and Seizure of

Papers, may perhaps *place our names among
them who have deserved well of mankind, by an
undaunted firmness, perseverance, and probity.*'
Here his vanity broke out, and was certain
never to let his exertions in this department
be forgotten. The rest was in a conventional
strain.

Parliament being dissolved. he appeared on
the hustings on March 15—which prompted
Burke's rather laboured classical pun—
'numerisque fertur lege solutis.' He obtained
the show of hands, but at the election found
himself at the bottom of the poll, having, however, received 1247 votes. Nothing daunted.
he appealed to another constituency, telling
them that he considered them all as electors
of Middlesex now, not of Westminster, and that
he would ask their votes in that capacity.

It would be difficult to give an idea of
the time of riot and mad disorder that now
set in ; intimidation and violence, with the
most extraordinary excitement. Wilkes had
of a sudden become an almost heroic
figure, his name was on almost every tongue,
and he must have felt for the first time the

stimulant of popular favour when he was
drawn in his carriage by the mob through the
streets of London. From that moment the
excitement seemed to kindle his enthusiasm,
and he saw the way not to success merely,
but to what was more important—cash, into
which all this popular admiration might be
transmuted. Private letters of the time are
filled with the one subject. There was
universal alarm and astonishment mixed.
A happy aid for Wilkes was the general display of the old number of the journal for
which he had been condemned, ' No. 45 '—
which served as a convenient and effective
badge, and was flourished everywhere. The mob
knew nothing of what it signified, nor of its
history. Everywhere it was chalked up :
all vociferated ' No. 45 ' until they were
hoarse. For some years this symbol was
to do Wilkes invaluable service.

During the polling that followed, mobs
lined all the roads that led to Brentford, where
the votes were taken. They took a particular
pleasure in forcing the superior classes to do
homage to their idol. No one was allowed to

pass without displaying the magic number in
his hat, and in default of which passport they
were dragged out, and the mystic sign chalked
upon their clothes or carriages. The Austrian
ambassador had to submit to the indignity of
having ' 45 ' marked upon the soles of his
shoes, and his angry complaints and demands
for a satisfaction which it was impossible to give
caused much amusement to his diplomatic
friends.   Ladies were forced to alight and cry
' Wilkes and Liberty.' The beautiful Duchess
of Hamilton, who refused to illuminate, had
her house battered with stones by the
mob.   Some were pelted, others dragged from
their coaches.

All this was deplorable, and owing to
' Wilkes and Liberty;' but after all it was only
a matter of police, and incident to a violently
conducted and popular election.   Wedderburn,
in a truly eloquent burst, dwelt upon the un-
meaning character of this folly.   He described
' the idle, beggarly, intoxicated mob without
keepers, actuated solely by the word ' Wilkes,'
which they use as other savages do a walrus,
to incite them in their attempts to insult

Government. Wilkes, I dare say, is vain
enough to imagine he has raised all this
tumult. but in my opinion he is as innocent
of it as the staff that carries the flag with his
name upon it.' But the King and Ministers
foolishly saw in it a revolutionary outburst,
and treated it as such.

' I went last week.' writes Franklin. on
April 16, 1768, ' to Winchester, and observed
that for fifteen miles out of town there was
scarce a door or a window-shutter next to the
road unmarked' (with 'No. 45,' and 'Wilkes,'
etc.). ' And this continued here and there to
Winchester, which is sixty-four miles. London
was illuminated for two nights at the command of the mob, who made their rounds at
intervals during the whole night, and obliged
those who had extinguished the candles to
light them again, their windows being smashed
if they refused.'

Wilkes' head was adopted as a tavern sign,
and he used to relate good-humouredly how he
had seen an old lady point to one of them, and
say. ' Aye, there he swings ! Everywhere but
where he ought !'

The poll was opened on March 28. He was opposed by Sir W. Proctor, and there was a third candidate, Mr. Cooke. Wilkes was returned triumphantly at the head, polling 1292 votes, Cooke following with 827, and Proctor with 807.

It may be imagined with what feelings of consternation the Court and Ministry regarded this ominous victory. The outlaw and exile was now heading the people, and it was evident that a most serious and critical struggle was at hand. But his case was every moment strengthened by some blunder of his enemies.

On his arrival he had sent notice to the Crown that he intended to surrender himself on the first day of term, viz., on April 20.* This was allowing himself a pretty long period for agitation, and it showed a strange weakness

* This notice was addressed to Nuthall, Solicitor to the Treasury, and he added : 'I pledge my honour as a gentleman that on the very first day of term I will then make my personal appearance.' It should be mentioned that some of the most interesting documents connected with Wilkes are to be found in the handsome folio published by Baldwin, without a date, and in no other of the numerous Wilkes collections.

on the part of the authorities that the ' outlaw ' was not at once arrested and brought up
for sentence.

He must have been particularly gratified by
receiving from one of the most distinguished
of his French friends the following letter of
congratulation :

'Paris, April 2, 1768.

' SIR,

' I received, with the greatest pleasure,
the news of your election. I happened to be
with the President when your letter was delivered to me. It was immediately read, and
the whole company, which was very numerous, was overjoyed at your success. Your
social virtues will, at all times and in all places,
render your memory dear and precious to your
friends ; and the justice which has been done
you in so public and distinguished a manner
indemnifies you sufficiently for the hardships
of your exile. How pleasing it is to reign in
the hearts of men ! You reign in those of
your fellow-citizens—you deserve to reign in
them ; you have supported their rights ; and,

genuine sons of freedom, as they are, they have crowned with applause the champion of their liberties.

' The uncommon unanimity with which the electors voted in your favour is an incontestable proof of their impartiality. The bribery, corruption and clandestine practices, which are so common in elections, had no place in yours. The love of liberty fired every breast, and procured the suffrage of the independent electors. And I doubt not but you might have been chosen for London itself, where the different interests arising from trade set so many secret springs in motion, had the electors been as free at Guildhall as they are interested in commerce ; but interest, you know, governs the world.

' Your quiet and peaceable demeanour does you infinite honour ; and your generous and patriotic principles will render your name immortal. You quitted Paris, that agreeable retreat, where your amiable and gentlemanlike behaviour hath gained you so many friends ; and notwithstanding all the amusements which we endeavoured to procure for you, in order to render your stay the more agreeable, you overlooked all dangers, and flew to support the rights of your country. Coriolanus meditated the ruin of his; and, under pretext of securing her liberties, proposed she should receive the galling yoke of slavery, after having demolished her walls. Actuated by a motive infinitely more noble, you go to yours in the character of a peacemaker; and, as a reward of all that you have suffered for her sake, you ask nothing but the power of being further serviceable to her.

· In the same instant London opens to you her gates, and the citizens their hearts; but the greater part of the electors, restrained or intimidated by the powerful influence of the other candidates, durst not venture to give you their votes. The independent and famous county of Middlesex, however, has indemnified you for the secret machinations of the one, and the base pusillanimity of the other. Europe will be surprised at your patriotism and your success; or, rather, Europe will admire the one, and rejoice at the other. I am the first to felicitate you on the occasion, ·

and to join my congratulations to those of all
the friends of the human race, which was certainly never intended to wear fetters.

' The august senate of Great Britain will
still count a Wilkes among its most illustrious
members ; and the liberty of your country
will still find in you a generous defender of
its rights and privileges.

  ' I have the honour to be,
    ' With the greatest sincerity,
       · DIDEROT.'

As in all confusion of the kind, some firmness and resolution at the opening would have
prevented all the mischief. The toleration
extended to the agitator seemed inexplicable.
When we look behind the scenes—that is, into
the council room—we find the explanation in
the uncertainty of Ministers, and chiefly in the
ignorance of their legal advisers. About the
middle of April, Mr. Whately, an acute observer, and one of the smaller official poli-
ticians, learned that one reason was that
Ministers were eagerly pressing the King to
pardon the agitator. And it has been always

agreed that this would have been the most prudent course. As another shrewd observer said, had Wilkes been allowed peaceably to take his seat, the House of Commons would have been the place where he would do the least damage.

The only opponent of Wilkes who was consistent throughout, and who all through was for dealing with the arch-agitator in the most summary fashion, was the King. In fact, the whole seemed to be really fought out between two men, his Majesty and Mr. Wilkes. The former identified him with the lowest scum of the population, and seemed to believe that he was ready to burn, sack and ravish. He held him accountable for the excesses of the mob. In alarm for the safety of the palace, he had sat up during the whole night, when the town was illuminated. He was even heard to express the wish that the mob would come, ' so that he might give them a warm reception with his Guards.' But he was infinitely disgusted at the unaccountable inaction of the Ministers in not arresting the outlaw on his arrival.

As he wrote to Lord Weymouth, his secretary, on April 25 :

' The Attorney-General's letter makes me imagine that Mr. Wilkes will not surrender himself; therefore, your having afresh insisted on the utmost being done to seize him, seems absolutely necessary. I cannot conclude without expressing my sorrow that so mean a set of men as the sheriff's officers can, either from timidity or interestedness, frustrate a due execution of the law. If he is not soon secured, I wish you would inquire whether there is no legal method of quickening the zeal of the sheriffs themselves.'*

These were the words of an undaunted spirit, of a man who knew his own mind. But he was in error in laying the whole blame of this supineness on the sheriffs and their men, others of higher degree being accountable. The lawyers were so ignorant, and so timorous, that they could not make up their minds as to the proper course to be pursued, and, as Mr. Whately learned, had to call in Sir Fletcher Norton to advise with

* Jesse, ' George III.,' i. 427.

them. To his astonishment, the latter found
that *their* idea of procedure was, that when
Wilkes chose to appear in the Court, they
were to appear, and that the Court, being
thus 'seized of the case,' would dispose
of it. Sir Fletcher asked them had they
ever been in the King's Bench, or they
must know that the judges never moved in
a case without formal application made to
them. After mentioning a number of 'points'
which showed the same ignorance, they at
last begged of him as a friend to say whether
they ought 'to take out a *capias*' to bring
Wilkes before the Court? Sir Fletcher answered them by putting a question : 'Why
hadn't they taken out a *capias* already ?'
Then they said they had no directions. Sir
Fletcher said it was no matter of directions
at all, but of execution. They finally returned to their first idea, which was to wait
the direction of the Court, and thus publicly
display their ignorance.

Wilkes, thus unmolested, carried out his
purpose of presenting himself, at his convenience, before the tribunal. On the day

he had fixed, he accordingly proceeded from his lodging in Prince's Row, Westminster, to a coffee-house, accompanied by friends, who enjoined order and quiet to the crowd. There was an immense concourse gathered round the house, and it was orderly enough. On his appearance in Court, Wilkes made a speech to the judges, offering to submit himself in everything to the laws. He added a short defence on the two charges, of publishing *The North Briton* and the ' Essay.' He complained also of the records being altered by Lord Mansfield. The points were shortly but forcibly urged, and he thus concluded :
' I have stood forth, my lords, in support of the laws against the arbitrary acts of Ministers. This court of justice, in a solemn appeal respecting General Warrants, showed this sense of my conduct. I shall continue to reverence the nice and mild system of English laws, and this excellent constitution. I have been much misrepresented, but under every species of persecution *I will remain firm and friendly to the monarch, dutiful and affectionate to the illustrious prince who wears the crown, and to*

the whole Brunswick succession.' These were becoming sentiments, if unexpected.

According to his favourite method, Wilkes thus contrived to turn his text to the usual self laudation, and draw attention to his own merits and services.

The case was then duly argued by counsel, and at the close a ludicrous position was reached, it being held by Lord Mansfield that he was ' *not before the Court.'* The only way in which they could be enabled to notice him was after action of legal process, that is, by being brought up formally ' before the Court,' under writ or warrant.

The law officers having thus displayed their ignorance, in spite of warning, Wilkes was suffered to depart, and thus added a fresh triumph to his score.

As it was anticipated that he might not be committed on that day, no less than seven sheriff's officers were drawn up outside the Court ready to seize him. When he left, they were brought round him, but could not be induced to do anything. Two of the men positively refused to be concerned in anything affecting Mr. Wilkes. They felt that it was too dangerous a service, after all the actions and mulctings their tribe had endured.*

The King, now more and more exasperated, began to press on Lord North ' that the expulsion of Mr. Wilkes appears to be very essential, and *must be effected.*' He quoted the case of Ward in the reign of his great-grandfather, which seemed ' to point out the proper course of proceeding,' and Wilkes's speech in the Court ' would surely be reason enough for not forgetting his criminal writings ;' for had he not declared ' No. 45 ' to be a paper that the author might glory in, and a blasphemous poem a mere ludicrous production ? This is scarcely a fair account of Wilkes's speech. But the fact remains, as may be seen by the King's letters, that it was

* After this the legal confusion became worse and worse confounded. Mr. Shebbeare, K.C., wrote an amusing account to a friend of the legal imbroglio or mess. The Attorney-General was refusing to grant Wilkes a writ of error, because, 'if granted, it would secure him from arrest in whatever situation he happened to be.' It was rumoured that he had gone into Surrey, so process had to be taken out for that county.

his Majesty who from the beginning sternly opposed granting a pardon, who had urged on to legal process, and was now the first to suggest his expulsion.

Lord Weymouth, who was very acceptable to the King, did not need any stimulating. He had already assumed that 'affairs were in a most critical condition,' and addressed a letter to the Lords-Lieutenant of the counties, enjoining on them measures of vigorous repression. In this extraordinary and suggestive document, after urging general steps of preparation, he says 'that after the recent alarming instances of riot and confusion, I cannot help apprising you that much will depend upon the preventive measures which you shall take, and much is expected from the vigilance and activity with which such measures will be carried into execution. When I inform you that every possible precaution is taken to support the dignity of your office; that, upon application from the civil magistrate, at the Tower, the Savoy, or the War Office, he will find a military force ready to march to his assistance, and to act accord-

ing as he shall find it expedient and necessary ;
I need not add that, if the public peace is not
preserved, and if any riotous proceedings
which may happen are not suppressed, the
blame will, most probably, be imputed to a
want of prudent and spirited conduct in the
civil magistrates. As I have no reason to
doubt your caution and discretion in not calling for troops till they are wanted ; so, on the
other hand, I hope you will not delay a
moment calling for their aid, and making use
of them, effectually, where there is occasion ;
that occasion always presents itself when the
civil power is trifled with and insulted ; nor
can a military force ever be employed to a
more constitutional purpose than in the support of the authority and dignity of magis-
tracy.'

This was certainly, in plain terms, im-
pressing on the magistrate that soldiers were
supplied to him for actual use and not for
mere show. It was little anticipated that
this monition was to add seriously to the
complications of the case.

Wilkes, whose good-humour was always

irrepressible, was now to infuse a little of the
spirit of comedy into the situation, and contribute to the harmless gaiety of the town by
one of his happiest sallies. A peculiar object
of his dislike had been the Speaker, Sir John
Cust, who had taken official share in his
expulsion. This personage he had already
stigmatised in coarse and unbecoming language in his letter to the Duke of Grafton.
The Speaker, it will be recollected, merely
pointed out that the certificate of the French
doctors as to Wilkes's incapacity to make the
journey to London was informal. In return,
Wilkes had described him as 'a person of the
meanest natural parts, and infinitely beneath
all regard, except from the office he bears,
with the utmost discredit to himself, with
equal disgrace and insufficiency to the public.'

But only a week or two after his arrival in
town he found an occasion to ridicule him in
the happiest manner.

To receive a rebuke from a parent or
guardian, head-master, Bishop, or chief
partner in the firm, are terrible things of
their kind. But there is something specially

uncomfortable in being ordered to the bar of
the House to be reprimanded by ' Mr.
Speaker ' in person, arrayed in his full or
fullest bottomed wig. Wilkes, who, like the
' sapper ' in Teresa's song, acknowledged
' nothing sacred,' now turned the august
ceremonial into fun. It seems that the
Mayor and Corporation of Oxford, being
much in debt and at their wits' end to extri-
cate themselves, proposed to re-elect the
sitting members on condition of their paying
down a sum of £7,500. The sitting members returned an ironical answer, thanking
them for ' the preference you are generously
pleased to give us,' but declining the offer as
' not being able to afford the purchase.' At
the same time they brought the matter before
the House, who directed the Speaker to
' reprimand ' the offenders. He accordingly
summoned ' Philip Ward, John Treacher, Sir
Thomas Munday, Thomas Wise, Richard
Tawney, etc., etc.'; and the Speaker, in im-
pressive language, administered a reprimand
ordered by the House, upon which they were
allowed to depart. It was on the Speaker

that Wilkes exercised his humour. The agitator caused much laughter by simply quoting the Speaker's grotesquely severe language, and adding some humorous comments of his own.

' I shall first (he says) consider the oration itself, as branched out under the four general heads of *Exordium ; Constitutio Causæ ; Insectatio ; Peroratio.* And then I shall examine the four other accessory circumstances of the *Personæ ; Tempus ; Locus ; Eventus.*

' I begin with the *exordium.* It is plain and simple, according to all the rules laid down by the ancients. It contains only these words, ' Philip Ward, John Treacher, Sir Thomas Munday, Thomas Wise, John Nicholls, John Philips, Isaac Lawrence, Richard Tawney, Thomas Robinson, John Brown.' No *exordium* was ever built on so firm a foundation. It stands on the legal base of the baptismal register itself. I do not believe anything happier could have been conceived. I must confess, with all my partialities about me, that the *constitutio causæ* is not so clear and full as I could wish. In the oration it is merely said, 'The offence of which you have been guilty has justly brought you under the severe displeasure of this House;' while the title is only, 'The speech of the Speaker of the House of Commons, when he reprimanded Philip Ward, etc., upon their knees,' etc., without saying for what crime. We are thus left to guess what it could be; and I own that when I read at the beginning that ' a *more* enormous crime they could not well commit,' I did not directly think of bribery and corruption. Although I was a little doubtful what enormous crime a man might *well* commit, yet when I heard that a *more* enormous crime they could not well commit, I own I was afraid that they had been guilty of murder, perjury, rape, etc., or some other crimes whose guilt I should imagine to be of a shade darker and deeper than even this of bribery and corruption. I was a little relieved, therefore, when I found that this was not the case, and that there was even somewhat of honesty in their proceedings; that they were endeavouring to pay off old debts, by trying to get beforehand a part of the money which such *country-puts* falsely imagine their representatives afterwards make of them.

'The *peroratio* is, alas! too short; but full of dignity, suited to the majesty of the Commons of Great Britain. '*I do reprimand you!*' The little word *do* is very emphatical here. As Pope says, 'feeble expletives their aid *do* join.' How weak would be the sense, and how poor the expression, without it! The last words, 'you are discharged, paying your fees,' I fear, will to many suggest an idea beneath the dignity of Parliament; and may make the world imagine that the fees were an illegal claim, not recoverable by action, and that therefore Mr. Speaker took the short way of keeping the parties in custody till his own and the clerk's fees were paid. But for my part I believe that, as an orator, he talked of the fees to add to the terror of the sentence and the weight of the punishment.'*

During the interval, while waiting sentence,

---

* Lord Brougham considers this piece one of the best of Wilkes' literary efforts.

he repaired to Bath, whence it was written to
Mr. Grenville that ' he had met with a very
mortifying reception, being universally avoided
by all degrees of men.' Mr. Grenville wrote
that it might possibly account for the firmer
tone of Ministers, and might have given
them courage. An amusing incident occurred.
The Chancellor, it was said, encountered
Wilkes suddenly in the Pump-room : ' Neither
of them bowed or spoke to the other, but
both stopped and stared, so as to set the
whole room in a titter.'

But now the law officers had at last discovered the proper mode of bringing Wilkes
before the Court, which, it seems, was by
a writ of ' *Capias Utlagatum.*' On April 27
he was actually arrested, and we find the King
writing his great satisfaction, on the same day.
Inquiry had been made of the Attorney-
General as to what were the next steps to be
taken. Wilkes's counsel had applied for a
writ of error ; and, in the meantime, application was made that he be admitted to bail.
This was refused, on the ground that no convicted person could be allowed out on bail.

Lord Mansfield accordingly committed him
to the King's Bench Prison, to wait the
argument on the errors submitted. This
decision was of ill omen for the good order of
the City; and the King, who was anxiously
following the proceedings, sent many missives
to the Secretary advising the ' keeping a careful eye upon the King's Bench Prison '; that
he was persuaded from the aversion of Wilkes
to being imprisoned, ' added to his not possess-
ing one grain of prudence,' that he would
encourage the mob not to let him be taken to
prison. As it is proved. Wilkes did all he
could to reach his place of confinement peace-
fully. He waited till 7 o'clock in the evening,
when with Parson Horne he set out in a
carriage. But on Westminster Bridge the
mob overtook him, took away the horses, and
drew the carriage in the opposite direction.
Enormous crowds followed, gathering as they
went. The procession passed through the
Strand, and up Fleet Street to Cornhill,
when it halted, and the mob opening the doors
turned out the two bailiffs. They then asked
Wilkes where he wished to be taken to. ' To

the King's Bench Prison,' he replied firmly,
‘ to which the laws of my country have sent
me!’ His admirers, however, refused to
comply with this request, and drew him away
till they reached the Three Tuns Tavern in
Spitalfields, where he entered ‘ amid the repeated hurrahs and acclamations of a triumphant people.’ The King, putting the worst
construction on these proceedings, ‘ was surprised that Mr. Wilkes should be so ill-advised
as to let violence be used to prevent the
officers of justice performing the duties of
their office.’ The truth being that Wilkes, so
soon as he got rid of his admirers, put on
a disguise, and set off to surrender himself at
the Bench Prison, to the great joy of the
Marshal.

Such was this eventful day, when this
strange London revolution had made an
enormous advance.

To understand Wilkes's behaviour, it must
be borne in mind what has already been
pointed out, that Wilkes was the most prudent
of demagogues, and seemed only anxious to
secure all free means of conciliation. He wished

to show what forces were at his command,
and that he was anxious to do his best to
keep them under control. In short, that,
Wilkes as he was, ' *he never was a Wilkite.*'

END OF VOL. I.